SEBASTIAN FITZEK

THE SOUL BREAKER

translated from the German by
John Brownjohn

First published in Germany as *Der Seelenbrecher* in 2008
by Droemer Knaur
First published in the UK in 2021 by Head of Zeus Ltd
This paperback editon first published in 2021 by Head of Zeus Ltd

Der Seelenbrecher copyright © 2008 Verlagsgruppe Droemer Knaur
GmbH & Co. KG, Munich, Germany

Translation © 2021 John Brownjohn

9 7 5 3 1 2 4 6 8

A catalogue record for this book is available from
the British Library.

ISBN (PB): 9781838934552
ISBN (E): 9781838934569

Typeset by Divaddict Publishing Solutions Ltd

Printed and bound in Great Britain by
CPI Group (UK) Ltd, Croydon CR0 4YY

Head of Zeus Ltd
5–8 Hardwick Street
London EC1R 4RG

WWW.HEADOFZEUS.COM

I'm not afraid of death; I just don't want to be there when it happens.

Woody Allen

Seventy-one days before The Fear

Page 1 ff. of patient's record no. 131071/VL

Luckily it was all just a dream. She wasn't naked, nor were her legs strapped to that antediluvian gynaecological chair while the maniac sorted out his instruments at a rusty side table. When he turned round she couldn't see at first what he was holding in his blood-encrusted hand. Then, when she did see it, she tried to shut her eyes but failed. She couldn't avert her gaze from the red-hot soldering iron that was slowly nearing the epicentre of her body. The stranger with the scarred, scalded face had folded back her eyelids and tacked them to her orbital ridges with a pneumatic stapler. She'd thought she would never experience greater pain than that in the little that remained of her life. But, when the soldering iron disappeared from her field of vision and the heat between her thighs steadily intensified, she sensed that the agonies of the last few hours were only a prelude.

Then, just when she thought she could already smell the stench of seared flesh, everything went transparent. The dank cellar into which she'd been dragged, the flickering halogen lamp above her head, the torturer's chair and the metal side table – they all dissolved. Nothing remained but a dark void.

Thank God, she thought, *only a dream*. She opened her eyes. And was mystified.

The nightmare in which she'd just been imprisoned had merely undergone a change, not lost its shape.

Where am I?

Judging by the decor, in a seedy hotel bedroom. The stained bedspread on the decrepit double bed was as filthy and as sprinkled with cigarette burns as the khaki-coloured carpet. The fact that she could feel its rough pile beneath her feet made her tense up even more on the uncomfortable wooden chair.

My feet are bare. Why aren't I wearing any shoes? And why am I sitting in some cheap hotel, staring at the grainy test picture on a black-and-white television?

The questions ricocheted around her skull like billiard balls. She gave a sudden start as if someone had hit her, then looked for the source of the noise. The door of the room. It shuddered once, twice, and burst open. Two policemen came dashing in. Both in uniform, both armed – that much she could see. They levelled their guns at her chest at first, then slowly lowered them, and the nervous tension on their faces gave way to horrified incomprehension.

'What the hell happened here?' she heard the shorter of the two exclaim – the one who had kicked the door open and dashed in first. 'Paramedics,' yelled the other. 'A doctor. We need help urgently!'

Thank God, she thought for the second time in a few heartbeats. She could still scarcely breathe for fear. Her body hurt all over and she smelled of faeces and urine. This, coupled with the fact that she didn't know how she'd got here, was driving her to the brink of insanity. Still, she was now confronted by two policemen anxious to summon medical assistance. That wasn't good, but it was considerably better than a maniac with a soldering iron.

A doctor – a bald man with an earring – hurried into the room moments later and kneeled down beside her. Evidently, the emergency services were already on hand with an ambulance. Not a good sign either.

'Can you hear me?'

'Yes…' she replied.

The dark rings around the doctor's eyes looked as if they had been permanently tattooed on his face. 'She doesn't appear to understand me,' he said.

'Yes, yes.' She tried to raise her arm, but her muscles refused to obey.

'What's your name?' The doctor took a medical

penlight from his shirt pocket and shone it in her eyes.

'Vanessa,' she said hoarsely. 'Vanessa Strassmann,' she added.

'Is she dead?' she heard one of the policemen ask in the background.

'Damn, her pupils barely react to light and she doesn't seem to hear or see us. She's catatonic, possibly comatose.'

'But that's nonsense!' Vanessa shouted. She tried to stand up but couldn't even raise her arm.

What's going on here?

She repeated the question aloud, doing her best to articulate the words as distinctly as possible. No one seemed prepared to listen. Instead, they all turned away and started talking to someone she hadn't seen yet.

'How long did you say it was since she left this room?'

The doctor's head was blocking her view of the door. A young woman's voice came from that direction: 'Three days at least, possibly longer. I thought there was something wrong with her when she checked in, but she said she didn't want to be disturbed.'

She's talking nonsense! Vanessa shook her head. *I'd never stay here of my own free will, not even for a night!*

'I wouldn't have called her even then, but that awful hoarse breathing got louder and louder, and—'

'Look!' The voice of the shorter policeman was right beside her ear.

'What?'

'There's something there. There!'

Vanessa felt the doctor prise open the fingers of her left hand and remove something with a pair of tweezers.

'What is it?' asked the policeman.

'A piece of paper.'

The doctor opened the slip of paper, which was folded in half. Vanessa squinted sideways in an attempt to look at it, but all she could see were some unintelligible hieroglyphs. The writing was in a wholly unknown language.

'What does it say?' asked the other policeman, who was standing by the door.

'Odd.' The doctor knit his brow: '"You buy it,"' he read aloud, '"only to throw it away at once."'

For heaven's sake... The fact that the doctor had read those few words aloud without a moment's hesitation brought home to her the full extent of the nightmare that held her captive. For some reason she had lost all ability to communicate. At this moment she could neither speak nor read. What was more, she suspected she was even incapable of writing.

Again the doctor shone the light straight into her eyes, and all at once the rest of her senses seemed to go dead. She could no longer smell the stench of her body or feel the carpet beneath her bare feet. All she noticed was that the fear within her was steadily intensifying and the hum of voices around her steadily fading, for scarcely had the doctor read out that brief sentence when an invisible power took possession of her.

You buy it, only to throw it away at once...

A power whose icy hand was reaching out and pulling her away. Back to the place she never wanted to see again for as long as she lived – the place she had left only minutes before.

So it wasn't a dream. Or was it?

She tried to give the doctor a sign, but the truth began to dawn on her as his figure slowly dissolved. Stark terror overcame her. They genuinely hadn't heard her speak. Neither the doctor nor the receptionist nor the policemen had been able to communicate with her. Why not? Because she had never woken up at all in that seedy hotel – far from it. As the halogen lamp overhead began to flicker once more, she grasped what had happened: she had fainted when the torture began. The hotel room, not the madman, had been part of a dream that was now retreating before the onset of brutal reality.

Or am I wrong yet again? Help! Help me! I can't tell reality from illusion. What is real? What isn't?

And then, all was just as it had been before. The dank cellar, the metal table, the gynaecological chair to which she was strapped. Naked. So naked, she could feel the madman's breath between her thighs. He was breathing on her – on her most sensitive spot. His scarred face came briefly into view, just in front of her eyes, and his lipless mouth said: 'I only marked the place. Now we can begin.'

And he reached for the soldering iron.

TODAY

Very much later, many years after The Fear

10:14 a.m.

'Well, ladies and gentlemen, what do you make of this introduction? A woman awakens from one nightmare only to find herself – from one moment to the next – in the throes of another. Interesting, no?'

The professor got up from the long oak table and surveyed his students' disconcerted faces.

It struck him only now that his audience had been more careful in their choice of attire than he himself. As usual, he had blindly grabbed some crumpled old suit from his wardrobe. A sales assistant had talked him into paying an exorbitant price for the dark double-breaster on the grounds that it went so well with his dark hair, which at that time, in a ludicrous fit of post-pubertal rebellion, he had worn somewhat longer than he did now.

If he were to buy a suit that went with his hair today,

many years later, it would have to be cigarette-ash grey, thinning in places, and display a sort of monk's tonsure at the back.

'Well, what do you think?'

He took an incautious step sideways and felt a stab of pain in his knee. Only six students had volunteered. Four female, two male. Typical. Women were always in the majority when it came to such experiments. Either because they were more courageous, or because they were in greater need of the fee he was offering for participation in this psychiatric experiment he had chalked up on the blackboard.

'Excuse me, but have I got this straight?' *Second on the left.* The professor checked the list in front of him for the name of the guinea pig who had just spoken. *Florian Wessel, 3rd term.*

While reading the introduction, Florian Wessel had skimmed the lines with the tip of an immaculately sharpened pencil. A small, crescent-shaped scar under his right eye denoted his membership of a duelling fraternity. He now deposited the pencil between the pages and closed the folder. 'Is this supposed to be a *medical record*?'

'It is indeed.' The professor smiled good-naturedly to convey that he could well understand the young man's mystification. It was all part of the experiment, so to speak.

'Soldering iron? Torture? Police? With respect, it

reads more like the start of a thriller than a medical record.'

With respect? It was a long time since the professor had heard that antiquated expression. He wondered if the youth with the razor-sharp parting always talked that way, or if the melancholy patina of their unusual surroundings had rubbed off on his turn of phrase. He knew that the building's horrific history had deterred some students from taking part, 200 euros or no 200 euros.

But that was the whole charm of the experiment: conducting it here and nowhere else. There could be no better venue for it, even though the entire complex smelled of mildew and it was so cold they'd briefly debated whether to clear the rubbish out of the fireplace and get a fire going. It was 23 December, after all, and the outside temperature was well below zero. They had eventually hired two oil radiators, but these were inadequate to heat such a lofty room.

'It reads like a thriller, you say?' the professor repeated. 'Well, you're not so wide of the mark.'

He pressed his palms together like a man at prayer and sniffed his withered fingers. His hands reminded him of his grandfather's clumsy paws, the difference being that, unlike him, his grandfather had had to spend a lifetime working outdoors.

'The document you're holding in your hands was found among the papers of a colleague of mine. Viktor

Larenz, a psychiatrist. You may have come across his name in the course of your studies.'

'Larenz? Isn't he dead?' asked someone else, a student who had volunteered for the experiment only yesterday.

The professor checked his list again and identified the youth with the dyed black hair as Patrick Hayden. He and his girlfriend Lydia were sitting close together. The gap between their bodies was so narrow, even dental floss would have had trouble insinuating itself between them. This was mainly down to Patrick. Whenever Lydia tried to acquire a little more elbow room, he tightened the arm draped around her shoulders and gave her a proprietorial hug. He wore a sweatshirt bearing the intellectually demanding slogan *Jesus loves you*. Just below it, in barely legible lettering, were the words *Everyone else thinks you're an asshole*. Patrick had been wearing it on a previous occasion, when he came to complain about some poor grades the professor had given him.

'Viktor Larenz has no bearing on this matter,' the professor said dismissively. 'His story is irrelevant to today's test.'

'So what *is* it about?' Patrick wanted to know. He brought his legs smartly together beneath the table. The laces of his leather boots were untied so his professionally ripped jeans couldn't cover the tongue, which was folded back. No one would have been able to see the designer label on the ankle otherwise.

The professor couldn't help smiling. Trailing shoelaces,

ripped jeans, blasphemous sweatshirts. Someone in the fashion industry must have made it his mission to turn conservative parents' nightmares into hard cash.

'Well, let me tell you...' He resumed his place at the head of the table and opened a scuffed leather briefcase that looked as if some domestic pet had used it as a scratching post.

'What you've just read really happened. The files I've distributed are merely transcripts of an authentic factual account.' The professor took out an old paper-back. '*This* is the original.' He deposited the slim volume on the table. Printed in red lettering on the greenish cover were the words *The Soul Breaker*. Above them was the shadowy figure of a man hurrying through a snowstorm to take shelter in a dark building.

'Don't be deceived by its outward appearance. It looks at first sight like a common or garden novel, but there's much more to it than that.'

He riffled the book's three-hundred-odd pages through his fingers, starting at the back.

'Many people believe that this account was written by one of Larenz's patients. He used to treat a lot of artists, writers among them.' The professor blinked. Then he added quietly: 'But there's another theory.'

All the students looked at him expectantly.

'A minority are of the opinion that Viktor Larenz himself wrote it.'

'But why?'

The speaker this time was Lydia. The girl with the light-brown hair and the mouse-grey rollneck was his most promising pupil. He couldn't understand what she saw in the unshaven student beside her, who had flunked more than once, nor could he fathom why she'd been refused a bursary despite her excellent grades on leaving school.

'You mean this man Larenz turned his notes into a thriller? Why should he have gone to so much trouble?'

'That's what we're here this afternoon to discover. That's the whole object of this experiment.'

The professor made a note on the pad beside the participants' list. Then he turned to the trio of girls on his right, who had still to utter a word.

'I shall quite understand if you're dubious, ladies.'

The redhead looked up. The other two continued to stare at the documents in front of them.

'You're all welcome to change your minds. The experiment proper hasn't started yet. You can pack up and go home right now. There's still time.'

The girls nodded irresolutely.

Florian leant forwards, running a nervous forefinger down his side parting.

'What about the 200 euros?' he asked.

'You get those only if you take an active part. And only if you adhere to the prescribed procedure set out in the original notice. You must read the entire document and can only take short breaks.'

'And afterwards? What happens when we're through?'

'That, too, is part of the experiment.'

The psychiatrist bent down and straightened up holding a sheaf of forms adorned with the independent university's coat of arms.

'I would ask all of you who remain to sign these.'

He handed around the declarations of consent. The guinea pigs absolved the university of all liability for any psychosomatic ill effects that might derive from their voluntary participation in the experiment.

Florian Wessel took the form, held it up against the light, and vigorously shook his head at the sight of the medical faculty's watermark. 'This is too dicey for me.'

He retrieved his pencil from the folder, picked up his rucksack, and rose to his feet.

'I think I know what lies behind this. If my assumption is correct, I'm far too scared to go through with it.'

'Your candour does you credit.' The professor took back Florian's form and folder. Then he looked at the three girl students, who were whispering together.

'We don't know what's involved, but if Florian's opting out we'd sooner give it a miss ourselves.' Once again, the only one to communicate with him was the redhead.

'As you wish. No problem.'

He collected up the girls' plastic binders while they were taking their coats from the backs of their chairs.

Florian was already waiting beside the door in his hooded anorak and gloves.

'What about you?' The professor looked at Lydia and Patrick, who were still leafing through their folders irresolutely.

At length they both gave an almost simultaneous shrug.

'What the hell,' said Patrick. 'Just as long as no one sticks a needle in me.'

'Yes, what the hell.' Lydia had at last succeeded in detaching herself from her boyfriend. 'You'll be with us the whole time?'

'Yes.'

'And all we have to do is read this stuff? Nothing else?'

'That's it.'

The door closed behind the others, who had left without a word.

'All right, count me in. I can use the money.'

Lydia gave the professor a look that set another seal on their unspoken vow of silence.

I know, he told her in his mind, and nodded to her. Briefly and unobtrusively.

It had been a sweltering April weekend when a wave of self-pity had washed him up on the shores of her private life.

His only friend had advised him, if he wanted final closure with the past, to break the bonds of his usual pattern of behaviour and do something he'd never done before in his life. Three drinks later they'd gone to this bar cum strip club. Nothing really exciting, just a boringly innocuous floor show. Discounting the fact that the girls danced topless, their gyrations were little more obscene than those of most teenagers at a disco. And, as far as he could tell, there was no back room.

But that didn't prevent him from feeling like a dirty old man when Lydia suddenly appeared in front of him bearing the cocktail menu. Without her rollneck pullover and Alice band, but clad in a schoolgirl's uniform skirt. Other than that, she wore nothing.

He paid for a cocktail but didn't drink it, walked out on his friend, and rejoiced to see Lydia in her usual front-row seat at his next lecture. They had never said a word about this incident, and he felt sure Patrick knew nothing of his girlfriend's sideline. Although he looked like someone who would be on first-name terms with the barmen in such establishments, he seemed pretty intolerant where his own interests were concerned.

Lydia gave a faint sigh and put her signature to the consent form.

'After all,' she said as she wrote her name, 'what can go wrong?' The professor cleared his throat but said nothing. Instead, he checked both signatures and looked at his watch.

'Good, so we're all set.'

THE DAY BEFORE CHRISTMAS EVE

Nine hours and forty-nine minutes before The Fear

5:49 p.m.

Page 8 ff. of patient's record no. 131071/VL
Only to be read under medical supervision

'Imagine the following situation...'

From where Caspar was kneeling at her feet, the old lady's voice sounded muffled, as if he were hearing it through a closed door.

'A father and son are driving through a forest at night. The road is dark and deep in snow. The father loses control of his car, which crashes into a tree. He dies instantly. The boy survives but is badly injured and taken to a hospital, where he's wheeled into theatre at once for emergency surgery. "Oh my God!" the surgeon exclaims on seeing him, frozen with panic. "I can't operate on this boy, he's my son!"'

The old lady on the bed paused for a moment, then

SEBASTIAN FITZEK

asked triumphantly: 'How can that be unless the boy has two fathers?'

'I've no idea.'

Caspar kept his eyes shut and relied entirely on his sense of touch as he tried to repair the television, so he could only picture her smiling roguishly behind his back.

'Oh, come on. A riddle like that shouldn't be too difficult for a man of your intelligence.'

He withdrew his hand from behind the bulky old valve TV and turned to Greta Kaminsky shaking his head.

The seventy-nine-year-old banker's widow had knocked at his door five minutes ago and asked if he'd take a look at her 'idiot box'. That was what she called the monstrous great set, which was far too big for her little room on the top floor of the Teufelsberg Clinic. He had naturally agreed although the medical director, Professor Rassfeld, had strictly forbidden him to leave his room unsupervised.

'I'm afraid riddles really aren't my thing, Greta.' He breathed in some of the dust that had collected behind the television and had to cough. 'Besides, I'm not a woman. I can't do two things at once.'

With the side of his head clamped against the TV once more, he tried to locate the tiny socket for the aerial lead by touch. The bulky set wouldn't budge a millimetre away from the wall.

'Fiddlesticks!' Greta smacked the mattress twice with the flat of her hand. 'Don't be so silly, Caspar!'

Caspar...

The nurses had christened him that. After all, they had to call him something until they discovered what his real name was.

'Go on, try! Perhaps you'll turn out to be a wizard at riddles. You can't remember anything, so who knows?'

'Wrong,' he grunted as he thrust his hand a bit further into the gap between the television set and the woodchip wallpaper. 'I know how to knot a tie, read a book and ride a bicycle. It's just my previous history that's a blank.'

'*Your factual knowledge is largely unimpaired,*' he'd been told by Dr Sophia Dorn, the psychiatrist in charge of his case, at the start of their very first session. '*But all that defines you emotionally – all that constitutes your personality, in other words – has unfortunately disappeared.*'

Retrograde amnesia. Loss of memory.

He had no recollection of his name, family or profession. He didn't even know how he had got to this luxurious private hospital. The Teufelsberg Clinic was situated on the outskirts of Berlin and at its highest point – more precisely, on a man-made hill created out of rubble from buildings destroyed by bombs in World War Two. The Teufelsberg was now a grassy mound on whose summit the US Army had installed its monitoring devices in the days of the Cold War. The four-storeyed building in which Caspar was undergoing treatment had functioned as the officers' mess of the US intelligence services until, after the fall of the Wall in 1989, it had been bought at auction by Professor Samuel Rassfeld. Rassfeld, a renowned psychiatrist and neuroradiologist, had modernised the premises and converted them into one of the foremost hospitals specialising in psycho-somatic disorders. Situated high above the Grunewald like a castle protected by a drawbridge, the clinic could only be reached via the narrow private road on which Caspar had been found lying less than ten days earlier. Unconscious, hypothermic, and covered by a thin layer of snow.

Dirk Bachmann, the clinic's porter and major-domo, had driven Rassfeld to an appointment at Berlin's Westend Hospital that night. If he had returned only one hour later, Caspar would have frozen to death beside the road. He sometimes wondered if that would have mattered.

After all, what's the difference between life without an identity and death?

'You mustn't torment yourself like this,' Greta Kaminsky said in a faintly reproving tone, as if she had read his gloomy thoughts. She sounded more like a psychiatrist than a fellow patient who suffered from spells of anxiety psychosis if left alone for too long.

'Memory is like a pretty woman,' Greta told him as

he continued his search for the elusive aerial socket. 'Run after her and she'll get bored and turn her back on you. Concentrate on something else and she'll get jealous and come back to you of her own accord.'

She uttered a high-pitched giggle.

'Just like our pretty therapist, who looks after you with such loving care.'

Caspar looked up at her in astonishment. 'What on earth do you mean?' he demanded.

'I may be an old crone, but I'm not blind. I think you and Sophia are well suited, Caspaarrr.'

Caspaarrr.

The long-drawn-out A and trilled R were reminiscent of German film divas of the post-war years. Greta had spent every Christmas holiday at this private clinic since her husband died of a stroke on the golf course seven years earlier. It provided her with company when the Christmas blues overcame her, and that was why it was such a disaster if her television didn't work. She left the 'idiot box' on all the time as an antidote to loneliness.

'If I was a bit younger,' she said, giggling, 'I'd happily let you squire me to a *thé dansant*.'

He laughed. 'I'm flattered.'

'No, I mean it. When my husband was your age – early forties, I'd guess – his dark hair flopped over his forehead just as attractively as yours. He had the same shapely hands, too. What's more...' – she couldn't help giggling again – '...he shared my passion for riddles!'

She clapped her hands twice like a schoolteacher signalling the end of break.

'That's why we're going to have another try...'

Caspar groaned in mock exasperation as Greta proceeded to repeat her riddle: 'Father and son have a car crash. The father is killed, the son survives.'

He broke out in a sweat, even though the pivoting window was open.

It had sleeted all that morning, but towards lunchtime the temperature had dipped below freezing. Out here in the Grunewald it had to be two degrees colder than it was in the city centre, but Caspar would never have known it at the moment.

Ah! His forefinger brushed against a circular metal ring in the plastic casing. *All I need do now is plug in the cable and...*

'The boy, who's badly hurt, is wheeled into the theatre for an emergency operation, but he's the son of the surgeon, who balks at operating on him.'

Caspar crawled out from behind the bulky set and got to his feet. He picked up the remote control.

'Well?' Greta asked impishly. 'What's the answer?'

'This is,' said Caspar, and switched on.

The screen flickered and the room was filled with the booming voice of a newsreader. When the corresponding image finally appeared, Greta clapped her hands in high delight.

'It's working again. Wonderful! You're a genius.'

I don't know what I am, thought Caspar, patting the dust off his jeans.

'I'd better get back to my room before the nurse gets angry...' he started to say, but Greta raised her hand for silence.

'*...more disturbing reports of the so-called Soul Breaker, who has now been terrorising female members of the population for several weeks...*'

Greta turned the volume up.

5:56 p.m.

'*We have just received a report that his first victim, the 26-year-old drama student Vanessa Strassmann, died this afternoon in the intensive care ward at Westend Hospital. She vanished without trace after a class two and a half months ago and was found exactly a week later in a seedy autobahn motel. Naked, paralysed and in a squalid condition.*'

The picture of a radiantly beautiful girl appeared on the screen, as if the newsreader's dramatic words were insufficient to convey the full extent of the tragedy. That photograph was followed by two more. Once again, someone had taken the trouble to obtain some particularly attractive pictures from the Strassmann family album.

'*Like the two subsequent victims – Doreen Brandt,*

a successful lawyer, and Katja Adesi, a primary school-teacher – Vanessa Strassmann was physically almost unscathed. According to statements made by the doctors who examined her, she had not been raped, beaten or tortured. Mentally, however, she was a wreck. Until her death earlier today, she reacted only to extremes of light and sound. At other times she remained in a waking coma.'

The photos disappeared, to be replaced by an exterior view of a modern hospital complex.

'The cause of death presents doctors with an additional mystery, because it's impossible to tell exactly what happened to the young women while they were in the perpetrator's clutches. One clue may be supplied by the little slips of paper found in the hands of all three victims, although the police are saying nothing about what was written on them. There have been no further reports of missing persons, fortunately, and we can only hope that this is the end of this horrific series of kidnappings, not just an intermission over the Christmas holiday. The finest Christmas present of all would be the news that the Soul Breaker had been arrested – wouldn't it, Sandra?'

The newsreader turned to his fellow presenter with a professional smirk and segued to the weather.

'You're right, Paul. Let's cross our fingers and hope that our other presents reach the foot of the Christmas tree safely and in good time, because the heaviest

snowfalls of the last twenty years have been followed by a flash-freeze that's bringing the traffic in many cities to a halt. What is more, fierce blizzards are forecast...'

Flash-freeze, Caspar thought as he saw the weather map of Berlin sprinkled with graphic warning symbols.

And then it happened for the first time. The memory assailed him so suddenly and violently, it was all he could do to retain it.

Flashback

'You'll come back soon, won't you?'

'Yes, don't worry.' He smoothed back her hair, which was moist with sweat and had flopped over her eyes during the convulsions.

'You won't leave me alone for long, will you?'

'No.'

He couldn't hear the little girl speak, of course. She'd been incapable of moving her tongue for some time, but he sensed an unspoken entreaty in the faint pressure of her fingers. He suppressed the agonising thought that it might only be a reflex like the uncontrolled twitching of her right eyelid, not a deliberate movement.

'I'm so frightened. Please help me.'

The whole of her frail, eleven-year-old body was crying out for help, and he found it an effort to hold the tears in check. To distract himself he stared at the little round mole that hovered above her right cheekbone like the dot of an exclamation mark.

'I'll get you out of there,' he whispered. 'Trust me.'

Then he kissed her forehead, praying that it wasn't too late.

'Okay,' she whispered without moving her lips.

'You're so brave, sweetheart. Far too brave for your age.'

'I know.' Her fingers detached themselves from his hand.

'But hurry,' she groaned mutely.

'Of course. I promise. I'll release you.'

'I'm scared, Daddy. You'll be back soon, won't you?'

'I will. I'll be back soon, sweetheart, then everything will be all right – everything'll be the way it used to be. Don't worry, okay? I made a mistake but I'll get you out of there, and then...'

'Well, what do you think?' Greta asked loudly, jolting Caspar out of his frightening daydream. Blinking feverishly, he swallowed the saliva that had collected in his mouth and opened his eyes. They promptly started to water as glare of the television smote his pupils. It was clear that Greta hadn't noticed his fleeting reverie at all.

'I'm sorry?'

A smell of burning lingered in his nostrils, as if the impact of that first fragment of memory had ignited something.

What was it? A genuine memory? A dream? Still shocked by the images that had unfolded before his mind's eye, he instinctively clutched his chest at the spot where his T-shirt concealed the freshly healed burns he'd discovered the first time he'd taken a shower at the clinic. Burns whose origin was as much of a mystery to him as his past in general.

'Interesting,' Greta said excitedly. 'What could be on them?'

She turned the volume down and the stench in his nostrils faded.

'On what?'

'Why, those slips of paper. The ones they found on the Soul Breaker's victims. What could they mean?'

'No idea,' he said absently. He had to get out of there. Collect his thoughts. Work out what it all meant and discuss it with his psychiatrist.

Have I got a daughter? Is she waiting for me outside somewhere? Sick and frightened and all alone?

'Perhaps you'd better turn off the television. You'll never get to sleep, listening to horror stories like that.' At pains to conceal his bewilderment, Caspar made slowly for the door.

'Go on, the Soul Breaker will hardly target me.' Greta gave him a mischievous smile and put her badly nibbled reading glasses on the bedside table. 'I wouldn't fit his pattern, even without my Zimmer frame, would I? You heard it yourself: all his victims were between twenty and forty, slim, blond and single. All the things that might have been said of me fifty years ago.'

She laughed.

'Don't worry, my dear. Tonight I'll go to sleep to a nice, cuddly animal film. They're showing *Silence of the Lambs*...'

'That isn't a...' Caspar started to say, then saw from her expression that she was pulling his leg. 'Touché,' he said. He couldn't help smiling in spite of his mental confusion. 'That makes us quits.'

He reached for the door handle.

'Quits? How do you mean?' Greta called after him, looking puzzled.

'Well, you had me just then, but I've cracked your riddle.'

'Fibber. You haven't!'

'Yes, I have: the surgeon was a woman,' Caspar said with a smile. 'The surgeon at the hospital was the boy's *mother*. That's why she wouldn't operate on him.'

'Well, I never!' Greta giggled and clapped her hands again like a schoolgirl. 'How come you knew it?'

No idea, he thought, smiling uncertainly, and said goodnight.

His smile vanished the moment he shut the door behind him and emerged into the passage. He briefly wondered whether he could dart back inside before he was spotted by the two psychiatrists who had just emerged from his room looking angry. Then he heard his name mentioned and decided to follow them unobtrusively.

6:07 p.m.

Rassfeld and Sophia were so engrossed in their argument, they failed to notice Caspar even though he was only a few metres behind them.

'I think it's far too soon,' Rassfeld's hoarse voice was saying. 'It could be too traumatic.'

The medical director had come to a halt and was fumbling with the woollen scarf around his neck. As usual, his appearance was one big contradiction. He wore a thick scarf even in midsummer for fear of colds, but this didn't deter him from venturing forth in winter with his bare feet shod in leather sandals. He set store by well-tended fingernails and a neat parting but ignored his facial hair. His beard and moustache displayed the same tendency to run wild as the hairs that sprouted from his nose and ears. And, although he had gained his doctorate with a dissertation on pathological obesity, his office was littered with empty fast-food cartons as well as stacks of books and papers. Although nowhere near as corpulent as his major-domo, Dirk Bachmann, he had enough of a paunch to make Sophia look like an anorexic patient beside him.

'You mustn't show it to him!' he commanded. Taking her by the arm, he steered her down the passage and away from the room they'd just left.

'Under no circumstances, is that clear?' he insisted. 'I forbid it.'

33

Caspar tiptoed after them.

'I disagree,' Sophia whispered somewhat less vehemently. She held up a slim folder. 'He has a right to see this.'

The medical director came to an abrupt halt, and for a moment it looked as if he might turn round. Caspar swiftly kneeled and untied a shoelace. But then Rassfeld opened the door of the nurses' kitchenette and drew Sophia inside. The door remained ajar, and Caspar, kneeling in the passage outside, could see through the crack. Rassfeld was outside his range of vision.

'All right, I'm sorry, Sophia,' he heard the professor say. 'I apologise if I overreacted, but we really don't know how much damage this information could inflict on him.'

'Or what memories it could trigger.' Sophia was leaning on the work surface beside the sink. As devoid of make-up as usual, she looked more like a first-year medical student than a senior psychiatrist. Caspar wondered why he felt sufficiently attracted to Sophia to be spying on her like this. Nothing about her was perfect. Every aspect of her appearance seemed to suffer from some minor defect: eyes too big, skin too pale, ears a trifle too prominent, a nose that would never have featured in a cosmetic surgeon's brochure. Despite this, Caspar simply couldn't feast his eyes on her enough. Every therapy session disclosed some new detail that fascinated him. At this moment it was the lone lock of hair that formed an inverted question mark below her temple.

'You're too impatient, Sophia,' he heard Rassfeld say in a low voice. Caspar winced as he saw the medical director's age-freckled hand creep slowly towards hers. The professor doubtless intended his tone of voice to sound seductive as well as confidential. 'All in good time,' he said softly, 'all in good—'

Just as Rassfeld stroked Sophia's wrist with the back of a hairy forefinger, Caspar acted on instinct.

He jumped up, pushed the door open, and promptly shrank back into the passage with a look of simulated surprise.

'W–what are *you* doing here?' Rassfeld snapped. It had taken him only a instant to regain command of himself.

'I came to get myself a cup of coffee,' Caspar explained, indicating the stainless steel thermos jug beside Sophia.

'Didn't I forbid you to leave your room unsupervised?'

'Erm, yes. I must have forgotten.' Caspar clutched his head. 'Sorry, it's been happening a lot lately.'

'I see, so you find it funny, do you? What if you suffered a relapse and sneaked out of the clinic un-observed? Have you taken a look outside?'

Caspar followed the direction of Rassfeld's gesture. The kitchenette window was steamed up.

SEBASTIAN FITZEK

'The snowdrifts are two metres deep out there. Bachmann won't be able to rescue you a second time.'

To Caspar's surprise, Sophia took his side.

'It's my fault,' she said firmly. She picked up the folder and came out into the passage. 'I told him he could, Professor.'

Caspar tried to conceal his astonishment. Sophia had, in fact, said the opposite. He was always to inform a nurse, even if he wanted to go to the toilet.

'If that's so…' – Rassfeld took a linen handkerchief from his medical gown and angrily mopped his brow – '…I hereby revoke that decision.'

Brusquely, he pushed past them and strode off without another word. '*You haven't heard the last of this*' hung unspoken in the air.

Sophia's expression progressively relaxed the further away he got. When he finally turned the corner she heaved a sigh.

'Come on, we must hurry,' she said after a short pause.

'Why?' Caspar followed her along the passage to his room. 'We already had our session today.'

'Yes, but you've got a visitor.'

'Who is it?'

Sophia turned to face him.

'Someone who may know who you really are.'

Caspar tensed. He halted abruptly. 'Who is it?'

'You'll see.'

His heart was still pounding, though not as fast as before. 'Does Rassfeld know?'

She frowned in surprise and eyed him suspiciously. Her searching gaze reminded him of his first moments of consciousness in intensive care, when he woke up and found himself staring at the image of a stranger reflected in her forget-me-not-blue eyes. He had initially been distracted by the amber glints that lent them additional depth, like pebbles lying on the bed of a transparent sea.

'Who are you?' she had asked him in a warm voice which, for all its professional tone, conveyed concern.

That was his earliest memory. Since then he had lived exclusively in the present.

'I thought the professor didn't want you to confront me with the truth too soon?' he said.

Sophia eyed him intently with her head a little to one side.

'I do believe you forgot your coffee, Caspar,' she said at length, trying not to smile. When she failed she turned round again and opened the door of his room.

6:17 p.m.

'Well?'

He leant forwards in the comfortable armchair. Like the bed, the luxurious carpet and the brightly coloured curtains, it would have looked more at home in an English country house hotel than a patient's room in a mental hospital.

'Do you recognise him?'

Caspar wished it were so. He wished it so much that he almost lied and said yes, just so as to not be alone any more. Desperately, he tried to recall some experience he'd shared with his unusual visitor as he looked him in the eye – the right eye. The left one wasn't there. It had been gouged out in some way, if he interpreted the scar correctly.

Unlike him, the dog seemed in no doubt at all. The shaggy mongrel was panting fit to choke, it was so delighted to see him again.

Caspar sighed. 'He doesn't ring a bell,' he said, taking hold of the dog's big paw, which was resting on his knee. The ball of tousled, sandy fur was having the greatest trouble balancing on its hind legs, it was wagging its tail so hard.

'Really not?'

Sophia, standing immediately in front of him and holding his file in both hands, looked down enquiringly at him and the dog in turn. The top button of her blouse had come undone, and a coin-sized pendant on a silver chain was glinting in her cleavage.

'Really not,' Caspar repeated, trying not to stare at the mother-of-pearl amulet in case she misunderstood his gaze. He heaved another sigh.

She confronted him with new fragments of his past every day. They were anxious not to rush things, she said, in case they sent his thoughts off on the wrong track and got them bogged down there. He called it 'jigsaw puzzle therapy'. Piece after piece had been handed him, and he felt more and more of a failure because he couldn't fit them together into a coherent picture.

His dirty clothes were the first thing they showed him.

Next, the crumpled first-class railway ticket, Hamburg–Berlin return, dated 13 October last. The only form of documentary evidence in his otherwise empty briefcase. That and the bruise over his right eye, which had since gone down, indicated that he had been the victim of a mugging.

'Where was the dog found?' Caspar asked.

'In the driveway. You probably owe him your life. Bachmann enjoys racing around in the jeep when Rassfeld's not at home. If the animal hadn't got in his way, barking like mad, he certainly wouldn't have got out and might well have failed to see you. It was dark already, and you were lying on the verge.'

Sophia kneeled down and fondled the dog, which licked the ID tag on her medical gown.

'Where's he been these last few days?'

'Bachmann's been looking after him.' She laughed. 'He says he doesn't care if you recover your memory or not, he won't give Mr Ed up. You can take his wife home instead.'

'Mr Ed?'

She shrugged. 'There used to be a talking horse called that on TV. Bachmann thinks the dog has the same woebegone expression – and he's even smarter.' She got to her feet again. 'Doesn't Mr Ed arouse any emotions in you?'

'Sure, I think he's cute, but maybe I'm just an animal lover in general. I'm not sure.'

Sophia leafed through his patient's record.

'All right... How about this?'

When she held out the photo it felt as if she'd slapped his face. His cheeks burned and the whole right-hand side of his face suddenly went numb.

'Where did you...'

He blinked, but he couldn't prevent a little tear from trickling down his nose.

'Was it... I mean...' He broke off and sniffed.

Sophia anticipated his question. 'Yes,' she said, 'Bachmann didn't find it until this morning, when he was clearing away the snow. It must have fallen out of your pocket and we overlooked it at the time.'

She handed him the enlarged colour print.

'Well, do you recognise her?'

The photo trembled in his hands.

'Yes,' he whispered without looking up, 'unfortunately.'

'Who is she?'

'I... I'm not sure.' Caspar stroked the mole on the little girl's cheek with his fingertip.

'I don't know her name.' He raised his head and forced himself to look into Sophia's eyes.

'But I think she's somewhere out there, waiting for me.'

6:23 p.m.

Mr Ed put his head between his big paws and imitated a hearth rug by lying flat on his tummy. His cocked ears made him look like an attentive listener.

'Your daughter? Why didn't you tell me before?' Sophia demanded when he'd finished telling her about the mysterious vision that had haunted him in Greta's room.

The little girl. Her twitching eyelid. Her look of mute entreaty.

'It was the first time, and I'm far from sure whether it's a genuine memory, or... or just a nightmare.'

You'll come back soon, won't you?

Caspar rubbed his tired eyes.

'And she looked ill?' asked Sophia.

No, worse than that.

'Perhaps she was just asleep?' he said without much hope. 'Her movements were convulsive and un-coordinated, like those of someone dreaming. But...'

41

'But what?'

'I felt I should have held the girl tight and prevented her from floating up to the ceiling like a helium balloon, she looked so weightless. As if someone had removed what lent her weight and left behind a soulless husk. You follow?'

'You often say that,' said Sophia.

'What?'

'"You follow?" You often use that phrase when we're talking together. Your profession is probably one in which you have to explain complex matters to non-professionals, for instance as a teacher, consultant, lawyer or the like. But I didn't mean to interrupt you. Can you remember exactly what the girl was lying on?'

'A bed or a stretcher. Something of the kind.'

'What did the room look like?'

'Bright. There were two big windows and the sun was shining in.'

'Were you alone?'

'Hard to say. I didn't sense the presence of anyone who…'

Who what? Had tortured, raped or poisoned her?

'So it was just you and the girl?' asked Sophia.

'Yes. She was lying there in front of me, breathing irregularly. Her hair looked damp with sweat and her eyelids were fluttering.'

'The after-effects of an epileptic fit, perhaps?'

'Perhaps.'

Or poison, shock, torture...

'But she spoke to you?'

'No, there was no direct communication. I couldn't hear what she said, only sense it.'

'Telepathically?'

Caspar shook his head vigorously.

'I know what you're getting at. But it wasn't a dream with supersensible elements, unless you include parental love. I held my daughter's hand and sensed what she was trying to tell me.'

I'm so frightened. Please help me...

'I feel she's somewhere out there, captured by someone who has done something bad to her, and I ought to get help before her condition deteriorates any further.'

'Were there bars?' Sophia's question rather put him off his stroke.

'I'm sorry?'

'Bars? On the windows? You said the sun was shining in.'

Caspar shut his eyes and tried to recall the scene.

I'm so frightened. Please help me...

The bright room did not, in retrospect, strike him as a prison or a secure hiding place.

'Hard to say.' He shrugged.

'Well,' Sophia said quietly but firmly, 'whoever this girl is, Caspar, you shouldn't worry about her too much.'

'Why not?'

'We sent her photo to the detectives working on your

case. They say no one of her age or appearance has been reported missing.'

Sophia brushed the strand of hair resembling a question mark behind her ear. Caspar gave a mirthless laugh.

'What does that prove? No one has reported *me* missing, if the police are to be believed, but here I am. So you can't guarantee me that my daughter...' – he hesitated, searching for the right words – '...that this girl isn't in danger. I mean, I *promised* her I'd go back there.' He paused for a moment, then added more quietly: 'Wherever "there" may be.'

'Very well.' Sophia turned the folder over in her hands. 'In that case, we ought to go public after all.'

'The press, you mean?'

She nodded.

'Yes, even though Rassfeld will man the barricades. He didn't even want me to show you the girl's photo. Personally, I think it's high time.'

'I agree,' Caspar said without hesitation. In any case, he was finding this bit-by-bit technique and Rassfeld's clinical isolation increasingly suspect. To the professor he was a welcome guinea pig, for Sophia had told him that cases of total amnesia were very rare in practice. That was the only reason why he had been permitted to stay at this exclusive clinic at all. Rassfeld wanted his case to be scientifically documented. This allegedly entailed that the cognitive process take place within himself and not be manipulated by means of outside influences. Rassfeld had even banned an interview with the police for that reason.

'The reporters can come any time, as far as I'm concerned,' said Caspar, even though he realised that he would be transferred at once if his photo was splashed all over the newspapers. The prominent patients who retired to the Teufelsberg Clinic because of drug problems or manic depression attached great importance to anonymity and peaceful seclusion. Camera crews outside the main entrance didn't fit in with that.

'All right, I'll arrange it. One more thing, though…' Sophia avoided his eye.

'Yes?'

'I won't be able to be with you when the media circus starts. From tomorrow, Rassfeld will be looking after you himself.'

Caspar digested this for a moment. Then he smiled.

'But of course, I understand. Have a good Christmas, Sophia.'

She looked up and shook her head sadly.

'No, it's not because of the holiday. This is my last day here.'

'I see.'

'I'm leaving.'

'Oh.'

He suddenly felt like an imbecile incapable of string-ing a whole sentence together. So that was why she could afford to ignore the medical director's instructions. She was deserting him.

'May I ask why?'

'No, please don't,' she said, and squeezed his hand – which made it all much worse.

He realised only now that she was the real reason why he hadn't packed his things and set off on a solo quest for his identity. In the few sessions they'd had together, Sophia had become a sort of sheet anchor in the ocean of his consciousness. And now she was going to sever the anchor chain.

'Is it to do with Professor Rassfeld?' he asked, although he knew that by asking that question he was leaving their therapeutic relationship behind and entering private territory.

'No, no.'

She replaced the girl's photograph in her folder and sat down at a small desk beneath the dormer window.

'Right.' Having inserted her latest treatment notes in the folder, Sophia closed it with a faint sigh and stood up. Caspar sensed her uncertainty as she debated whether to say goodbye with a handshake or a hug. She plucked at her right forefinger in embarrassment, then stepped aside and stood looking down at his bedside table.

'But you must promise to go on using your eye drops regularly when I'm no longer here to check on you. You will, won't you?'

She picked up the little plastic bottle and shook it. Caspar wore contacts. When they found him the lenses were stuck to his eyeballs like discs of desiccated chewing gum – yet another indication, in addition to his hypothermia, that he must have been lying in the open for a considerable time.

'I don't think I need them any more,' he protested.

'Oh yes, it's the same with the ointments. You mustn't stop using them just because the itching has subsided.'

She patted the edge of the bed. Obediently, Caspar sat down beside her.

He preserved a discreet distance, but she moved nearer. Now it was his turn to avoid her gaze. He still hadn't got used to the sight of the stranger who had been reflected in her eyes since his rebirth a few days earlier.

'What do you think?' he asked while she was un-screwing the top of the eye drop bottle. 'Could she be my daughter? Does she resemble me at all?'

Sophia held her breath for a moment, then sighed.

'Hard to tell at that age.'

Caspar could sense what an effort she was making not to deprive him of his first memory and last hope.

'I don't know what to think,' she went on. 'Anyone would be happy to be the parent of such a sweet-looking child. As a mother, though, I find it heartbreaking that she may be waiting for her father to return at this very moment.'

He glanced at her left hand.

'As a *mother*?' He couldn't see any wedding ring. The only jewellery she wore was the mother-of-pearl charm on the thin chain around her slender neck.

'Well, let's say I applied for that job in my daughter's case and failed miserably.'

Caspar had more than once sensed the latent melancholy in her tone during their sessions, but never as clearly as he did now.

'I worked too hard and neglected Marie. That's why he found it so easy to take her away from me.'

So that's it, he thought. *That's why I feel there's a bond between us. We've something in common.*

'Who took her away from you?' he asked softly.

'My ex-husband. He managed to get sole custody.'

'How?' He bit his lip, but it was too late. His question was too stark, too insistent and demanding. It reminded her that he wasn't entitled to pry into her private life.

'He has his methods, let's say,' she said curtly, wiping her cheek on her sleeve. 'Damn it!' She cleared her throat. 'I've already said too much.'

He tried again. 'You're welcome to talk about it.'

She withdrew the pipette.

'No. Talking doesn't make mistakes any better, only action does. That's why I'm leaving: to get ready.'

'What do you have in mind?'

'I'm going to fight him. I've got an important date in court soon. Cross your fingers for me.'

'I will.' Caspar looked at her encouragingly. 'Besides,

who knows? I may turn out to be a attorney specialising in custody cases. Then I can repay you for your
excellent treatment.'

'Yes, who knows?' She gave a sad little laugh. 'But
now, please put your head back.'

He obeyed. The strand of hair behind her ear escaped
as she bent over him. Caspar hoped it would brush his
cheek as titillatingly as her faint perfume had been
caressing his nostrils.

We've never been so close before, he thought as she
gazed at him and the first drop formed at the end of the
pipette.

Just then Mr Ed scented danger. He uttered a yelp,
leaped over the bed and barked up at the open swivel
window. His instincts had alerted him before the sound
waves did. Now they, too, could hear it: a splintering
crash followed by a screech of metal. And then, for
one brief, terrible moment, it sounded to Caspar as if
something down in the driveway had been cut in half.
Something alive.

6:31 p.m.

He wondered briefly whether he ought to follow Sophia,
who had hurried out of the room with Mr Ed on a
lead. Something had happened outside. An accident,
presumably.

49

He went right up to the dormer window, but there was little to be seen from there. In daytime the top floor of the clinic afforded a breathtaking view of the wooded nature reserve that stretched away to the prosperous Berlin suburbs, but darkness and sleet had long ago swallowed up the wintry, concrete-grey afternoon. This made the unnatural light source seem even more ominous. Red and blue emergency lights were flashing at regular intervals amid the snow-laden conifers flanking the road that zigzagged up from the valley to the entrance of the Teufelsberg Clinic.

Caspar pushed the window wider open and put his head out. The snow was falling more heavily. Some distance away he could hear a monotonous hum. Then, four floors below him, the massive front door opened and two men came out into the cold.

'Did you see what happened?' he heard Rassfeld ask. Although the medical director was standing outside the faint glow escaping from the reception area, his hoarse voice was unmistakable.

'No, I was taking a break,' Bachmann replied, 'in the library. You know, I was returning that book on public speaking you recommended.'

Public speaking? Caspar was puzzled.

Bachmann was normally known for trying to cheer patients up with a repertoire of feeble jokes. In Rassfeld's presence he sounded like a nervous schoolboy who has turned up late for class without a letter of excuse from his parents.

'These damned flash-freezes,' the professor grumbled. 'Was anyone hurt?'

'Hard to say. The vehicle's lying slewed across the entrance. The CCTV cameras don't give a complete view of it.'

The wind blew a cloud of moist snowflakes into the room, completely obscuring Caspar's view.

'How the hell are we going to get down there?'

At that moment the window slammed shut with a loud bang.

Caspar swung round to see Linus standing in the doorway. His fellow patient was looking startled, bewildered and curious all at once, as if he had just discovered he could shut windows by telekinesis.

'It was only the wind,' Caspar told him reassuringly. 'What's happened?'

'Accibad,' Linus murmured softly. 'Overtip.' A permanent patient, the professional singer not only lived in a world of his own but communicated in a language of his own invention.

For years Linus had mistaken his head for a mixing bowl to be filled by way of his mouth or nose with an inexhaustible supply of pills, potions and powders. No one could say exactly which drug had eventually turned the blender to maximum revs, but after the paramedics had resuscitated him backstage after a concert he could no longer string words together in the correct order. Even the letters became jumbled.

'Fallenshit yessalam!' he exclaimed with a smile. Although Caspar had interpreted 'accibad' as 'bad accident', these neologisms defeated him.

Linus's grin seemed to denote that he welcomed the unexpected distraction. On the other hand, it was unwise to infer his state of mind from his facial expression. The last time Caspar had heard him laughing, he had just been handcuffed to his bed to prevent him from tearing out his hair and eating it in another of his psychotic fits.

'Shall we go and see?' Caspar asked. For a moment Linus looked as if he had never been so insulted in his life. Then he gave another laugh and scampered out of the room like an exuberant schoolboy. Caspar shrugged and set off after him.

6:39 p.m.

Linus had pinched the lift from under his nose, so he decided to go down the old-fashioned wooden stairs that spiralled around the lift shaft like a liana. The worn treads creaked at every step, and since Caspar was in his stockinged feet he felt like a youngster sneaking out of the parental home at night.

Did I do that once upon a time? Or was I a goody-goody who always came home punctually?

For days he had spent every spare minute scouring the cathedral-like void of his memory for answers to the most trivial questions. What was the name of his first cuddly toy? What make of car was in his garage? What was his favourite book? Was there a song he listened to on special occasions only? Who was his first love? His greatest enemy? He couldn't say. His memories were like pieces of furniture in an empty house whose previous owner had shrouded them in dust sheets. Until yesterday he'd tried to tear the dust sheets off. Today he was afraid they might be concealing some terrible truth.

I'm so frightened. Will you be back soon, Daddy?

Linus had disappeared by the time Caspar reached the ground floor, still engrossed in his depressing thoughts. Instead, he saw Yasmin Schiller coming towards him.

'Yes, yes, I will. Who else?' the young psychiatric nurse said irritably. She was evidently responding to some request by Rassfeld, who was standing a few metres away in Bachmann's office.

Yasmin's annoyance at being demoted yet again to errand-boy status was written all over her face, two-thirds of the lower half of which disappeared beneath a pale-blue balloon of bubble gum as she strode past Caspar without acknowledging his presence.

'*I'm only doing this temporarily – I'm really a singer,*

not a psycho-nanny,' she'd told him on his second day at the Teufelsberg, clearly relieved that he could pee without assistance. She certainly did seem quite out of place here, with her acrylic red fringe, thumb adorned with barbed-wire ring, and eternal ill temper, but Caspar had since gathered why Rassfeld permitted her within his elitist orbit despite her tongue stud and ink: Yasmin liked her job. She was good at it, too, but she didn't want anyone to register the fact.

On his way to the reception area, Caspar's feet sank into the thick pile of the carpet that covered the entire entrance hall. This floor covering made a homely, reassuring impression on new arrivals, quite unlike the antiseptic lino more commonly found in hospitals. The same went for the porter's office. Dirk Bachmann was a fan of Christmas. Although his marriage had so far been childless, he celebrated the family festival with an obsessive attention to detail, almost as if there were a prize to be won for the most elaborate decorations. His lair beside the main entrance, which was partly enclosed by glass, displayed such a clutter of Father Christmases, gilded angels, strings of coloured bulbs, Nativity figures and gingerbread houses that one almost failed to see the tinsel-festooned Christmas tree squeezed in between his metal desk and the safe.

'Professor?' Although Caspar spoke quietly so as not to startle him, the medical director gave a jump.

'You again?' There was something vaguely guilty

about Rassfeld's expression, but it swiftly evaporated. 'I thought I'd made myself clear. You should be in bed.'

So should you, thought Caspar, trying not to stare at the dark rings around the medical director's eyes.

'The others are very agitated,' he lied. In fact, the only patients in residence apart from himself were Greta and Linus. The old lady was watching the early-evening programme at full volume on her resuscitated television set. As for Linus, he appeared to have lost interest in the latest happenings. At all events, he was nowhere to be seen.

'What's going on out there?'

Rassfeld hesitated. Then, reluctantly, he jerked his head at the monitor. It seemed he hoped to get rid of Caspar the sooner by answering at least one of his questions.

'An ambulance skidded off the road outside the entrance to our drive. It crashed into a phone box and tipped over.'

Caspar glanced at the flickering screen. So those were the flashing lights he'd seen through the trees. The ambulance's blue light was still rotating on its roof.

If the entrance is covered by CCTV there ought to be a shot that shows how I got here, he thought, but decided this wasn't the time to question Rassfeld about it.

'Anything I can do to help?' he asked instead.

The clinic was understaffed tonight. Since there were

only three patients on the premises, all the medical staff except Sophia had taken the day off. The major influx of holiday depressives wasn't expected until tomorrow afternoon, when their last-minute fear of spending yet another lonely Christmas became an unendurable certainty.

'No thanks, we'll manage on our own.' Rassfeld contrived a sarcastic smile. 'Dr Dorn and Herr Bachmann have gone down there in the snowmobile.'

As if in confirmation, Sophia came into view on the CCTV screen, closely followed by the porter.

'It's the only way to get down the icy slope,' said Rassfeld, 'let alone up it.'

A radio beside the monitor crackled and Bachmann's voice made itself heard. 'I think the driver was on his own.'

Rassfeld took the flashing walkie-talkie from its holder. 'Is he injured?'

'Hard to tell.' That was Sophia. 'I suspect he's in shock. He's sitting down in the snow beside the wrecked phone box. One moment...'

Rassfeld's back was completely obscuring Caspar's view of the screen. 'Damn it,' said Sophia's crackly voice, 'there's someone inside. The ambulance was carrying a patient.'

Caspar stood on tiptoe.

The vehicle's frosted glass side window had been smashed. If his eyes hadn't deceived him, he'd just seen a bloodstained hand emerge from it and wave in a helpless sort of way.

Startled, Rassfeld recoiled a step.

'Bring them both up here,' he said into the walkie-talkie.

'Hm, I don't know,' said Sophia. 'Wouldn't it be better to—'

'Better to what?' barked Rassfeld. 'Send for a helicopter? Call the fire brigade? The ambulance wrecked the phone box, you know that as well as I do.'

And mobile phones don't work in the clinic or the grounds.

Caspar's mouth went dry. He gave a sudden, involuntary cough as if he'd choked on the thought. This was one of the last remaining areas without mobile phone coverage – a topographical advantage in Rassfeld's eyes, given that one important aspect of his psychiatric treatment consisted in shielding patients from negative outside influences.

The radio started flashing again.

'Dirk has prised the doors open and I'm now with the patient. Oh no! Good God!'

'What? What is it?' Rassfeld peered at the monitor, trying to make out what was going on.

'Sorry, but the patient has a knife stuck in his throat.'

'Is he dead?'

'No, the windpipe has been punctured but he's conscious and breathing steadily. But…'

'But what?' Rassfeld demanded, utterly unnerved. He gestured brusquely to Caspar to clear off.

'You'll never believe who it is.'

6:56 p.m.

Yasmin, who had returned, was curtly instructed by Rassfeld to escort Caspar back to his room, where a supper tray was already waiting on his desk. The cook, Sibylle Patzwalk, had as usual devoted almost more care to the appearance of his meal than to the meal itself. The solid silver cutlery was flanked by a linen napkin deftly folded into the shape of a swan, the bowl of soup was adorned with sprigs of parsley, and a white orchid reposed beside the cut-glass tumbler. As Caspar removed the cloth from the bread basket, hunger smote him like a watchdog taking scent. He hadn't eaten a thing for hours.

He had only just put a morsel of bread in his mouth when he heard a mechanical hum outside the window. It sounded like a ride-on mower, and its swelling roar drowned the rumbling of his stomach. He replaced the baguette in the basket and went over to the dormer window. The dense snowflakes were already building up on its lower edge and would soon obscure the pane altogether. He could hardly make out the snowmobile in which Sophia and Bachmann were transporting the accident victims to the clinic.

He opened the window a crack. The cold that hit him was so intense, he was half afraid the tears in his eyes would freeze. *What on earth am I doing here?* he wondered. His breath, which was escaping from his lips like tobacco smoke, reminded him of the smoke he thought he'd smelled in Greta's room when the vision of the sick girl had suddenly imposed itself on his mind's eye.

You will come back soon, won't you?

Caspar pulled the swivel window shut. Back in the middle of the room, he turned on the spot, sensing that his inner disquiet was reaching fever pitch. This told him something about himself that was almost more important than a distinct recollection: that it wasn't in his nature to stand around idly. That realisation was more significant than the many little personal characteristics he'd discovered in the last few days. For instance, that he wore his watch on his right wrist, that he salted his food as a matter of course, even before tasting it, or that he found it hard to read his own handwriting.

The fact that everything within him cried out to leave this clinic at once must also mean that he was prone to self-delusion. He had chosen to wait for a therapeutic miracle instead of taking things in hand himself. The truth was, he had hidden himself away, not in this clinic, but in a place where no one could find him: inside himself.

He opened his wardrobe. Only four of the eight hangers were in use, and only because he'd hung up the jacket and trousers of his suit separately. He wouldn't have to take much luggage with him if he decamped tonight.

Caspar sighed as he spread out his few possessions on the bed. Most of them had been either borrowed from the clinic or bought for him in town by Sophia so that he at least had a change of clothes: half a dozen pairs of socks and pants, two pairs of pyjamas, a tracksuit and some slippers, toilet articles, and a historical novel which he really ought to return to the clinic's library.

My life fits into a plastic bag, he reflected when he'd stowed away everything he didn't intend to wear. Not possessing a rucksack or other form of luggage, he had to use the sturdy plastic bag that lined his rubbish bin.

Then he put on the dark suit he'd been wearing the day he arrived. His fur-lined overcoat he draped over the arm carrying the plastic bag. In his other hand he carried his heavy lace-up boots. He wouldn't put those on until he'd negotiated the wooden stairs.

Right, that's it.

Caspar refrained from taking a last look round his cosy room. He turned off the light and padded out into the silent passage, intending never to return.

He crept slowly down the stairs, relieved that the clinic was so understaffed tonight that he was unlikely to bump into anyone. When he got to the first floor, however, it was brought home to him that he couldn't have picked a worse time to try to cross the reception area and make his exit unobserved. He leant over the banister. From below came the sound of a loud voice he didn't recognise – evidently that of the paramedic who had been driving the ambulance. Contrary to Sophia's initial assumption, the man certainly wasn't in shock; he was speaking far too articulately.

'Jonathan Bruck, age forty-seven, height one metre eighty-five, weight around ninety kilos.' He reeled off these particulars in a pleasant baritone that would have sounded as unremarkable as a newsreader's, had it not been for the puzzling noises that accompanied them, which reminded Caspar of an espresso machine frothing milk.

'Probably under the influence of alcohol or drugs. The proprietor of the Teufelssee Motel summoned an ambulance after one of his cleaners found Bruck unconscious in his room.'

Caspar heard the rattle of a metal gurney whose wheels were probably leaving ruts in the cream fitted carpet, and the significance of the bubbling sound suddenly dawned on him: it was issuing from the patient's throat.

'And the tracheotomy?' Rassfeld asked as if in confirmation.

'Self-mutilation. I thought he was unconscious, you see. It was my last trip of the night – all I wanted was to get him to Westend Hospital as quickly as possible. But then, just as we were passing the entrance to your private road, I glanced in the rear-view mirror and thought my eyes were playing tricks on me. This lunatic got to his feet, let out a yell, and drove the pocket knife into his throat. I slammed on my anchors and skidded into that transformer box, or whatever it was. The rest you know.'

Rassfeld and the paramedic had wheeled the gurney over to the lift during this recital and were now standing immediately below Caspar. He was so close to them he could distinctly hear Bruck's breathing, which was now reminiscent of someone sucking up coffee dregs through a straw.

'I would ask you not to refer to the patient as a *lunatic*,' said Rassfeld, sounding as if he'd been personally insulted.

Caspar gave a start. He had glimpsed a movement in his immediate vicinity.

Then he realised it was just a reflection in the big picture window in the outer wall a few steps below him. The storm outside had taken only a few minutes to develop into a regular blizzard. The feeble rays of the garden lights in the hospital grounds were no match for the coin-sized snowflakes. Their glow bounced off the swirling flurries, briefly and unpleasantly putting Caspar in mind of a swarm of white bees coagulating into a solid mass before his eyes. And then, as he concentrated on the reflection in the window pane, he caught a momentary glimpse of a weird group picture: two thickset men flanking a trolley on which lay a motionless figure with a Swiss pocket knife protruding from its throat. The lift doors opened with an indignant squeak and the image vanished as swiftly as the smell invaded Caspar's nostrils. A smell of fire. Of burning. Of smoke.

Will it herald another memory?

Instinctively, he shrank away from the lift shaft as if the memory might ascend inside the cabin and leap out at him unexpectedly. He shivered, then uttered an involuntary cry as he backed into the gaunt figure that had been secretly watching him from the shadows all the time.

7:10 p.m.

The man was chewing gum and wearing thin leather gloves, but his freshly washed hair gave him away. Nor did it help that he must have smoked his cigarette by an open window. The tobacco smoke had lodged in his few remaining hairs, and when he shook his head he scented the air around him with its rather stale residue.

'It's all right, I won't tell on you.'

A strict smoking ban was in force throughout the clinic, and it was ironic that Linus had chosen to light up on the floor devoted to physical fitness.

So it didn't herald another memory...

'Cummussi showthing!' The corners of Linus's mouth twitched. He sounded more scared than a simple breach of the rules would have warranted. He flapped his hands uneasily as though trying out sign language – not a bad idea, thought Caspar, in view of his limited ability to communicate.

'What's the matter?' he asked.

In lieu of a reply, Linus grabbed the hand that was carrying the plastic bag and towed Caspar behind him. He opened the door facing them, which bore a sign inscribed 'Fitness Centre'. In any other establishment it would simply have been called the gym.

Caspar hadn't been inside there before, so he was rather surprised to see all the modern high-tech equipment distributed around the mirror-lined sports hall. His eyes roamed over the treadmills, rowing machines and press benches, and he was just speculating on the purpose of the rubber Stepmaster flashing away in the corner when Linus put a finger to his lips and turned out the lights, then opened a glass door leading to a small balcony. It seemed suddenly to become lighter, but this was an optical illusion created by the snowflakes whirling around their legs and the flashing lights of the electronic gym equipment.

Okay, so this was where you had a quick drag, thought Caspar. He paused on the threshold, but Linus gave his arm another tug. He obviously wanted Caspar to follow him out onto the balcony, whose timber floor was covered with frozen mush.

'Hey, see these?' Caspar pointed to his feet and shook his head. 'I'm not going out there with no shoes on.'

'Cummussi showthing,' Linus hissed, more nervously and impatiently this time. He backed out onto the balcony and gave Caspar a nod. A moment later he disappeared into the darkness.

'Come back,' Caspar called. *You'll catch your death.* He shivered at the thought before he could articulate it.

What now?

He had no time to lose. Right now, Rassfeld and the rest of the staff would have their hands full with the new arrival. An ideal moment to sneak out of the clinic unobserved. On the other hand, he suddenly thought he'd interpreted Linus's gibberish.

Cummussi showthing: Come with me, I must show you something.

Damn it. If he didn't comply, Linus might come running after him, shouting, and he could dispense with that form of attention.

He slipped his feet into his boots and pulled on his overcoat. The steel roller shutters over the windows and doors had been lowered almost a third and he was two heads taller than Linus, so he had to bend double in order to follow him outside. The icy wind buffeted him like an invisible doorman trying to repel an unauthorised intruder into his glacial domain. Caspar bent even lower, hugging his chest. A projecting wall on his left provided some shelter from the driving snow, but not from the Siberian temperature. Linus, who was also standing in its lee, put a finger to his lips again.

'Lookitair,' he whispered, pointing to the red snowmobile parked at an angle outside the entrance. Most of the vehicle was beneath the reception area's sheltering canopy. Only the tapering snout protruded into the snow-covered driveway. It was still warm, so the snowflakes were melting as soon as they landed.

'Well, what about it?' Caspar leant forwards, but he could see even less because he was more exposed to the wind. The snow blew straight into his eyes. Blinking, he ducked his head and cursed himself for being such a fool. Instead of sneaking past Bachmann and out of the clinic, he was standing beside a psychotic patient on a dark, icy balcony.

Just as he was about to beat a retreat, the wind veered and restored his vision. All at once he spotted it.

A patch in the snow. It originated immediately beside

the rear of the snowmobile's right-hand track and was spreading in the direction of the entrance. In the faint light issuing from the porter's lodge it looked like a puddle of golden-yellow urine, but Caspar knew at once what it really was.

Petrol.

Either the tank's fuel hose had become detached by itself, or someone had given it a helping hand.

But why? Why should anyone have immobilised the only means of transport capable of battling its way through this blizzard?

He was about to ask Linus if he knew who had been tampering with the vehicle when the musician yanked him back into the lee of the wall. Just in time, or Bachmann might have looked up and seen them as he emerged from behind the snowmobile.

7:18 p.m.

Caspar had really returned to his room only to wait until the porter left the reception area and set off on his rounds, but tonight nothing seemed to be following its usual pattern. He realised that his escape, if it merited that description at all, was becoming more and more difficult. He was stuck up here, cut off from every form of telecommunication, and now, for some unknown reason, the porter appeared to have sabotaged the vehicle he'd intended to borrow for his descent through the blizzard. Never mind. He would make it down the hill even so, if need be, sitting on his plastic bag.

He wouldn't spend another night here under any circumstances, and not just because he was haunted by the possibility that he'd abandoned a daughter who urgently needed his help. He also sensed that the mysterious newcomer had been accompanied into the clinic by something he would be well advised to avoid: a threat as invisible as a virus. It was spreading, disrupting the little hospital's well-established early-evening routine, and he now discovered that it even seemed to have found its way into his room.

What's going on here?

The closer he got to the door, the slower he went. It was open, and the light was on although he'd turned it off only a few minutes earlier.

What on earth…?

The sound of two raised voices was spilling out into the passage. One of them belonged to Sophia, who took the words out of his mouth by asking: 'What are you up to?' He was equally mystified by the sight that met his eyes when he reached the door of his room. Why was a young man in muddy boots standing on his desk with one hand extended towards the window?

'I think I got one just then,' he said with a laugh.

Caspar recognised him as the paramedic by his voice, which didn't go with his outward appearance. Somehow, he had entertained a different picture of the ambulance driver. More of a rough diamond, with eyes tired and puffy from responding to emergency calls at night. Instead, he was confronted by an archetypal yuppy who would have looked more at home behind the wheel of a flashy sports car than that of an ambulance.

'One what?' asked Sophia.

'One bar on the display.' The paramedic jumped down from the desk and showed her a minuscule mobile phone. 'I thought I might get a signal up here on the top floor. Sorry.' He treated Caspar to a buddy-buddy smile, but his eyes strayed back to Sophia at once. 'The door was open. I was checking to see if I could get a signal, that's all.'

Sophia almost inaudibly clicked her tongue and brushed some mud off the desktop with an air of disapproval.

'Mobile phones won't work anywhere in the grounds, no matter what contortions you get into.' Sophia's body language betrayed what she thought of the paramedic.

Caspar, too, eyed him like a prospective opponent in the boxing ring, even though he looked quite innocuous with his slim build, beardless chin and flue-brush hair, which was gelled in front. He wouldn't normally have given the youngster a second thought, but he disliked the flirtatious way he kept looking at Sophia.

'Please go downstairs and get Herr Bachmann to show you your room,' she said.

The young man smiled. 'You really want me to spend the night with you, doctor?'

Sophia almost imperceptibly rolled her eyes. 'Want doesn't come into it, Herr Schadeck. You're stuck here, unfortunately.'

To Caspar's pleasure she ignored the paramedic's request to call him Tom.

'Won't your dispatcher send someone to look for the ambulance if you fail to report back tonight?'

'Not a chance.' Schadeck shook his head. 'This was my last trip – I was to take the bus home after delivering the patient. Headquarters don't expect me back till lunchtime tomorrow.'

Sophia shrugged her shoulders. 'Well, be that as it may, it seems pointless to try to fight your way through a blizzard in the dark on your own. According to the weather forecast, conditions will have improved by tomorrow morning and the roads will soon be cleared and salted. We can all go down together when daylight comes.'

Down, thought Caspar, dumping the plastic bag beside his bed.

On Sophia's lips the word sounded as if they were on the summit of a towering, vertiginous cliff with the waves of a dark and mighty ocean breaking against its foot.

'So you aren't joking? Do I really have to spend the night in this...' It was obvious how hard he found it to swallow the words on the tip of his tongue. The 'loony bin' remained unspoken.

'You don't *have* to do anything,' Sophia retorted. 'We're less than half an hour's walk from the nearest house. You can always try, but I reckon you'd have to wade there through waist-deep snow. The temperature is seven below and falling.'

'And if something happens?'

'Meaning what?'

'What if Bruck's condition deteriorates? How do we get help?'

Schadeck's question sounded plausible enough, but Caspar guessed he was getting at something else.

'Don't worry, we're well equipped here,' Sophia replied. 'The knife didn't inflict any life-threatening injury, from the look of it, just damaged his vocal cords at most. The professor is dealing with the wound at this moment, and Dr Bruck will be medicated to prevent his windpipe from becoming occluded. He'll be in pain when he recovers consciousness, and he'll probably be unable to speak, but he'll survive.'

Dr Bruck?

'And now, if you wouldn't mind…' Sophia jerked her head at the door.

Schadeck smiled as if she'd asked him out on a date. 'By all means,' he said, giving her a mock salute. 'But I may at least borrow your snowmobile and see if I can get to my radio.'

'The best of luck,' said Caspar. He was going to mention the pool of petrol Linus had just shown him, but the moment passed.

Sophia, who was following Schadeck out, squeezed Caspar's hand as she passed him.

'Sorry about the intrusion,' she whispered with a rueful smile.

His melancholy mood vanished, but only for an instant. It returned abruptly when Schadeck paused in the doorway.

'Or maybe I could move in with you, doctor? I'm scared of being on my own in the dark.' He laughed and raised both hands in surrender. 'Hey, only joking.'

Caspar was about to make some suitable retort when his eye was caught by some scars on the inside of Schadeck's wrist. They resembled the burns on his own upper body, except that, unlike those random disfigurements of the skin, they formed a geometrical pattern.

He wasn't sure, but it looked as if Tom Schadeck had had a swastika tattoo burned off in a rather amateurish fashion.

7:24 p.m.

He had been on his own for only a minute when Sophia put her head round the door.

'The same applies to you, by the way.'

'What do you mean?' he asked, shoving the plastic bag under the bed with his foot. Too late. She came in.

'Please don't do anything stupid tonight,' she said, pointing to his boots and his overcoat, which he'd forgotten to replace in the wardrobe.

He didn't even try to deny his intentions. 'I've got to, Sophia. I've already been here too long.'

'Where would you go? In a lounge suit? In this weather? Without any money?'

'I'll go to the police,' he said. It was a plan he'd only just thought of. Foresight wasn't one of his most conspicuous characteristics, he had to admit.

'But we discussed that earlier. Rassfeld has agreed to your speaking to the police and the press.'

'Yes, but when?' Caspar got up off the bed, scratching the scars beneath his T-shirt. 'Tomorrow? The day after? After the holiday? It's all taking far too long. I may not have that much time to spare.'

Sophia shook her head so vigorously, a lock of hair fell over her eyes. She brushed it aside.

'Look, I'm not in favour of Rassfeld's delaying tactics either, but I share his opinion in one respect: in your present condition, it's still far too dangerous for you to leave the clinic unsupervised.'

'Perhaps, but I can't afford to think of myself alone.'

'You're talking about the girl?'

Caspar nodded. 'I'm sorry, but ever since I had that

vision of her I've felt I'm stifling in here. I simply have to go at once.'

'But we've no idea if she really is your daughter. She may not even exist.'

'Perhaps, but...' He wondered briefly if his next words would overstep the mark. 'But if you're leaving tomorrow I'll be on my own anyway. I won't have anyone to confide in.'

Sophia gave him a long look. Then she smiled sadly.

The telephone in the pocket of her gown rang, but she ignored it. Evidently, the internal phones were was still working.

'I understand,' she said, when it had stopped ringing. 'For all that, Caspar, I'd like to ask you a favour.'

'Yes?'

'Sleep on it for one night. We'll have another word together before I leave.'

'What good will that do?'

'Tomorrow morning, if you're still absolutely set on going, I won't try to dissuade you.'

'But...?'

'I'll give you some information first. You mustn't leave the clinic without it under any circumstances, least of all if you're going to the police.'

Caspar opened his mouth to speak but failed. His head was filled with a sudden whistling sound, as if a tiny blood vessel had burst inside his ear. He felt utterly helpless, like a patient who has just been told he hasn't long to live.

'What sort of information?' he whispered.

She shook her head, then looked at the telephone, which was ringing again.

'Tomorrow morning, Caspar. Not now.'

The whistling in his ear grew louder, as did his voice.

'I want to know now!'

'I realise that, but I can't tell you.'

'Why not?'

'I have to make sure first.'

'Of what?' demanded a voice from the doorway.

They both gave a start. The ringing of the phone had drowned Rassfeld's footsteps.

'What do you have to make sure of?' the medical director asked suspiciously, holding out a cordless phone and disconnecting it. Caspar swallowed hard, but Sophia seemed to have recovered her composure.

'The patient was asking for a barbiturate, but I said I'd have to check with you first.'

Rassfeld nodded, evidently satisfied that his authority wasn't being undermined.

'Good, but that can wait, Frau Dorn,' he said in a voice that brooked no contradiction, and led the way out into the passage.

'I've been trying to reach you for some time,' Caspar heard him say. 'You're needed in theatre.'

* * *

Long after Sophia had followed Rassfeld out, leaving Caspar alone with his nagging uncertainties, her mysterious promise continued to ring in his ears: *'I'll give you some information. You mustn't leave the clinic without it under any circumstances.'*

Her voice was still as insistent two hours later, when he lay down on the bed and shut his eyes, trying to sort out his thoughts. What could be in his file that Rassfeld was so reluctant to divulge?

'I have to make sure first.'

He was about to get up and go and look for Sophia when he found he couldn't open his eyes.

He made a final effort, straining all his willpower, but it was no use. The events of the day had proved too much for his already overwrought mind. He had fallen asleep.

CHRISTMAS EVE

Three hours and twelve minutes before The Fear

12:26 a.m.

The smoke was a living creature, a swarm of microscopically small cells that permeated his skin and corroded him from within.

The particles concentrated their attack on his lungs, finding their way down his windpipe and into his bronchial tubes. He coughed.

That was usually the moment when he awoke from this nightmare – a nightmare in which his memories encompassed only the last ten days – but tonight he slept on as if the burning car in which he was trapped would not release him. Not tonight.

Not before he had cast a glance at the photograph lying on the passenger seat. The heat was already so unbearable that the edges were curling upwards, making it even harder to recognise the man's face.

Restlessly, Caspar lashed out with his legs. He was in the unpleasant state of suspension between sleeping and waking, in which consciousness makes only a sluggish return to reality. He strove to hasten that transformation and cast off the shackles of the nightmare.

That was why he unbuckled his seat belt. Immediately in front of him, flames were darting out of the dashboard at chest height and beginning to lick at his shirt. His mind's eye caught a momentary glimpse of Schadeck's scarred wrist as he thrust his hand into the blaze, hoping that the imaginary pain would finally wrest him from the clinging embrace of sleep.

In the end, however, it was actual pressure – violent shaking – that woke him.

He opened his eyes. The burning car had disappeared, to be replaced by Linus's anxious face and staring eyes. He was bending over him, so close that Caspar could have put out his tongue and licked the little singer's nose.

'Phosia!' he said. It was little more than a croak – the sort of sound someone makes when they whisper but would really like to shout.

'Not again.' Caspar yawned wearily. Linus, who suffered from insomnia, tended to roam the passages at night when he couldn't sleep.

'Phosiapatikil.' Linus was now tugging at his arm and trying to haul him out of bed. The fact that he was half naked, dressed only in stained pyjama trousers

78

that were almost slipping off his skinny hips, made the situation even more absurd.

'Look, you can't just...' Caspar broke off. He had heard it too: a muffled crash from the floor below, as if someone had lifted the end of a heavy table and then let go. The sound was repeated. Caspar looked at his watch. Twenty-seven minutes past midnight. Hardly an appropriate time to move furniture.

'What's going on down there?' he asked, wondering who or what was on the floor below.

'Phosialp... phosialp...' Linus repeated the word several times, but he let go of Caspar's arm when he saw him extricate himself from his crumpled bedclothes and stand up.

'Cumpliss!'

'Yes, yes, I'm coming.'

Caspar looked for his slippers. The crashes below him gave way to a dull, scuffing sound like someone laboriously dragging a wet carpet from one room to another, so he decided to waste no more time. Unlike Linus, who went thundering down the stairs, Caspar tried not to make too much noise in case there was an innocuous explanation for these nocturnal sounds – not that he himself believed this after the events of the last few hours, especially as Linus's original wake-up call flashed through his mind just as he reached the landing.

Phosialp!

He pounded down the stairs himself. *Sophia... help...*

Turning the corner into a gloomy passage, he wondered why the sensors weren't working. The ceiling lights normally came on automatically if someone walked along it, but now the only light came from one of the rooms at the far end. Linus was standing outside the open door with both hands clasped above his head, trembling violently.

And then, just as he felt the bitter cold seeping out into the passage, he interpreted the rest of Linus's cryptic gibberish:

Phosialp. Patikil... Patient. Kill.

He peered into the room. Of course! The third floor, which Linus thought was vacant tonight, was where the 'difficult' cases were housed. Intensive medical care. Lockable rooms with hydraulic beds and electronic gauges beside them.

Sophia. Help. Patient. Kill.

Caspar shivered when he saw the tube dangling unattached from the drip stand positioned beside the empty bed like a dumb waiter. He was aware of his breath steaming. And then everything seemed to go into slow motion. He now felt like an uninvolved but interested observer examining a photo album, each page of which had to be turned before his eyes could transmit yet another frightful image to his brain:

The open window... the man with one foot on the radiator, the other leg already outside... Linus trying

to push past... the man, his face contorted into an
agonised grin... turning once more... pointing to the
bandage around his throat... shaking his head... and
leaping into the void.

Just as the escaping patient was engulfed by snow-laden darkness, everything sped up again and the first palpable recollection lodged in Caspar's defective network of memories. He recognised the man who had just jumped out of the window. His face was as familiar as the smell of burned paper that was once more filling his nose. He had often seen Jonathan Bruck in the past – most recently just before Linus shook him awake. His face appeared in that ever-recurrent nightmare of the blazing car, clearly visible in the scorched photo on the passenger seat beside him.

'What's going on here?' he demanded. Linus was leaning out over the window sill, shivering with either cold or fear, Caspar wasn't sure which.

'Phosiapatikil,' came the repetitive reply, but Caspar couldn't see Sophia anywhere. What about Sophia? He could understand neither Linus nor himself. How did he come to know Bruck? Why was the man now fleeing into the blizzard dressed only in a thin hospital gown? And why was Linus running out of the room with mortal terror in his eyes?

It was several seconds before he heard the reason. He couldn't say, afterwards, whether the bathroom tap had been running all the time, but it was only now that he became aware of the muffled, irregular gushing of water in the room next door.

12:34 a.m.

She looked lovely despite everything. For one brief moment Caspar felt he was gazing at an inanimate statue exhibited in the little bathroom by some untalented and patently demented sculptor.

Although her face was set in an expressionless mask and her right leg twitched uncontrollably as she lay in the bathtub, he was alive to Sophia's beauty. That was just what rendered the sight of her torment so unbearable.

'Sophia?' he said, far too quietly. His hoarse voice was washed away by the gushing water. She seemed unaware both of him and of the icy puddle that had formed beneath her limbs.

'What's the matter with you?' He was almost shouting now, but she didn't even blink. Her head merely flopped sideways at a precarious angle and her eyes seemed fixed on some imaginary point far beyond the tiled surface of the bathroom wall. Her nipples were visible beneath the sodden white nightdress that clung to the upper part of her body, which had ridden up to reveal that the pubic area was inadequately covered by a torn pair of panties.

'Can you hear me?' Caspar asked. He might have

been trying to communicate with a corpse. There was no blood to be seen, nor could he detect any obvious injuries. She was still breathing, yet she looked dead. Not even the fact that her foot collided at irregular intervals with the bathtub's enamel side was a reliable sign of life. It was reminiscent of the last, reflex twitchings of a crash victim when the neural tracts between the brain and the spinal cord have already been severed.

A terrible thought flashed through his mind when he grasped the parallels between his memory of the little girl and this grisly scene in the bathroom.

You will come back soon, won't you?

Yes, don't worry.

All at once he thought of a title for the horrific vision which the psychotic artist had exhibited here: *Buried Alive.*

That was just what she was: walled up and left to die inside herself.

He put out his hand to touch her hair, which had brushed against him so gently only a few hours earlier, and which now clung to her pale throat like blond seaweed. Then he pulled himself together. He'd already spent far too long in shock.

'I'm going for help,' he whispered. He was just turning away when it happened: life shot back into Sophia's body. It was even more terrible than her previous inertia. Her entire frame vibrated like a tuning fork. Caspar instinctively recoiled as she raised her right arm with a jerk. At first he thought she was trying to show him something.

I have to make sure first.

He turned to look at the open bathroom door, but there was nothing to be seen.

Then his eye fell on her left arm, which was draped almost voluptuously over the edge of the bath. Her knuckles, he saw, were white as snow. She seemed to be trying to squeeze the blood from her fist, her slender fingers were so tightly clenched.

'What have you got there?' He was about to ask that question when another tremor ran through her body. Her fingers uncurled little by little, as if in slow motion, until the mysterious object she was clutching finally fell to the floor.

Before Caspar could verify his alarming suspicion, someone grabbed his shoulders from behind, swung him around, and pinned him face down on the tiled floor.

12:36 a.m.

'What's going on here?' he heard Rassfeld ask. The medical director's white health shoes strayed into his restricted field of vision.

'No idea what he's done to her,' replied Bachmann, whose weight on his back felt like a ton of bricks.

'Absolutely nothing,' he tried to say, but there wasn't enough air in his lungs.

'Good God! Frau Dorn?' He heard Rassfeld click his fingers and someone turned the tap off. The sudden silence was so complete, he could hear the hum of the halogen lights overhead.

'Suspected stroke. Yasmin, get the scanner ready,' Rassfeld ordained with professional composure. 'I'll also need a blood count.'

Somewhere behind him Caspar heard the receding squeak of Yasmin's rubber-soled shoes hurrying off. He felt a sharp pain between the shoulder blades as Bachmann hauled him to his feet and applied a headlock. Although the porter's massive forearm was clamped across his face, he desperately tried to establish visual contact with Rassfeld, who was now kneeling beside the bath at the spot where himself had been standing a minute earlier. The medical director was shining a penlight in Sophia's eyes.

'Pupillary reflexes present,' he muttered. 'But... What the devil...?'

He shook his head and turned to Caspar without removing his left hand from Sophia's carotid.

'What did you give her?'

'Nothing,' he gasped. Bachmann relaxed his grip, enabling him to take a couple of whistling breaths. 'It was Bruck,' he said eventually.

'Bruck?'

'His bed is empty,' the porter confirmed.

'He jumped out of the window.'

Rassfeld stood up, his eyes narrowed to slits. He must have given Bachmann an invisible sign, because Caspar was now hauled backwards out of the bathroom. At the same time, a shadowy figure smelling of aftershave pushed past him.

'What do *you* want?'

'I came to help,' Caspar heard the figure reply.

Tom Schadeck's image swam into view like a slide in an old-fashioned slide show.

It was clear that the entire clinic had now been roused by the commotion. Rassfeld did not seem averse to accepting the paramedic's help. A sound of splashing came from the bathroom, and Caspar felt sick at the very thought of the two men trying to lift Sophia's limp, wet body out of the tub.

'Look, we're wasting precious time,' he told Bachmann. The porter had allowed his captive to sit down on the vacated bed, probably because this left him free to push the wheelchair standing beside it over to the bathroom door.

'We may be able to catch him if we're quick.'

'Who?' Bachmann scratched his head. Unlike his body language, which had been extremely forceful hitherto, his expression was rather apprehensive.

'Bruck, of course.' Caspar jerked his head at the open

window. The porter shut it, shivering, but the room seemed suddenly colder, perhaps because of the sight that now met their eyes. The bedraggled bundle of flesh and bone which Rassfeld and the paramedic were just heaving into the wheelchair looked more like a dummy than a human being.

'Come on, come on, down to the basement,' said Rassfeld, and Schadeck set off with an almost bored expression. He might have been pushing a supermarket trolley, not a patient.

Rassfeld followed him, then paused in the doorway as if he'd forgotten something.

'Bruck?' he said incredulously.

'Yes.'

Rassfeld came back into the room and stood over Caspar. His furrowed brow was beaded with droplets, either bathwater or sweat.

'Linus can confirm that,' Caspar said, realising even as he spoke how absurd he must sound. It was like citing a blind man as an eyewitness.

Rassfeld expelled a deep breath. 'All right, now listen. I could detect no external injuries, but Frau Dorn appears to be severely traumatised. I don't want to waste time on unnecessary enquiries, so if you know anything – if you saw anything – you must tell me at once, or—'

'No, I didn't see anything.' Rassfeld was already on

the point of hurrying off to radiology, so Caspar blurted out the next words fast: 'But I *found* something.'

He opened his hand and showed Rassfeld the object he'd picked up just before Bachmann overpowered him.

'I don't know if it's important, but Dr Dorn was holding this in her hand.'

'Oh no, please not...' Rassfeld stepped forwards and took the little slip of paper – gingerly, as if it might burn him.

It looked entirely innocuous, like one of those missiles schoolchildren fire across a classroom with the aid of a rubber band. The medical director's hands started to tremble as he deftly opened the little piece of paper, which had been folded twice in half.

'"It's the truth, although the name is a lie,"' he read in a whisper. Then he tilted his head back and looked up at the ceiling with his eyes shut. That was when the full horror of the situation dawned on Caspar. It might have been Bachmann's headlock that had extruded the memory. It might also have been the mysterious sentence Rassfeld had just read out, which reminded him not only of Greta Kaminsky's love of riddles but also of the newsreader's voice:

'*One clue may be supplied by the little slips of paper found in the hands of all three victims, although the police are saying nothing about what was written on them...*'

'The Soul Breaker,' said Rassfeld, articulating the

thought that was bellowing aloud in Caspar's head. He glanced at the window, which was now shut.

'You know what you have to do now?' he said to Bachmann.

The porter nodded slowly. 'A total lockdown.'

'I'm afraid we've no choice.' Rassfeld mopped his furrowed brow once more, and this time the moisture that came away on the sleeve of his gown was definitely sweat.

'We must lower the shutters at once.'

12:41 a.m.

For the second time within a few hours Caspar was standing in the porter's office, staring at Bachmann's monitor.

This time, however, he was barefoot and the overturned ambulance captured by the CCTV was buried beneath half a metre of snow. Thanks to the image intensifier, this looked on the screen like a greenish, shimmering mass.

'Happy Christmas Eve,' growled Bachmann.

His attention was focused on a grey fuse box on the wall, which had not become visible until he'd pushed the heavy Christmas tree aside.

'The shutters? What did Rassfeld mean?' It wasn't the first time Caspar had asked that question since the medical director had ordered him not to stir from the porter's side. Bachmann grunted. This time, however, he proved unexpectedly informative.

'It's a security precaution. Only three institutions in the world have installed it, and the Teufelsberg Clinic is the only one in Germany. See that thing there?' Breathing hard, he lifted the box's hinged plastic cover to reveal a row of identical trip switches. Then he drew in his substantial paunch so that Caspar could see the only odd one, which was green. Written in black felt tip on the metal plate below it was the word 'GINA'.

'Throw that switch, and GINA automatically seals off all the exits. Two dozen massive roller shutters come down over every door and window.'

Caspar remembered the heavy shutter he'd had to duck beneath when following Linus out onto the balcony.

'Gina?' he said.

'My wife's name,' said Bachmann. 'She also battens down the hatches when we have a row.' He gave a mirthless laugh.

'But what's it for?'

'Preventing dangerous patients or potential suicides from escaping. It's never happened yet, of course, but we get all new arrivals to sign a consent form permitting us to implement a lockdown in an emergency.'

Caspar wondered if he himself had signed one. Leaning on the desk with one hand, he felt a faint vibration under his fingertips.

'Fair enough, but Bruck has already escaped. We can't stop him getting to the nearest housing development and finding himself another victim.'

'That's not the point.' Bachmann's paunch bulged beneath his overalls, once more obstructing Caspar's view of the fuse box.

'So what *is* the point?'

'You've heard of the Soul Breaker?'

Caspar nodded warily.

He may even be a personal acquaintance of mine, he thought, but decided at the same moment to keep that knowledge to himself. At least until he'd discovered what reason there could be for Bruck's picture to have haunted him in his dreams.

'The professor was consulted by the police. As a psychiatric expert. He examined the victims, including the woman who died today, so he's better qualified than any of us to know what the Soul Breaker is capable of. That's why he told me to lower the shutters. Rassfeld doesn't want to shut the madman in; he wants to stop him getting back inside. With us!'

Caspar cleared his throat. The vibrations around him seemed to intensify in proportion to the growing uneasiness he felt at Bachmann's words. The porter stepped back from the fuse box, and Caspar saw that the green switch had already been tripped.

'Help!'

The woman's voice rang through the reception area.

It wasn't until she shouted again that Caspar recognised it as belonging to the young nurse. Yasmin came running towards them.

Bachmann looked startled. 'What is it?' he called.

In the glow of the dimmed ceiling lights Yasmin's red fringe made it look as if her forehead were wet with blood.

'It's the professor,' she said breathlessly. 'He's disappeared.'

'Disappeared?'

'Yes. The earplugs had run out, so he sent me off to get some more.'

She opened her right hand to reveal two yellow foam earplugs. They were evidently intended to protect Sophia's ears from the noise of the scanner.

'He was gone by the time I got back.'

'Damn it.' Bachmann bent down and opened the middle one of three drawers in his desk. His hand emerged holding something that resembled an outsize, transparent toy pistol.

'Damn it,' he said again, and hurried off with Caspar at his heels.

As they were crossing the reception area the ambient light underwent a change. It seemed to become brighter. In reality, the darkness was being excluded. The ceiling lights were suddenly reflected more strongly because they had encountered a form of resistance: the shutter that was coming down over the entrance hall's big picture window. Like those that were descending over every other window in the Teufelsberg Clinic.

The shutters...

They were halfway down when Sophia started screaming in the basement.

12:43 a.m.

The agonised, panic-stricken cries were almost unbearable. More dreadful still, however, was the sudden silence that fell when one such scream had risen in a crescendo. It was as if someone had severed Sophia's vocal cords with a pair of scissors.

They pounded down the stairs with Bachmann in the lead. Caspar followed close behind, his bare feet slapping the stone steps that led to the clinic's upper basement level.

'Hello?' Yasmin had paused at the top, but her apprehensive cry went echoing along the narrow, tunnel-like passage that stretched away on either side at the foot of the steps. Both ends of the passage terminated in emergency exits: glass doors beyond which the shutters had completed all but the last few millimetres of their descent.

There was a click. The louvres reversed their angle and the shutters finally obstructed any view of what lay beyond the doors.

'Oh no!' Bachmann pointed to a bloody footprint on the floor. They hurried down the passage to the right, making for the second door from the end, above which was an illuminated sign reading 'Radiology. No admittance'.

Bachmann's heavy boot thudded against the metal-bound door as he kicked it open and dashed into the neuroradiological control room. Caspar followed him in.

'Where are they?'

Rassfeld, Sophia!

Their eyes met for a moment as they turned on the spot, feverishly scanning the room. There was no one and nothing to be seen except the big glass window that reflected their weary faces.

Bachmann went over to it and threw all the light switches with one sweep of his hand. Their reflections vanished, giving them a view of what had been in darkness beyond the glass.

Those legs. Those twitching feet.

'Is it her?' Caspar asked. It was a superfluous question. Sophia's shapely form was jerking around inside the tubular scanner as if in contact with a live power cable.

Bachmann hurried into the scanner room with Caspar at his heels. They had to force themselves not to avert their gaze.

Sophia's fragile-looking limbs were strapped to a sliding stretcher. Having withdrawn her from the tube, Bachmann found that her spastic convulsions had already loosened one wrist strap. He proceeded to release the Velcro restraints with which Rassfeld must have immobilised her for the scan, but her left leg lashed out so uncontrollably that Caspar thought he felt the wind of it on his cheek. She began to whimper, too, and a smell of old copper coins filled the air. Caspar guessed what he would see next if he looked down. His assumption proved to be correct.

'There's some blood here too.'

'Where?'

'There.'

He indicated the floor at his feet. Several big drops of it could be seen leading out of the scanner room. Two of them were smudged as if someone had trodden on them in bare feet.

'Okay, I'll stay with her.' Bachmann mopped the sweat from his bullet head. 'You go and look for Rassfeld and Linus. And fetch the others. Yasmin, the paramedic, even the cook for all I care. We need everyone we can...' He broke off.

'What is it?'

'Hear that?'

Caspar cocked his head.

What was it?

A new noise could be heard over Sophia's whimpers. To Caspar it sounded as if a giant was tightening a wire noose immediately overhead.

'Is that the…?' Caspar didn't wait for Bachmann to complete his question. He dashed out of the room and ran back along the passage. The sound grew louder the nearer he got to the aluminium doors.

It *was* the lift!

He came to a halt beside it and looked at the electronic floor indicator. Someone had just left the basement and was on his way up.

12:47 a.m.

Caspar developed a stitch between the first and second floors, but he resisted the urge to stop.

Although the hospital lift ascended the shaft at a tai-chiesque crawl, it would still get there before him if he didn't put in a final spurt. He gritted his teeth and began taking two steps at a time.

Ping.

He'd made it. He reached the second floor and debouched from the stairwell just as the bell over the lift doors tinkled, but his sense of triumph at having won the race by a short head gave way to fear. The instant light showed through the crack between the aluminium doors, he realised he was about to face the Soul Breaker at any moment – unarmed.

A final jerk and the doors began to open. Little by little, they disclosed a view of the big mirror on the back wall of the cabin. Suppressing an urge to run, Caspar raised his arms defensively in front of his face and saw...

Nothing!

'What are *you* doing here?'

He spun round so fast, most people would have recoiled instinctively. Not so Tom Schadeck, who stood his ground. He didn't even blink.

'Come on, out with it. What are you doing here?'

The paramedic had evidently changed his clothes. He'd still been in a bathrobe when he wheeled Sophia out of Bruck's room. Now he was wearing a pair of white jeans and the rollneck sweater he'd arrived in. His hair looked as if it had been freshly gelled.

'I could ask you the same thing,' Caspar retorted. 'Was it you that...?'

'Huh?' Schadeck stared past him into the empty lift.

'I mean, did you...?' Caspar groped for the right words, realising how idiotic he must not only sound but look, in his present get-up. Standing on the landing barefoot, unshaven, and dressed only in a pair of mint-green pyjama trousers and a faded T-shirt, he was the image of a mental patient who had been overlooked when the medication was doled out that evening.

'It doesn't matter, I'll explain later. First we must find Rassfeld.'

'Rassfeld?'

'Yes, he's gone missing.'

Caspar shivered. Looking down at his bare feet, which were so cold he could hardly feel them, he realised his mistake. He wasn't cold because of his thin night attire – the clinic was well heated – but because of the icy draught swirling around his ankles.

'What's it to you?'

Caspar, still looking down at the floor, didn't answer.

The spot of blood on the polished linoleum was claiming his full attention.

'Hey, psycho, I'm talking to you!'

He left Schadeck standing there and followed the trail of rust-coloured spots along the passage, which kinked to the right after twenty metres.

The paramedic's angry voice faded and the cold draught intensified as he turned the corner. At the same time, a metallic clicking sound came to his ears. And then he saw why.

The shutter over the emergency exit at the far end of the passage wasn't quite closed. Like a fly that keeps forgetting it has flown into a window pane a hundred times before, it persisted in its vain attempts to slot into place. A thin metal bar was preventing it from descending the last two centimetres, and the glass door itself had been smashed.

Caspar turned round, intending to call Schadeck, but it turned out to be unnecessary because the paramedic was already standing behind him with Bachmann, who must also have hurried upstairs and joined them.

He was about to ask after Sophia, but the porter got in first.

'Have you found Rassfeld?'

'No, but look.' Caspar pointed to the metal bar that had been wedging the roller shutter open. 'He probably used that to smash the window.'

'And cut himself on the glass.'

Schadeck kneeled down and examined one of the numerous spots of blood to be found here too. 'Shit,' he said. The word conveyed what they were all thinking.

The nature and direction of the spots of blood allowed only one conclusion.

The Soul Breaker had jumped out of the window of his room and landed on the balcony one floor down. He had smashed the glass emergency door and wedged the roller shutter open before it could descend all the way. Having sneaked back into the clinic, he had kicked the bar away and the shutter had descended to within two centimetres of the bottom of the frame.

'Does that mean we're...?'

'Yes,' Caspar said in answer to Bachmann's unfinished question.

'Then raise this thing! At once!' Schadeck demanded, indicating the shutter. He had previously made a vain attempt to lever it up with the bar.

'No can do.' Bachmann shook his head.

'What do you mean? The blood leads away from the door. We've shut the bugger in, not out.'

In here. With us.

'No can do,' Bachmann repeated, looking as resigned as he sounded. 'It's not possible.' He heaved a sigh. 'I can't cancel the lockdown just like that.'

Two hours and twenty-six minutes before The Fear

1:12 a.m.

Caspar knew that the whirling snowflakes being blown against the shuttered windows of the Teufelsberg Clinic had a long journey behind them. High overhead, at a temperature of minus fifty, water droplets of moisture had frozen onto particles of dust. While falling through the clouds these little frozen nuclei had a radius of only one-tenth of a millimetre, so their tiny surface area was insufficient for the friction of their descent to make them melt. Not until they passed through a layer of air registering minus fifteen, where more and more water vapour had frozen around the condensation nuclei, did they assume their typical stellate shape. Caspar also knew that the six points of each star were identical despite exposure to turbulence and winds of varying direction. Yet never since man first trod the planet had two identical snowflakes fallen to earth, a marvel of nature in which Aristotle himself had taken an interest. Caspar could remember all these useless facts, yet his own provenance remained a mystery to him. How had he got here? Why did he know the man who had just tried to kill Sophia? And whom had he left behind outside after promising to summon help? His heart ached at the thought that the external situation had become a reflection of his personal predicament. A total lockdown was preventing him from breaking out of this prison and going in search of his nameless daughter.

'Well, I don't know about you guys...'

He strove to concentrate on Bachmann's deliberately cheerful tone.

'...but the last time I was up this early at Christmas, I'd asked my mummy and daddy for a Scalextric set.' The porter's attempt to dispel the tension misfired. Nobody laughed. On the contrary, four suspicious pairs of eyes were staring at him. Schadeck was regarding him with derision, whereas the cook looked as if she was about to burst into tears at any moment. Yasmin, too, had dropped her habitual air of indifference and was nervously scratching the inside of her wrist.

'Cut the crap, Bachmann,' she said. 'Just tell us what the plan is.'

'Take it easy, Yasmin. We're safe for the time being, here in the library.'

The porter produced a pair of rimless reading glasses from the breast pocket of his overalls and put them on his nose. Presumably he thought a somewhat more intellectual appearance would boost his credentials as a crisis manager. In fact, they looked as out of place on his shaven head as a set of traffic lights in the desert, nor did they conceal his extreme anxiety. In order to control his sweating, trembling hands he tightened them on the plastic handles of Sophia's wheelchair and pushed it forwards a couple of centimetres.

'This room is protected by a heavy oak door. No one's going to get past that in a hurry, so there's no need to panic.'

'No need to panic?' Yasmin said with a sarcastic laugh. 'Dr Dorn is in a waking coma, Rassfeld has disappeared, and I've had to lock the patients in their rooms upstairs because some bloodstained psychopath is rampaging around the clinic. Call me a drama queen, but if that isn't reason enough to panic, why have we barricaded ourselves in here?'

Yasmin's angry gaze swept her surroundings like the invisible beams of an infra-red alarm system. The ground floor room in which they'd assembled was used as the clinic's dining room, and most patients capable of taking their meals down there did so. However, the bookshelves that lined the walls from floor to lofty ceiling made it look more like the smoking room of a London club, so everyone referred to it as 'the library'.

Every corner extended an invitation to take one's ease, whether it be on the comfortable sofa, the wine-red leather armchairs or the cream-coloured dining room chairs, but most patients and their visitors favoured the Regency-striped wingback chairs in front of the open fireplace. At the moment they were all standing around a massive table so long that it would readily have lent itself to a reproduction of the Last Supper.

'What was that about a bloodstained psychopath?' demanded Sibylle Patzwalk. The cook had taken a sleeping pill and slept through the recent commotion. No one had yet explained to her why she'd been yanked out of bed in the middle of the night and hustled into the library in her nightdress. She was ignored yet again when Schadeck cornered everyone's attention.

'I still don't understand. Why don't we simply raise the shutters and send for help?'

He clumped to the far end of the room in his heavy shoes. In warm weather the French windows facing the garden stood open. Now, any view of the snow-covered grounds outside was obscured by the mouse-grey slats of the roller shutters.

Bachmann cleared his throat and instinctively felt for the gas pistol he'd armed himself with before leaving his office. It was only loaded with 9mm blanks, but he'd assured Caspar that they could inflict serious or even fatal wounds if fired at very close range.

'I don't know the code.'

'What? I thought all you had to do was throw a switch?'

'Yes, when lowering them fast – for instance to prevent a potential suicide from breaking out. Raising them is another matter. The patient mustn't be able to free himself until we've sedated him. That's why the lockdown has to be deactivated by means of a code.'

'And you don't have it?' Schadeck stared at the porter in surprise. 'That must contravene every fire safety regulation in the book!'

'We have an emergency plan, of course. For reasons of security, two doctors per shift must always know the current combination. Trouble is...' – Bachmann cleared his throat again – '...one of them has disappeared and the other can't communicate.'

Caspar looked down at Sophia, whose head had lolled sideways. She seemed to be immersed in an everlasting, dreamless sleep.

'But even if she wakes up,' said Bachmann, 'what good will the code do us? There's the mother of all blizzards raging outside.'

'So we're stuck here?' said Yasmin.

'Only for another six hours. Then the day shift comes on. They'll send for help when they see something's wrong in here.'

'That's a lousy plan.' Schadeck shook his head vigorously. 'We'd do better to get out of here and collar that madman. After all, he's got your boss in his clutches.'

'And Linus,' Yasmin put in.

'Linus?' said Caspar. At the thought of the little musician, a vague sense that he was forgetting something quite else stole over him.

'Yes, he wasn't in his room when I went to lock him in. Unlike Greta. She was asleep already, lucky old thing.'

Yasmin glared at Caspar as if to remind him that she thoroughly disapproved of his presence down here. He had refused to remain alone in his room and Bachmann had eventually allowed him to join the others, probably because he needed another man to offset Schadeck if he wanted to retain his spokesman's role during the night.

'All right,' said the porter, 'Rassfeld and Linus have disappeared, but if we go looking for them we'll make ourselves a target for the Soul Breaker.'

'The Soul Breaker?' gasped Frau Patzwalk. She shivered, hugging the massive bosom whose outlines were visible beneath her nightdress. Despite her repeated enquiries, she didn't look as if she really wanted enlightening about the horrific goings-on in the clinic. Caspar could tell what an effort she found even looking at the figure in the wheelchair.

'Does that mean…?'

'Afraid so, yes.'

Bachmann shrugged and drew a deep breath. Then he picked up a newspaper at random from the coffee table in front of the festively decorated fireplace. He didn't have to search for long.

'Here: three women, all young, good-looking and in the prime of life.'

Like Sophia, Caspar amplified in his head as he bent over the dining table, like the others, and examined the victims' photos.

'All were abducted, one after another. They turned up again only a few days later, out of the blue. No physical injuries could be detected, but their minds had been completely destroyed. Nobody knows what the man did to them – what mental torture he subjected them to. Take a look at this picture.'

Bachmann tapped a black-and-white photograph captioned 'Vanessa Strassmann'. The first victim to die.

'See? She has the same apathetic expression as Dr Dorn here.'

'And Bruck is supposed to have done that? Never!'

All eyes turned to Schadeck, who had propped his bottom against the dining table and crossed his legs. If recent events had unnerved him, he was concealing it brilliantly. There was even a faint smile hovering on his thin lips.

'Why not?' Bachmann coughed nervously into his fist.

'Bruck was lying in a pool of vodka when I got to

the motel. He's a drunk – a bum. The manager wanted him out of his establishment before the holiday. In the ambulance service we're human garbage collectors pre-Christmas.'

Schadeck's smile widened, but the porter shook his head.

'That doesn't add up. Professor Rassfeld referred to him as *Dr* Jonathan Bruck, and Dr Dorn seemed to know him too.'

'In that case,' sneered Schadeck, 'they ought to choose their colleagues more carefully.'

'I don't understand it all myself, I grant you,' said Bachmann. 'What was Bruck doing drunk in that motel? Why did he stick a knife in his throat? Why did he escape and then come back?' He drew a question mark in the air with a fleshy forefinger. 'No idea, but one thing I know for sure: Dr Dorn is the Soul Breaker's fourth victim.'

Caspar guessed what was coming. Although none of them wanted to hear it, Bachmann was going to conclude his speech for the prosecution with a convincing piece of evidence.

'Each of the women was holding a slip of paper.' He felt in his pocket. 'Like this one.' He handed it to Schadeck, who read the words aloud.

'"It's the truth, although the name is a lie."'

'Yes. It's a riddle.'

'It fell out of Sophia's hand when I found her in the bath,' Caspar put in.

'Oh my God!' Sibylle Patzwalk's voice failed her. Presumably she'd seen the breaking news broadcast Caspar had seen in Greta's room hours earlier. To his surprise, she wiped away the tears that were coursing down her veiny cheeks and kneeled in front of the wheelchair.

'The poor girl,' she sobbed, squeezing Sophia's limp hand. 'Why her? Why?'

'Yes,' said Yasmin. 'What does he want with us?'

'With us? Nothing.' Caspar's whispered words attracted everyone's attention. He put out two fingers and tapped the newspaper lying open on the dining table in front of them. 'It says here that all his previous victims have reacted only to stimuli of the most extreme kind. They're completely mute. Dr Dorn's case is different. She was trembling earlier on. We even heard her scream, and Rassfeld found that her pupils reacted to light. According to this report, such reactions were extremely limited in all the other cases.'

'So maybe it wasn't the Soul Breaker at all,' said Frau Patzwalk, clutching at straws. 'Perhaps it was an accident?'

'No, it simply means that he isn't through yet. Linus interrupted him. I think he wants us out of the way, so he can get Sophia alone again. That's why he came back: to finish what he started. Whatever that may be.'

Caspar was surprised he had the strength to voice this terrible suspicion so calmly. If he was right, and if they failed to protect Sophia from the Soul Breaker, it would deprive him of far more than the code to the building in which they had imprisoned themselves. He would never learn what she had discovered about his identity. And about his daughter.

First I must make sure...

As if Sophia were applauding this dreadful realisation, the wheelchair's metal frame abruptly rattled beneath her violently twitching body. And then something far more startling mingled with her weird token of approval: she opened her mouth and began to speak.

1:22 a.m.

Sop... Just one word, and as short as it was unintelligible. She didn't enunciate it clearly – it might have been *zop* or *shop*. Caspar hadn't understood it, nor had his involuntary companions in misfortune, who exchanged mystified glances. Kneeling down in front of Sophia, he gingerly touched her cheek. She responded to this cautious form of contact by exerting pressure on his palm with her chin. Then she opened her lips, which were dry and cracked.

'Dr Dorn? Sophia?' Caspar's voice seemed to penetrate her consciousness for the first time, but he wasn't sure whether this was grounds for rejoicing. Any

THE SOUL BREAKER

reaction from a coma patient was accounted a mile-
stone on the road to recovery. But what if this was just
a brief convulsion, a final flicker of life?

'Can you hear me?' he asked softly.

The eyeballs beneath her closed eyelids rolled to and
fro like marbles under a taut sheet.

Bachmann appeared at his side, looking concerned.

'She's cold,' Caspar said.

Someone, presumably Yasmin, had fetched Sophia's
medical gown and pulled it on over her thin nightdress,
but she was shivering nonetheless. The porter silently
nodded and stepped aside.

'Did you understand what she was trying to say?'
Schadeck said in Caspar's ear. Not that Caspar had
noticed him until that moment, he had come over and
was kneeling down beside him.

'No, it was…' Caspar gave a start and almost lost his
balance.

Sophia had abruptly turned her head towards him
like a barfly who, after staring into his glass for minutes
on end, suddenly decides to strike up a conversation
with the person beside him.

What is she trying to tell me?

He stared into her eyes, which had focused for the
first time since the incident in Bruck's room. Blank until
now, their gaze had acquired an intensity that could
have driven nails into a plank of wood.

'Sophia?' he said again. Schadeck flapped his hand

to and fro between their faces like a windscreen wiper, trying to draw attention to himself.

'Sop... zop...' she croaked hoarsely. It was as unintelligible as before.

For a moment Caspar had the unreal feeling that the mysterious sounds issuing from Sophia's lips were dissolving into smoke in front of his eyes. Smoke that smelled of birchwood. Then he saw flames reflected in her eyes. Bachmann had lit a fire.

'Good idea.' Caspar stood up. He gave the porter an approving nod and pushed the wheelchair over to the fireplace. Yasmin had dug out a brown bedspread from somewhere. She draped it carefully around Sophia's shoulders, softly singing a tune which Caspar found strangely familiar. Although he couldn't attribute it to any particular band, he could have joined in and sung the words by heart.

> *Yesterday I got so old*
> *I felt like I could die*
> *Yesterday I got so old*
> *it made me want to cry*

The song seemed to have a soothing effect on Sophia. She shut her eyes.

'I hope she's not in pain,' said Yasmin, and went on singing softly.

Go on, go on
just walk away
Go on, go on
your choice is made

The scene was becoming more and more unreal. The nurse singing, the blazing fire, the mantelpiece adorned with sprigs of fir and Christmas tree baubles, the woman wrapped in a bedspread in front of it. Everything looked infinitely peaceful all of a sudden, but that in itself intensified Caspar's sense of foreboding.

He brushed Sophia's parched lips with his fingertips. 'She's dehydrated,' he said.

'There's no water in here,' the cook piped up. She had stopped crying, at least for the moment, and seemed to have recovered her composure. On the other hand, she might only have been reacting mechanically like a person in shock after an accident.

'Water on its own is no good,' said Yasmin. 'She's incapable of drinking – she needs a drip.'

'Sounds sensible,' said Schadeck. 'An electrolyte infusion, preferably.'

'I don't know.' Bachmann kneaded the back of his shaven head, looking worried. 'Is it really necessary?'

'No idea. Hard to tell, not knowing what Bruck did to her.' Caspar felt Sophia's forehead. 'A physiological solution of common salt wouldn't hurt, but if she's

suffering from toxic shock she should have some cortisone urgently.'

'No, I don't think we should run any risks.' Bachmann
nervously rubbed his eyes under his glasses. 'I say we sit
it out in here for the time being.'

'Balls!' Schadeck said loudly. 'I'm not skulking in
here like some gutless faggot!'

Caspar saw Bachmann almost imperceptibly flinch
as if he felt personally affronted by Schadeck's coarse
language. Perhaps he did. The reading glasses, the intellectual pretensions, the veiled allusions to his marital
difficulties – all these pointed to a person ill at ease with
himself. In denial, perhaps.

Schadeck took a step towards Bachmann. 'Let me tell
you what I learned from my father. He was a professional boxer.'

'I can guess.'

'No, wait. My dad never lost a fight. Know why?'

'No, but you really think this is the time for personal
anecdotes?'

Schadeck ignored this. 'Because he always picked on
weaker opponents. My mother, mostly.' He smiled like
someone screwing up the suspense before getting to the
punch line. 'Once, when I was twelve, he went too far.
He said the mashed potato wasn't salty enough, so he
reached across the kitchen table and slammed Mum's
head into the bowl. Wham!'

Schadeck made the corresponding movement with his arm.

'I honestly thought she'd never lift her head again, it made such a crack. The whole kitchen was splattered with mashed potato. I was standing at the sink, but I got some in my hair.'

His ironic grin had vanished.

'But then Mum looked up. Blood spurted from her nose and soaked the rest of the potato. I don't know which was broken into more pieces, the bowl or her jaw. The old man just laughed and said she'd overdone it this time: the potato was *too* salty now. Then he told me to look in the phone book and find the address of a hospital we hadn't been to before.' Schadeck looked round at the others. 'You know, because of the silly questions they ask when a wife has two accidents in quick succession.'

'Okay,' Bachmann put in, 'it must have been awful, but what does it have to do with our present situation?'

'That night I swore to myself I'd never again take anything lying down. I mean, we were only children, but there were four of us including my mother, and only one of him. Get the picture?'

'What did you do to him?' Sibylle Patzwalk asked softly.

'Everyone has at least one dark secret.' Schadeck shot a sudden glance at Caspar, smiling sardonically.

'Nice story,' said Bachmann, 'but I still think we should wait...' He broke off, and they all stared nervously at the ceiling. '...till morning, when the day shift... What the devil's that?'

Caspar had heard it too now. The sounds were issuing from what he'd previously thought was a smoke alarm: a small plastic box on the ceiling. Metallic overtones rendered the bubbling hiss even more unintelligible than the pathetic noises made by Sophia. It sounded like someone imitating an espresso machine at its last gasp.

'Where's it coming from?' asked Schadeck.

'That's our public address system,' said Bachmann. 'There's a loudspeaker in every room.'

'Good God,' exclaimed the cook. 'Is that *him*?' Caspar nodded instinctively. Of course it was. His vocal cords were damaged. That must be how someone sounded when he'd punctured his windpipe with a knife.

'It's the Soul Breaker!' Yasmin cried with a note of mounting hysteria in her voice. 'He's telling us something!'

'Shush, all of you! Quiet!' said Schadeck, gesturing impatiently. He climbed on one of the dining room chairs and cocked his head. 'There's something else,' he said at length, looking down at them. 'In the background.'

Damnation, I can hear it too, thought Caspar. He felt suddenly sick as he realised whom he'd forgotten in all the excitement, and whose tormented whimpers were issuing ever more loudly from the public address system.

He hadn't recognised him earlier on, when he'd been sitting so close to him, but now that those anguished howls were coming from a distance, 'alienated' by a loudspeaker, he felt certain he'd heard them once before. Not through a loudspeaker but issuing from the boot of a derelict car on the outskirts of a flea market. He shut eyes and the whimpering grew louder.

It was summer again, and the wreck's silver paint-work reflected the dazzling sunlight so strongly, he had to shade his eyes with his hand as he looked in its direction. All four wheels had been stolen, so the car's disintegrating remains reposed on its bare hubs. There was nothing that hadn't already been kicked in or smashed. Headlights, windscreen and rear window, side windows – even the boot looked as if someone had dropped a refrigerator on it. Caspar could hear a hubbub of foreign voices in the background, a young woman laughing at a successful business transaction, and the recurrent tooting of delivery vehicles. Two grimy children ran off as he came over to examine the length of coarse string with which the lid of the boot had been lashed to the rear bumper. He touched his lighter to it, the boot sprang open, and he found himself looking death in the face. Four dogs. Young ones, dehydrated and dead of thirst – burned up inside. The outside temperature was about thirty degrees.

Inside the boot it must have been at least twice that. They had all died a slow, agonising death. All except one, whose left eye had been poked out with a stick.

The dog everyone at the clinic called Mr Ed. The one that was whimpering over the public address system as pathetically as it had as a puppy, during the first few minutes after its fortuitous release.

1:31 a.m.

The darkness had a clarifying, almost cleansing effect. They had been stealing across the pitch-black reception area for several seconds, but it might have been floodlit, Caspar could hear, smell and feel their surroundings with such intensity. The Soul Breaker had destroyed every light source in this part of the ground floor.

'Keep left,' Schadeck whispered as the agonised howls overhead ceased for a moment or two. He was close behind Caspar, having insisted on accompanying him to the clinic's dispensary.

'Is it true, what Yazzy says? You're a blackout case?'

They groped their way cautiously along, one hand brushing the wall so as not to lose their bearings in the gloom. Caspar didn't know what surprised him more, that the paramedic was taking advantage of their excursion from the library to indulge in small talk, or that he was already calling the indiscreet nurse by her nickname.

'Mental blackout, amnesia. It goes with the whole situation, don't you think?' Schadeck chuckled. 'I hope that maniac doesn't have night vision goggles. If he does, we can forget about our brilliant plan right now.'

'We'll simply fetch the bare essentials for Dr Dorn, look for Mr Ed and switch off that damned loudspeaker system,' Caspar had told Bachmann. The porter had nodded grimly when they set off, but not without uttering a warning:

'Rassfeld's office is right next door to the dispensary. One of the public address system's two mikes lives on his desk, so there's a fifty-fifty chance Bruck'll be waiting for you in there.'

Tiptoeing slowly on, Caspar almost collided with a water cooler. The plastic dispenser was very near their destination, if he remembered rightly. Only two more doors to go.

The whimpering above their heads had grown fainter the further they got from the entrance hall. Not so Caspar's mental image of an animal expiring in an overheated boot, which was becoming ever more vivid.

'Look!' Schadeck's hand abruptly descended on his shoulder.

'What?'

'That.'

Okay, so he's seen it too.

Caspar had thought at first that the flashing red light was an illusion – the sort that occurs when you screw up your eyes too tightly in the dark. But it was evidently real. A red glow was flashing on and off at regular intervals in the crack beneath the door to Rassfeld's office. It was as if someone were lying on the floor and signalling in Morse with a remote control's LED.

'That wasn't there just now, was it?' said Schadeck. Caspar shook his head, too strung up to reflect that his response would be invisible in the dark.

'What now?' he asked, guessing what the paramedic's answer would be.

'What do you think? We go in.'

1:33 a.m.

No remote control, no torch, no Morse. For one horrific moment Caspar mistook the harmless object for a bomb with a flashing detonator waiting to explode in the middle of Rassfeld's desk. Then he identified it.

'The rotten bastard!' Schadeck exclaimed. Casting caution to the winds, he pressed the switch beside the door. Caspar's eyes soon became accustomed to the ceiling lights, which bathed the medical director's spacious but cluttered office in a dazzling glare. Apart from mountains of patients' records, tottering stacks of books, an empty pizza carton and two grossly overcrowded bookshelves, there was nothing to be seen. Nothing alive, at all events. There was no one there but them. Neither Rassfeld nor the Soul Breaker.

'He's playing with us.' Schadeck had picked up the dictating machine beside the microphone. Its LED flashed every time the random generator selected and played one of several recordings.

'Here...' he tossed the gadget to Caspar. 'He must have tortured the poor beast and recorded it on tape.'

Caspar examined the mobile-sized recording machine. Without thinking, he pressed a well-worn knob on the side. Mr Ed's howls ceased. He felt faint and had to hold onto the desk with both hands. The recording machine fell to the floor.

'What's the matter?' asked Schadeck.

'I...' Caspar hesitated, not knowing what to reply. Then he opted for the truth: 'I don't know.'

He didn't know this room and had never been here before, yet everything seemed so familiar. Like most of the larger rooms in the building, the medical director's office was equipped with a fireplace. Hanging above it were numerous framed diplomas and one or two family photographs which Caspar seemed to recognise despite their unfamiliarity. He took a step towards the fireplace, drew a deep breath – and then...

It happened without warning. A biochemical signal-man in the siding of his memory switched the points. The train of recollection was approaching fast – far too fast for the disused track along which it was eating its way through his consciousness. But then the locomotive slowed down. The dense smoke from its smokestack – smoke that smelled of burning paper – ascended from the depths of his buried long-term memory, rising higher and higher until it materialised in his mind's eye. *Into a desk! A desk at which he saw himself sitting with a dictation machine in his hand like the one Schadeck had just tossed him.*

'It's time. Your daughter is ready for you,' he heard a woman's voice say over an intercom. And he saw himself get up, straighten his chair and cast a last glance at the photograph in the folder he was just closing. It showed a girl with curly fair hair. His daughter?

'All the preparations are complete, Doctor...'

'Hello, anyone at home?'

'What? Er... yes, I'm fine,' Caspar said unconvincingly, and the intercom in his ear fell silent.

Schadeck eyed him suspiciously. 'Remembered something, did you?'

'No, I... Feeling a bit nervous, that's all.'

He didn't want to unsettle anyone until he'd made some sense of his slowly returning memory, least of all a person who radiated latent hostility.

'You're hiding something, aren't you?' Schadeck insisted.

'No.'

'Yes, you are.'

Caspar had no wish to become involved in an argument. He pushed past Schadeck and made for the door between Rassfeld's office and the dispensary. It was locked, but Bachmann had given them a key.

Activated by a sensor, the ceiling light came on automatically when Caspar entered the windowless room. He stood irresolutely in front of the medication arrayed in glass-fronted cabinets and on metal shelves.

'Here's what we need.' Schadeck, who had followed him in, opened a refrigerated cabinet with a glass door. He took out two infusion bags and shook them like a barman, then tried to resume the argument he'd started just now.

'For instance,' said the paramedic, 'I'd lay odds we're in the same line of business.'

'Why?'

'Dehydration, infusion, toxic shock, cortisone?' Schadeck quoted as he looked for needles and plasters in a drawer. 'All your own words, so you're either a medical man or a hypochondriac. Besides, it all looked thoroughly routine somehow.'

'What did?'

'The way you felt her forehead and took her pulse. I'll bet you've given a transfusion before now.'

Schadeck slipped several cannulas into his trouser pocket and turned to look at Caspar. 'Just so you know,

I've got my eye on you. I know about that CCTV video, you see.'

'What video?' asked Caspar, although he guessed what Schadeck was alluding to.

'You hung around in the driveway and didn't come up here with your dog until that big baby Bachmann had driven the boss off the premises. To me, that proves you aren't here by chance. You had something in mind.'

'Oh yes? Did "Yazzy" tell you all that?' It irked Caspar that he didn't sound anything like as bored as he meant to, but he was feeling far too tense. The ironic thing was, he could neither deny nor confirm Schadeck's imputation.

'Yes, and she had it from Bachmann.'

'Great sources.' Caspar glanced at his wrist, forgetting that he wasn't wearing a watch. 'Don't let's waste any more time. We'd better head back as soon as possible. You realise why the Soul Breaker planted that tape recorder here?'

'To lure us out of our bolthole!' Schadeck turned to face him.

'Correct.'

As though in confirmation, a door slammed somewhere near the library. Then the cook's piercing screams came echoing down the passage.

They ran back along the passage, which now looked to Caspar like a dark tunnel with a miner's lamp swaying at the far end. On the outward journey the entrance hall had threatened to engulf them like a black hole, whereas now they had a faint glow to guide them – a guide that shouldn't have been there if the library door was still shut.

'Careful,' Caspar said warningly as they neared the corner where the passage turned right. Towards the library. And the light source.

Why had Bachmann done it? Why had he left the door open?

Sibylle Patzwalk had stopped screaming – an ominous sign, thought Caspar. Screaming entailed breathing, and pain could only be felt if the brain was supplied with blood. He felt ashamed of his perverse desire to hear the woman's laboured breathing, if nothing more. Then they turned the corner and he recognised his mistake: the library door was shut. The light was coming not from the library, but from a small room across the way.

'It's a trap,' Schadeck whispered, producing a longish object from his pocket. It glinted silver in the dim light. He must have taken the paper knife from Rassfeld's desk while Caspar was engrossed in his mysterious memories. Then he lay down flat on the ground and started crawling with an agility that suggested he practised close combat in his spare time. All he needed to complete the picture was the paper knife gripped between his teeth.

This is insane, thought Caspar. He turned right and rattled the handle of the library door.

'Hey, open up!'

'Are you alone?' Bachmann's response was instantaneous. He had obviously been listening with his ear glued to the door.

'Yes, no. I don't know,' Caspar replied, glancing at the room across the way. Issuing from it was a sound like rats scurrying around inside a cheap plastic bag. He recalled that the kitchen was on this floor.

'Let me in.'

'Where's Sibylle?' Bachmann's voice was muffled by the heavy oak door.

'No idea. You should…'

Caspar swung round. The rustling noise had grown louder and altered its character. It now sounded like a overloaded garbage sack being dragged across a stone floor.

Schadeck, too, was taken aback. Like a startled gecko, he froze in mid movement only a metre from the doorway. He raised his head and cocked it with his right ear just clear of the floor, then drew up one knee. He was about to crawl forwards for a better view of the room when darkness swallowed everything in sight.

Nocturnal gloom filled every nook and cranny on the

ground floor even before the fragments of the shattered light bulb could fall to the floor of the room.

Nothing. Not a glimmer. Not a flicker. Caspar could see nothing at all, he could only hear. The slithery sound was heading straight for him. Just that, no footsteps. He had a horrific vision of a maggot-filled garbage sack twitching convulsively as it writhed its way along the passage on its own.

He tried to shout, only to discover that he was already doing so. His lungs were hurting. So were his toes, bruised by all the kicks he was aiming at the library door in the hope that Bachmann would open up at last and let them in out of the night, out of the darkness that seemed to grow more intense the louder the slithering noise became. It had now been joined by a sibilant choking sound. Caspar hoped Schadeck would grapple with the Soul Breaker – hoped it was the paramedic who was producing those strangled, gurgling sounds by squeezing Bruck's throat. But then he realised it might just as easily be the other way around, and if Schadeck was losing the battle, he himself would be the maniac's next victim.

What's the matter? Why won't Bachmann open up? Caspar's mouth was pervaded by a metallic taste. He'd bitten his tongue, but he felt that as little as he did the brass door handle he was rattling so desperately. 'What do you want with us?' he shouted, far more softly than he'd intended, and all at once events sped up.

It began with a flash that singed his hair and missed his temple by millimetres. He jerked his head sideways, wondering why he lost his balance instead of hitting his forehead on the door. And then, as he fell forwards into the light, he caught another glimpse of the pale green cotton material that had shown up in the muzzle flash. *A hospital gown. Bruck!*

Someone hauled him backwards and a pair of heavy boots flew past his head. One of them trod on the pit of his stomach, the other on his upper arm.

Later on, when the bruises were forming, Schadeck would apologise for trampling on him in a panic as he fled into the library, but at that moment Caspar felt no pain, just boundless relief that Bachmann had opened the door at last. It was a euphoric sensation to have escaped death in the nick of time, but it only lasted until the porter had locked the door behind them and burst into floods of tears.

TODAY

Very much later, many years after The Fear

12:34 p.m.

No snow had fallen yet. The weather forecast had announced that it would snow this afternoon, but all that the wind had so far blown across the frozen ground were some dead leaves and a torn plastic bag.

Winter makes for clarity, thought the professor. He leant against the frame of the French windows that led out into the grounds. Or into what the years had left of them. The once immaculate lawn resembled a muddy football pitch.

Cold strips the leaves off the tree of knowledge and reveals what lies beneath.

Resting his hand against the glass, he surveyed the few remaining trees. With the exception of one indestructible weeping willow, they had either died or were under attack by fungus. A gale had snapped a birch tree in half, but no one had bothered to reduce its trunk to firewood. Hardly surprising, he thought. The fireplace hadn't been used for years.

Not since...

'Professor?'

He gave a start and turned round.

'Yes?'

For a moment he'd completely forgotten about the two students.

Patrick Hayden shut his folder and stood up. He pointed first to the empty bookshelves against the grimy wall, then to the chairs stacked in front of the fireplace with heavy dust sheets draped over them. Finally, he rapped the tabletop with his knuckles.

'This is the library, isn't it?'

'I'm sorry?'

'Caspar, Schadeck, the Soul Breaker – they were here in this room. This is where it all took place!'

It sounded more like an accusation than a question or a statement.

'Genius!' Lydia said scathingly before the professor could reply. 'The location was a building on the Teufelsberg, that was clear from the first few pages.'

'Really?' Patrick fished an untidily folded sheet of paper out of his hip pocket. 'It said nothing about that in the invitation to take part in this experiment.' He waved the paper in the air. It was printed on both sides, the front being occupied by a map in two colours. 'All the uni gave me were these directions on how to get here. No street names, no Teufelsberg, and I don't recall seeing a signpost at the bottom of the drive.'

'You aren't from Berlin?' The professor picked up his reading glasses. He had returned to his place at the head of the table.

'No,' Patrick said curtly.

'Then you couldn't have known. The drive is a private road and the Teufelsberg isn't marked on every street map, not by name.'

'Great.' Patrick clapped his hands and reached for his rucksack, which he'd deposited on the chair beside him. 'First we have to read this mysterious text, which was obviously written by a lunatic, and then it turns out we're sitting on the very chairs these people sat on while waiting for their executioner.'

'What are you doing?' Lydia asked tensely. She sounded far more nervous than she had at the start of the experiment.

'I'm going.'

'What?'

'Going outside for a smoke,' Patrick explained. He clamped the rucksack between his knees so as to free both hands and started to pull on his dark-blue quilted jacket. 'And when I come back,' he said, one arm already in the sleeve, 'I want to hear what this experiment is really about.'

'I fear that won't be possible,' the professor said

amiably but firmly. He rubbed his weary eyes without removing his glasses.

'Why not?' Patrick demanded. 'Is smoking banned in the grounds as well?'

The professor smiled indulgently. 'No, but I'm afraid you can't leave the room at this stage in the experiment.'

'Why not?' Lydia and Patrick asked almost in unison.

'Not until you've read to the end.'

'You can't keep us here against our will, surely?'

'Well, you may have overlooked this, but you agreed to that condition when you signed your consent form. Quite apart from that, the experiment would be far from over even if you both went home right now. You can't terminate it unilaterally.'

'Why not? I don't understand.' Patrick replaced his rucksack on the chair.

'It's part of the experiment,' the professor said with a smile. 'For it to succeed you mustn't take any long breaks – you must read on to the end without stopping. I strongly advise you to do so, but from now on in a rather more concentrated manner.'

'How can you tell how hard I've been concentrating?' Patrick demanded, though less aggressively than before. He seemed to have become infected by Lydia's uncertainty. 'You've been staring out of the window all the time.'

'I can tell by your reaction. You'd never have wanted to take a break now if you'd been concentrating hard from the first. The truth…' – he picked up the original copy of the Soul Breaker record – '…the truth is to be found in every single sentence on every single page, but you've skimmed over it.'

'That's nonsense.'

'Find it out for yourself.' The professor picked up the bottle of water he'd placed in the middle of the table for communal use. He poured himself a glass and proffered the bottle to Patrick with a look of enquiry.

'All right,' said Lydia. She tugged at the empty sleeve of her boyfriend's jacket. 'Let's carry on. You'd like to know how it all turned out, wouldn't you?'

Patrick hesitated, running his fingers through his dyed black hair. He tried to break Lydia's grip, but she held on tight and gazed deep into his eyes. No one spoke for several seconds.

Patrick shuffled towards the door in his boots with the trailing laces. Two metres from it he came to a halt. Then, picking up the bottle of water without a word, he returned to his place and sat down. 'What the hell,' he said. 'An hour or two won't matter.'

I'm afraid the people in this library took a rather different view, thought the professor, his eyes misting over. He looked down to conceal how exercised he was by the whole situation, and how much a part of him had wanted Patrick to keep his jacket on and leave the building, preferably hand in hand with his girlfriend. But he pulled himself together and drew a deep breath.

'All right,' he said hoarsely. 'After this unscheduled break I would ask you to continue the experiment without further interruption.'

He cleared his throat, but it seemed to tighten still more as he watched first Lydia and then her boyfriend reopen their folders and turn over. To page 124 of the patient's record.

One hour and fifty-seven minutes before The Fear

1:41 a.m.

Page 124 ff. of patient's record no. 131071/VL

'It's all my fault,' said Bachmann. He spoke with surprising clarity and his tears had ceased by the time Caspar had scrambled to his feet and patted the dust off his pyjama trousers.

'What the devil happened?' asked Schadeck, who was standing beside the dining table, holding something that looked at first sight like a gym bag.

The porter put his reading glasses away and uttered a dry cough. 'The thing is, she wanted... well, she wanted to pay a quick visit to the storeroom, that's all.'

Schadeck and Caspar stared at each other. Bachmann had no need to say her name, it was obvious who he meant. Not only had they heard the cook's screams, but the chair Sibylle Patzwalk had been sitting on was unoccupied.

'But what on earth did she want from there?' asked Caspar.

'This,' said Schadeck, emptying the contents of the bag on the polished tabletop. 'This is what she risked her life for.'

A dented can of ravioli came tumbling out along with several other tins. Caspar watched incredulously as they went rolling across the table.

'And where did *you* get all this stuff?' he demanded, looking bewildered.

Schadeck groaned and slapped the table with the flat of his hand. 'Hell, that's beside the point now. The Soul Breaker smashed the light bulb and dragged her out of the room. She must have clung to the bag in her death throes – how should I know? I grabbed the maniac by his ankles, but they were so...' – he displayed his bloodstained palms – '...so slippery I couldn't hang onto him. Then this bag landed right on my head. I thought it must be full of guns or something, so I brought it with me. Who cares, though? What matters far more is how the woman came to be roaming around out there by herself.'

Schadeck took a step towards Bachmann and squared his shoulders menacingly like a striker about to head the ball. 'Hey, Bachmann, I'm talking to you.'

The paramedic's white jeans displayed a damp patch

at crotch level. For a moment Caspar wondered if he'd wet himself with fear. Then he remembered the infusion bags Schadeck had attached to his belt before they left the dispensary and hurried back to the library. One of them must have burst while he was crawling across the floor.

'She started trying to talk again while you were away,' Bachmann said hesitantly, looking over at Sophia's wheelchair. '"Sop", or something – you know what I mean. Sibylle thought she might be hungry.'

Caspar nodded. It was quite possible that the speech centre in Sophia's brain had been affected. He sensed that he was overlooking something important but suppressed the thought when Bachmann went on speaking.

'I was against it at first, of course, but the storeroom is immediately opposite and Sibylle said there'd be a bag of supplies handy, so I let myself be talked into it.'

'I don't believe it!' Schadeck flung up his arms theatrically. 'You drove a defenceless woman into the Soul Breaker's arms for the sake of some tinned food?'

'Take it easy,' Caspar started to say, but Bachmann cut him short.

'No, not defenceless. I gave her the gun just in case.'

'What?!' Caspar was also infuriated now. He clutched his head.

'Jesus,' Schadeck exclaimed, looking as if he might spring at Bachmann at any moment, 'you're even crazier than the patients in here!' The veins in his temple were throbbing wildly. 'That madman out there has now got another weapon!'

'It's only a gas pistol.'

'That's enough!' Caspar shouted. 'Bad as the situation is,' he went on more quietly, 'we can't turn the clock back.' He looked Schadeck in the eye. 'Besides, we left the dispensary unlocked. I'm sure there's enough stuff in there for him to do damage with.'

'True,' Bachmann said in a subdued voice. 'There's even a tranquilliser gun in there.'

'Shit, *now* you tell us!' Schadeck kicked the newspaper rack, scattering several tabloids across the herringbone parquet.

'And now?'

'Now we should do what we set out to do in the first place: attend to Sophia.' Caspar gestured to Schadeck to detach the still intact infusion bag from his belt, which he did with ill grace.

'Here, you'll be needing these too.' Schadeck took a hypodermic needle plus syringe from his pocket and tossed them onto the table.

Caspar picked them up and went over to the fireplace, where Yasmin was sitting cross-legged in front of Sophia, stroking her hand. His eye lighted on the strips of sticky tape that had been used to attach a string of coloured lights to the mantelpiece. He peeled off two of them and told Yasmin to turn the wheelchair away from the fire. Then, with some difficulty, he rolled up Sophia's sleeve. She seemed totally unaware of what was happening.

'We ought to help Sibylle,' Yasmin said as he was tapping the crook of Sophia's arm. 'Perhaps we could free her?'

'I'm afraid it's too late,' Schadeck said behind them. His voice sounded several degrees friendlier, and Caspar could hear the unspoken 'Yazzy' at the end of his interjection. Caspar attached the needle to the syringe and, almost without thinking, inserted it in Sophia's readily visible vein.

I really must have done this before...

'I got a momentary glimpse of the storeroom before the light went out,' Schadeck went on. 'It didn't look good. I think he broke her neck.'

Yasmin recoiled a step. 'Sibylle's dead, you mean?' she exclaimed in horror.

'No, I doubt that,' Caspar said without looking up. He had removed the syringe and attached the infusion tube. Sophia still hadn't displayed any reaction throughout this procedure. 'Why would he have killed her and then dragged her away? Why hasn't he simply left her, Linus and Rassfeld lying there?'

He got Yasmin to hand him a tissue, folded it several times, and taped it over the needle with the two strips of plaster.

'Shit, how would I know?' Schadeck said angrily,

flaring up again. 'Maybe he's a goddamned corpse collector.'

'No, I think he's more of a gambler; that's why he leaves those riddles behind. Hence the dictating machine, too.' Caspar looked up. 'He's gambling with us, and Sophia is the stake.'

'Okay, let's give her to him.' Schadeck raised his hand. 'Hey, only joking.' His smile was surprisingly genuine – it even carried a hint of melancholy. He also surprised Caspar by offering to hold the infusion bag from which the first drops of saline were rolling into Sophia's bloodstream like marbles, one after another.

'Thanks.' Caspar handed him the infusion bag and went to stand at the head of the table.

'Right, I'll sum up. We don't know the Soul Breaker's motives. We don't know how he puts his victims into a coma or why he picked on Sophia. Further questions are raised by Rassfeld, Linus, Patzwalk – even Mr Ed. Where has he taken them? Are they dead? Are they still alive?'

Bachmann uttered an audible sigh, but Caspar ignored the interruption.

'We don't have answers to any of these questions, but we mustn't risk our lives again in order to go looking for them. From now on we must stick together and devote the time to helping Dr Dorn.'

Even as he spoke, he felt he'd been stabbed in the chest. Then he realised, with terrible clarity, that this sensation had been triggered by a single idea: What if the Soul Breaker were after him, not Sophia? What if he wanted to prevent her from revealing what she'd discovered about him and his daughter?

'We must all help Dr Dorn to survive the next few hours,' he went on, trying not to show anything, 'until help arrives. She's also our key to freedom. She knows the code.'

The key to my identity.

'And she's trying to tell us something.'

First I must make sure...

'Perhaps we'll succeed in fathoming her secret before—'

He stopped short in mid sentence and looked down at his bare feet, wondering why he had suddenly broken out in a sweat although he was wearing nothing but some thin pyjama trousers and a T-shirt. He felt his forehead to see if he was feverish, knowing at the same time that the cause of his hot flush was a single word: a word he had heard a few minutes ago but failed to understand until now.

'Are you feeling all right?' he heard Bachmann ask.

'I, er... Please could you say that again?' He looked first from Bachmann to Schadeck and then at the bookshelf behind Sophia's wheelchair.

'I asked if you were feeling all right.'

'No, no, I didn't mean that. What did Dr Dorn say while we were gone?'

'The same as ever. Just one word, if it *is* one.'

No. It wasn't the same.

'Please say it again, for all that. Please.'

'"Sop" something, but what...?'

'Good God.' At that moment Caspar didn't know who frightened him more, the Soul Breaker or himself. He had suddenly grasped what Sophia had been trying to tell them all the time.

1:49 a.m.

The treads of the library steps creaked loudly beneath Caspar's unaccustomed weight. It was unlikely that they had been used in recent years because the upper shelves held books that served decorative purposes only. Caspar would never have thought of searching them for medical reference works if Bachmann hadn't told him that Professor Rassfeld kept some of his discarded volumes up there.

'What are you up to now?' asked Schadeck.

Standing beside Yasmin, he was trying to wedge a poker in the wheelchair's headrest for use as a drip stand.

'I'm not sure,' Caspar replied without looking round. He pulled out the penultimate volume of an old medical dictionary on the uppermost shelf and leafed through it to the letter S. He found the entry he was looking for within seconds.

'So that's it.'

'What?'

'Dr Dorn is a psychiatrist. She knows her own diagnosis.'

'Which is?'

Bachmann looked up at him enquiringly and Schadeck stopped work on his makeshift drip stand.

Caspar turned sideways on the ladder, supporting the open volume with one arm. '"Sleep paralysis,"' he read out. '"Those affected remain in a state intermediate between sleeping and waking from which they can be roused only by means of powerful, mostly negative stimuli such as pain, violent shaking, shouting, et cetera."'

He raised his head and quoted the last sentence of the entry without looking: '"This disorder is also known as *sopor*, the Latin for..."' – he hesitated – '"...for deathlike sleep."'

'Deathlike sleep?' Bachmann said incredulously. 'Does that mean we simply have to wake her up?'

Schadeck laughed derisively, but Caspar nodded. Then, leaning precariously over to the right, he took another book from the shelf. It was a bulky volume, and its cover bore the words *Fundamentals of Human Neuropsychology. Fifth Edition*. It was too big and too cumbersome to open on the ladder, so he climbed down and deposited it on the table in front of the mound of tinned food. After consulting the index he opened it at page 720 and tapped the second paragraph:

'"Sleep paralysis is an episode of paralysis in the transition between wakefulness and sleep. The period of paralysis is usually brief but can last as long as twenty minutes. Sleep paralysis has been experienced by half of all people, if classroom studies are a true indication of its frequency."'

'I've had it myself,' Yasmin said excitedly. 'It's really awful. One time I dreamed there was a man in my bedroom. I knew he'd be gone as soon as I woke up but I simply couldn't open my eyes. I couldn't move and had to shout myself awake.'

Caspar nodded. 'So you released yourself from sleep paralysis.'

'Come off it, all of you!' said Schadeck, looking at Sophia. He still hadn't managed to attach the drip to the poker, so he'd pushed the wheelchair over to the table and thrust the bag into Yasmin's hand. 'Twenty minutes! Our patient must have exceeded that time limit long ago.'

'You're right,' said Caspar. 'That's why we now know what the Soul Breaker does to his victims.'

'Yeah?'

'He puts them into a deathlike sleep. I've no idea how he does it, but he must have discovered some psychological method of keeping them permanently in the paralytic phase between dreaming and waking.

Sophia is in a never-ending, horrific cycle. That's what she's been trying to tell us all the time.'

Schadeck knit his brow and looked sceptical. He ran his fingers through his gelled hair, then smoothed it down and clicked his tongue contemptuously.

'Okay, Sherlock Holmes, then tell me something else.'

Caspar braced himself in expectation of the question to which he had no answer. *Not yet…*

'How do you know all this? How come you're so good at first aid? How come you've just given an intravenous infusion and can quote blind from psychiatric textbooks?'

'I've no idea.' Now it was Caspar's turn to raise his hands in surrender. 'Perhaps I really am a doctor. Perhaps I'm a pharmacist or a psychologist. We could be in the same line of business, you said so yourself. On the other hand, perhaps I simply paid special attention on a first aid course. I wish I knew.'

'Oh, sure, hide behind your amnesia. I just don't buy it.' Schadeck turned to Bachmann. 'When was he admitted?'

The porter scratched his sideburns thoughtfully. 'Around ten days ago, I think.'

'And when exactly did the Soul Breaker's series break off?'

'What are you insinuating?' Caspar demanded angrily. He slammed the book shut and jumped up from the table. '*You* brought that madman here! *You* made sure we couldn't send for help because *you* crashed your ambulance into that phone box!'

Caspar emphasised each 'you' with a furious chopping movement like a referee counting a boxer out, but his verbal onslaught seemed to bounce off Schadeck. He didn't even blink, but Bachmann thought it advisable to separate the two gamecocks and interposed himself between them, breathing heavily.

'Hey, hey, hey, this'll get us nowhere. We must stick together. And trust each other.'

Trust? Caspar couldn't help recalling how Bachmann had suddenly appeared from behind the snowmobile when Linus had shown him that the fuel hose had been tampered with.

I can't trust anyone here, he thought. *I don't know anyone here. Not even myself.*

He resumed his seat at the table, pressed his trembling knees together with both hands and stared at the news magazine which Bachmann had left lying open.

The print swam before his eyes as Schadeck and Bachmann continued to argue behind him, but he didn't want to listen or speak or read. He felt infinitely weary all of a sudden. His brain badly needed to change down a gear – or, preferably, a short spell in neutral before he re-engaged it and ventured back into the fray.

He forced himself to think of nothing, and at first it actually seemed to work. But then he made the mistake of shutting his eyes, and because he'd spent too long staring at the magazine's picture of the second victim, the schoolteacher, her image continued to glow on his retina and his respite was short-lived. This time he heard the screech of metal on metal even before the locomotive's acrid smoke filled his nostrils – even before he opened his eyes and the memory train pulled in.

Flashback

'She's always been a very quiet girl. Too quiet. I've been worried because I had no need to worry, if you know what I mean.'

'Yes, of course.'

He stared at the rusty ring the tea had left on his empty cup and declined a refill.

'Here, take a look.' The woman opened a laminated folder. She must have got it out specially for her visitor and left it ready to hand on the coffee table. There was even a little slip of paper between the pages.

'See what I mean? All the others are laughing, but she isn't even looking at the camera.'

She turned the yearbook to give him a better view, but it wasn't necessary. He knew the girl with the curly fair hair and the braces on her teeth. He always kept a photo of her in his wallet. A passport photo, but she wasn't smiling in that one either.

He shut his eyes. The sight of his daughter hurt, he missed her so much.

'Everything all right?' she asked, her lips twitching

SEBASTIAN FITZEK

uncertainly. He didn't answer. Looking again at the group photograph in the yearbook, he saw that the woman was also in it. She was standing right on the edge of the group wearing tight jeans and black knee boots. There was a little asterisk floating beside her head. He found its twin at the bottom of the page and read the small print in the footnote:

Katja Adesi, form mistress of 5B.

'Is something wrong?'

'No, it's just that...'

Feeling in his trouser pocket for a handkerchief, he came across the crumpled railway ticket he'd bought in Hamburg that day. He longed to ask the teacher all the questions that were troubling him: When did you first notice this? How many of these disturbing pictures has she painted in art class? Are there any other indications?

'I think you'd better go now.' Katja Adesi stood up. 'I've already said too much. I'm not accusing anyone, you understand? Perhaps I'm simply imagining things.' She looked at him almost pityingly, then shrugged her shoulders. 'I'm sorry.'

He found he lacked the strength to ask even one of his questions. His tongue refused to move.

'You understand?' Her smile had vanished.

'Hello? Anyone at home?' The teacher's regular features became distorted, and Caspar gave a start – almost of disgust – when her voice changed too.

1:58 a.m.

'Hello, I'm talking to you, psycho!'

Caspar opened his eyes and was abruptly catapulted back into reality. A reality in which Schadeck had just squared up to him with a challenging air.

'What was it this time?' sneered the paramedic. 'Julius Caesar, were you? Or were you remembering your days as a film star?'

Yasmin unexpectedly took Caspar's side before he could reply. 'Leave him alone, Tom! Caspar wasn't putting on an act – he was in another world. He's a patient!'

She moved away from Schadeck, nervously twisting the ring on her thumb. Then, remembering her duties as a nurse, she carefully wheeled Sophia back in front of the fire.

Caspar followed her with Schadeck's irate gaze boring a hole in his back. 'How is she?' he asked in a low voice.

'Not too good. You can hear for yourself.'

It was true. He wondered how long he'd been 'away', Sophia had gone downhill so badly in the interim. Her once regular breathing now sounded like the panting of an asthmatic dog. She coughed from time to time, causing the infusion bag, which had at last been suspended from the poker, to sway precariously. Her hands were icy cold and her pulse seemed far weaker than it should have been.

'The fire's going out,' Caspar said. Schadeck got up and came over with the cook's food bag. Removing a small bottle of brandy, he unscrewed the top and poured some of its high-proof contents on the embers, then tossed a birchwood log into the blaze.

'Here,' he said, looking at Caspar's bare feet, 'you could also do with something to warm you up.' He held out the bottle, which still had a little brandy sloshing around inside it.

'No thanks, I don't drink,' said Caspar. Surprised by the feeling of malaise that was taking root in him like an incipient bout of depression, he attributed it to Sophia's condition.

'Well, you should,' Schadeck told him with his hands still in the bag. 'The day shift won't be coming on for another five hours, and these things…' – he pulled out another miniature – '…may make the wait a bit more tolerable.'

Five hours?

Damn it, that was too long. Time was oozing away with the sluggishness of molten glass while the lethal spiral of deathlike sleep was inexorably winding its way around Sophia. Vanessa Strassmann had taken two weeks to die, but who could tell how far gone Sophia already was, and when she would cross the frontier beyond which it would be impossible for her to escape from the prison of her body? She would then take her knowledge of his daughter to the grave.

'Hey, what's this?'

Schadeck let the jute sack fall to the floor. Looking round at him, Caspar saw a hint of fear in his eyes for the first time. He reluctantly let go of Sophia's hand and stood up.

'May I see it?'

Schadeck handed Caspar the little slip of paper. 'I think it's another greeting from our friend the Soul Breaker,' the paramedic said in a low voice, more to himself than the others.

'Where did you find it?' Bachmann asked excitedly.

'Here in the bag with the food. Bruck must have put it in there after he overpowered the cook.'

Caspar nodded.

That makes sense. Bruck is sticking to his established method. A victim in exchange for a riddle.

Caspar's fingers were trembling. The slip was folded just like the others. The Soul Breaker's choice of paper seemed a deliberate gibe at his victim. He had clearly been in Sophia's office and scrawled the words on one of her prescription forms, and the handwriting was an ominous indication of his state of mind.

'What does it say?' Bachmann asked impatiently.

'I don't want to know.' Yasmin clamped her hands over her ears and turned away, but Caspar unfolded the paper and read the mysterious text aloud:

FINISHED FILES ARE THE RESULT
OF YEARS OF SCIENTIFIC STUDY COMBINED
WITH YEARS OF EXPERIENCE

'Huh?' Schadeck grunted irritably, but Bachmann's voice vibrated with tension.

'What does it mean?'

Caspar looked up. He brushed an eyelash out of the corner of his eye with the back of his hand and drew a deep breath.

'I've no idea,' he said truthfully, lowering the hand that held the slip of paper. 'But there's someone we can ask.'

2:07 a.m.

The lift, which had been installed when the building was converted to its present use, was big enough to accommodate a hospital bed, so there was plenty of room for them all. Caspar had insisted that they stay together. Even in the wild, animals milled around in a group that presented a predator with no clear target – as long as none of them possessed some special feature that marked it out from the anonymous herd.

Looking at the shiny chrome spokes of the wheelchair, Caspar knew who would be the predator's first victim unless they kept Sophia in their protective midst.

'What's that?' asked Caspar, pointing to the '-2' beside the lowest brass button.

'It's the lower basement level,' Bachmann replied. 'Rassfeld's laboratory. Bruck must be hiding down there, I reckon.'

'Why?' asked Caspar, pressing the '4'.

'To get right down there you need a special key, and only Rassfeld has that. You see?' Bachmann pressed the lowest button while the doors were closing, but the light beside it flickered briefly and went out.

'I'd sooner not go up *or* down,' Yasmin grumbled as the lift began its leisurely ascent. 'We'd do better to remain in the library; you said so yourself.'

Caspar sighed. 'No, I only said we shouldn't split up.' At least the others didn't attack him, Bachmann because he was relieved not to have to make any decisions of his own after the disaster with Sibylle, and Schadeck because he preferred to remain on the move rather than cower passively in a potential trap.

'You may be right, Yasmin,' Caspar went on, 'but do you know the poem about wrong decisions?'

The nurse blew her fringe out of her eyes and stared at him uncomprehendingly. 'No, should I?'

'It goes like this:

> *Yes?*
> *No?*
> *Yes?*

No?
Yes?
No?
Yes?'

He paused for an instant, then added:

'*Too late.*'

Yasmin glared at him as if he'd just spat at her.

'What I mean is: If we go on twiddling our thumbs in the library and watching Sophia sink deeper and deeper into herself, we'll be giving the Soul Breaker the run of the hospital. He can arm himself, and I'm not just talking about anaesthetics or scalpels. I mean inflammable cleaning fluids, containers of formaldehyde and medical alcohol – stuff he can use to make Molotov cocktails and smoke us out. What would we do then? An oak door two centimetres thick wouldn't be much good. This place is hermetically sealed – we'd grope our way aimlessly through the smoke and suffocate.'

They passed the third floor.

'It may be that Bruck has something quite different in mind, but I'm afraid that, unlike us, he *does* have a plan of some kind. That leaves us with only two possibilities. Either we discover what it is, or we find ourselves a safer bolthole than the library.'

The scanner room, Bachmann had suggested just before they set off. It was equipped with fireproof doors and its own ventilation system.

'Yes, yes, all right,' Yasmin sighed. 'I understand, but all the same…'

She ceased her objections once the lift had juddered to a stop and the doors slid open.

Fourth floor.

In contrast to the situation downstairs, the motion sensors were working perfectly up here. The passage light came on as soon as the first member of the party left the lift.

'All right,' said Caspar, 'we'll do what we agreed – nip in, get her, and go back down at once.'

'Shit,' said Schadeck, who had gone on ahead.

'What is it?' asked Bachmann, but he saw it at the same instant as Caspar.

The door.

'Oh no…'

The door of Greta Kaminsky's room was wide open.

2:10 a.m.

'Is she dead?'

'I don't know.'

Reflected by the attic room's slanting white walls, the faint light from the passage imparted a waxen tinge to the face of the motionless figure. The old lady was lying in the middle of her bed like a saint on a tomb. From his angle, Caspar couldn't tell whether the body beneath the blanket was moving or not.

He tiptoed another step into the room. Why were they whispering? he wondered. If the Soul Breaker had done something to her, they need hardly worry about invading her privacy.

There! Had he seen something? Had her thin, almost translucent nostrils quivered?

'I think she's…' Yasmin spoke so softly, Caspar didn't catch the last word. He had no need to, though – he'd seen it for himself. There was no doubt about it: Greta Kaminsky had opened her eyes.

'What is it?' she demanded, turning on her bedside light. Her tone was quite unruffled, and if she was surprised to find members of the staff and a fellow patient standing over her bed in the middle of the night, she managed to conceal the fact extremely well.

'Something's happened,' said Caspar, wondering how best to explain the lunatic events she'd obviously slept through until now. 'Put some clothes on. You must come with us at once.'

'Says who?'

'I'll explain when you've—'

'Nonsense, my boy!' she broke in. 'I like you, Caspar. You repaired my television set, but that doesn't mean I'm traipsing around after you at two in the morning

– least of all with a horde of strangers in tow.' She gave Schadeck an icy look. 'Who are you, may I ask?'

'Tom Schadeck. I'm a paramedic, and I delivered an accident victim here a few hours ago: the Soul Breaker.'

'Who?'

Schadeck stepped aside and Yasmin pushed the wheelchair over to the bed so that Greta could see the figure slumped in it.

'Good God!' She clapped both hands over her mouth. 'This isn't a joke, is it? Is it part of my anxiety therapy?'

'I'm afraid not.'

Caspar recounted how he had seen Jonathan Bruck escape from his room, how they had lowered the shutters after finding Sophia in the bath, and how Rassfeld, Linus, Sibylle and Mr Ed had all disappeared. He even managed to summarise their death-sleep theory in a few words.

'And you left me lying alone up here the whole time?' With an agility surprising for someone of her age, Greta jumped out of bed and slipped her bony feet into a pair of slippers adorned with pink bobbles.

'You were locked in,' said Caspar, simultaneously wondering why the door had been open. If the Soul Breaker had taken the trouble to open it, why had he spared the old woman's life? He got the answer quicker than he'd expected.

'No, she wasn't,' Yasmin said sheepishly. 'I didn't come here at all.'

'What?' Bachmann and Caspar exclaimed in unison.

'I was too scared. Hey, no need to look at me like that – you made a balls-up yourself!' she said, jerking her chin at Bachmann. 'I was in Linus's room,' she went on, pouting like a little girl, 'and someone suddenly banged on the shutter.' She pointed to the dark window. 'From outside! There was someone out on the balcony.'

'Now you tell us?' said Caspar.

'It scared me to death. I didn't dare look in on Greta after that – I came straight downstairs.'

No wonder she'd wanted to stay in the library.

'Look, let's not waste any more time arguing,' Schadeck said soothingly, springing to his *Yazzy*'s defence.

Greta had pulled on a silk dressing gown and was standing there with her hands on her plump hips. 'All right, so you thought I was safely locked in up here. In that case, why come to fetch me now?'

Caspar handed her the slips of paper found in Sophia's hand and Sibylle's bag. 'We need your help.'

Greta shuffled over to her bedside table and fitted the nibbled ends of her reading glasses over her ears. '"It's the truth, although the name is a lie"?'

'Yes, that was found in Sophia's hand. We think the solution to the riddle could rouse her from her torpor.'

'Poor thing,' Greta sighed, looking at Sophia. Then she shook her head regretfully. 'Well, I'm an old hand at riddles, but I pass on this one.'

Schadeck clapped his hands. 'Fine, so we've wasted another twenty minutes. Let's get down to the basement before—'

'But *this* one is an oldie,' Greta broke in. She flapped the second slip of paper like someone waving a handkerchief in farewell.

'Really?'

'Yes. In fact I think it comes from one of my old books of riddles.'

'So what does it mean?'

FINISHED FILES ARE THE RESULT
OF YEARS OF SCIENTIFIC STUDY COMBINED
WITH YEARS OF EXPERIENCE

Caspar had the text off pat, he'd read it so often by now.

'The meaning is irrelevant to solving the riddle.'

'How so?' asked Bachmann.

'You have to count the Fs.'

'The Fs?'

'Yes, the letters. How many Fs occur in the text?'

Schadeck took the slip of paper from Greta and read out the words once more.

FINISHED FILES ARE THE RESULT
OF YEARS OF SCIENTIFIC STUDY COMBINED
WITH YEARS OF EXPERIENCE

'Three,' he said. He passed the paper to Bachmann and Caspar in turn.

'I count four,' said Caspar. Yasmin declined it with a gesture, so he handed it back to Greta.

'That puts you in the top ten per cent of the population. It's an intelligence test, you see. Members of the common herd...' – she gave Schadeck another withering glance over the top of her glasses – '...see three. A few people, like you, Caspar, see four. In fact, there are six.'

'Six?' scoffed Schadeck. 'Ridiculous! Where are the others?'

She handed the slip back, this time with an air of triumph. 'In the word "of", which so many people simply overlook.'

Caspar peered over Schadeck's shoulder and, sure enough, all six Fs suddenly caught his eye like beacons.

FINISHED FILES ARE THE RESULT
OF YEARS OF SCIENTIFIC STUDY COMBINED
WITH YEARS OF EXPERIENCE

'Well, I'll be damned,' muttered Schadeck.

'Yes, the human brain always thinks in images, and it can't think of a suitable one for the word "of", so we overlook the letter even though it's right in front of our eyes.'

Caspar shook his head, wondering for an instant

which Greta was talking about, the riddle or his memories.

'Six Fs?' Schadeck still couldn't believe it, apparently. He counted them again. 'Okay, but what does that tell us?'

'I only saw three, but for once I think I know the answer.' Bachmann produced a big bunch of keys from his overalls and thumbed through a number of different plastic tags. 'This,' he said eventually, holding up a key with a green tag, 'is the key to Room 6F.'

'Room 6F?' Yasmin said incredulously. 'Never heard of it. We've only got four floors here, so where is it?'

'Well, this is a little in-joke between Rassfeld and me. Six F stands for "six feet under". Believe it or not, he's got a sense of humour: "six feet under" means down in the basement.' Then, when he saw that the others still hadn't caught on, Bachmann added: 'It's the key to the pathology lab.'

2:16 a.m.

The room was about as welcoming as a disused slaughterhouse. Although Rassfeld and his students had only occasionally used it for purposes of dissection, it seemed to Caspar as if the bone punches, brain spatulas, retractors and scalpels had eaten into its walls as well as their objects of study. *The room's wounded soul...* He must once have read those words in a popular science magazine, and the quotation had lodged in his memory: pointless knowledge of *feng shui* as opposed to useful information about his true identity.

Caspar felt inwardly torn, like a pre-school child unable to name the street Mummy and Daddy live in but capable, for some reason, of delivering an off-the-cuff lecture on negative energy – on those who believe that traumatic events leave their mark not only on the psyche of the living but also on the inanimate material that surrounds them. Like an invisible fingerprint left by the evil one instantly senses in a hospital's A & E ward or at the scene of a crime. An imprint which esoterics describe as an aura and realists as an atmosphere, and which, depending on the beholder's sensitivity, can generate apprehension, gooseflesh or fear. Most of those in the basement seemed to feel all three at once. Even Sophia's breathing quickened, becoming almost jerky, although her blank, apathetic expression hadn't changed.

'I wouldn't like to lie here when I'm dead,' Yasmin whispered. She parked the wheelchair right beside the handbasin at the head of the dissecting table. In the gloom of the emergency lighting the rectangular room might, with a touch of imagination, have been mistaken for an eccentric futurist's kitchen, with its grey stone floor, white tiled walls, and central working surface of brushed aluminium, except that the ventilation cowl was really a bank of halogen lights and the refrigerated, chromium-plated lockers were intended for body parts, not food.

Bachmann turned on the ceiling lights, which accentuated the sinister atmosphere.

'Well, what are we looking for?' Schadeck demanded.

'Another clue.'

Caspar was examining the floor for spots of blood, but the Soul Breaker didn't seem to have left any traces as he had in the scanner room next door.

'Why does a private loony bin need a morgue like this?' asked Schadeck.

Bachmann thoughtfully scratched his shaven head. 'I think it's regulations. Every hospital has to be prepared in case a patient dies – not that it's ever happened here.'

Until now, thought Caspar.

'But what about these nine refrigerated lockers? Goddammit, you don't have that many patients here!' Schadeck tapped his forehead derisively.

'Rassfeld is a virtopsy specialist,' said Bachmann. He looked pleased when Schadeck obviously didn't know the term. 'Virtual autopsy. To cut up a corpse you need either a court order or the consent of the next of kin,' he explained. 'But a lot of people don't want their nearest and dearest mutilated, so it's becoming more and more common to put bodies through the tube. The trouble is, a full scan can take several hours – all night, sometimes – and normal MRI scanners aren't programmed to operate for so long. Added to that, there's the noise. That's why hospitals like to farm such examinations out. Rassfeld was quick to see that virtopsies can be a nice little earner. Sometimes all our fridges are occupied.'

Clang!

Caspar gave a start and spun round. Greta Kaminsky had just opened one of the refrigerated lockers in the wall behind him.

'What the hell are you doing?' demanded Schadeck, who was just as startled.

'What does it look like, young man?' Greta slid a long metal stretcher out of the wall. 'Anyone'd think this was a cathedral, the way you're standing around whispering. It can't be respect for the dead. The truth is, you're just plain scared, but if the Soul Breaker has left us another clue, it'll be in one of these things, won't it?'

Clang! She slid the stretcher back into the wall, slammed the door and opened another locker.

The paramedic laughed drily. 'I thought you said you were having anxiety therapy.' He turned to the others and cocked an eyebrow.

'I'd like some of those pills myself,' Bachmann chimed in.

Like Yasmin, Caspar smiled despite himself. He sensed that they were lapsing into a silly mood like mourners who swap jokes after a funeral, hoping that forced gaiety will enable them to traverse the vale of tears confronting them.

Clang!

'Nothing in there either.' Greta had slammed the third of the nine locker doors. They all gave a start, this time at a new and different sound coming from the opposite wall. Caspar was the first to shake off his immobility.

'What's that?' he asked, pointing to the oblong plastic box butted up against the end wall of the path lab. It reminded him at first sight of a chest freezer.

'Just another icebox,' said Bachmann.

'I can see that. I meant the noise.'

He made his way past the dissecting table.

'It's the coolant.' Bachmann tried to inject a reassuring smile into his voice. 'Sounds like a lawnmower sputtering, I know, but this one is pretty ancient. I thought it had been disconnected. Rassfeld doesn't use it any more.'

'Really?' Schadeck had followed Caspar over. 'So why is it plugged in?'

Caspar took hold of the lid with both hands. It opened with a sound like someone smacking their lips and icy vapour flowed out over the rim. He instinctively put a hand to his mouth, but it was too late. The acrid stench had already taken a short cut to his brain. Via his nose.

He coughed and his eyes watered, but not because of the sweetish, pungent gases. The sight that met them was unbearable.

'Well?' Schadeck said from behind him. The

paramedic came a step closer, holding his nose. 'What's *that*?' he asked, sounding as appalled as Caspar felt.

The chest freezer possessed no internal light, so he couldn't make out whether the bloodless corpse still had all its extremities. All he saw for certain before Yasmin and Bachmann, too, came up behind him, was that someone had half flayed the dog's eyeless skull.

2:18 a.m.

'Mr Ed,' Yasmin groaned.

Caspar, who had come to the same conclusion, felt ashamed because the sight of the mutilated creature left him completely unmoved.

Perhaps it was only a stray. Perhaps it isn't Mr Ed at all, he thought, trying to appease his guilty conscience. Perhaps he was reacting so unemotionally because he'd been expecting something far worse.

No, it isn't that.

'Shall we take it out of there?' Bachmann asked irresolutely.

It doesn't add up.

'The Soul Breaker cut off his paws, didn't he?' Yasmin couldn't tear her eyes away from the dog's remains. She didn't seem to mind the sickening smell, either, because she bent even lower over the chest. Much to his unspoken relief, Caspar had to make room for her.

'Yes,' she said, 'the skin has been pulled over its right ear and its paws are missing. Good God, what kind of sick pervert would do such a thing?'

'Rassfeld,' said Bachmann. To the nurse's horror, he extracted a flat bone from the chest. 'Here, take a look.'

Yasmin and Schadeck stared at the porter in bewilderment.

'This is the dog's hip bone. Rassfeld sawed it off personally, but there's nothing perverted about it.'

Caspar nodded. He was beginning to understand why he'd remained so unmoved. Why he hadn't mourned Mr Ed's death. It was because...

'It isn't Mr Ed at all,' said Bachmann. 'Rassfeld sometimes works down here with his students, as I told you. This was a demonstration piece.' He tossed the bone back into the chest and shut the lid. 'The dog was run over. A vet supplied it to us.'

'How can you be so sure?'

'You didn't look closely enough, Yasmin. Mr Ed was a mongrel, this one's a Labrador, and the stuff that smells so bad is formalin. The animal's floating in it, it's completely bloodless – all its bodily fluids have been replaced. Even if the Soul Breaker is a taxidermist, he couldn't have done all that in the time.'

'B-but...' Yasmin said haltingly. 'What's he trying to tell us?'

'Nothing. Don't you understand. He wants to—'

'—kill us,' said Greta from the other end of the room.

It didn't sound like her voice at all. She was whispering now.

Everyone turned to look at her. No one asked any questions – it wasn't necessary. The ninth refrigerated locker, now open, demonstrated what the old lady had been doing while they were wasting time on a dog's cadaver.

'Is he... I mean, is that *him*?' Greta asked, pointing down. She no longer looked undaunted. Her forehead was deeply furrowed and her complexion had taken on a greenish tinge in the merciless overhead lighting. Caspar was afraid she would be sick. Then, as he took a step towards her, he revised his opinion: she would probably be all right, but he wasn't so sure about himself. He gulped to keep down the meagre contents of his stomach, which were already trying to force their way up his gullet. Then he looked more closely at the head protruding from the lowest refrigerated locker.

Yes, it was him.

Rassfeld hadn't been a good-looking man in life, but death had made a monster of him.

2:20 a.m.

He looked as if he were in still in the process of dying. As if he had only been waiting for them to open the refrigerated locker and witness his final moments. His head was bent backwards like that of a child trying to watch the progress of an aircraft across the sky without turning round.

Rassfeld was screaming. Not with his mouth, from which a swollen, violet tongue was lolling, but with his dead, staring eyes, which had never before protruded so far from their sockets. He was screaming silently, yet so loudly that Caspar couldn't hear the agitated voices around him. He even found it hard to understand his own thoughts.

Puffy cheeks, bluish, waxen skin, dark blotches on the throat. Post-mortem lividity normally becomes visible in places where the blood settles most quickly after death. Not on the face but on the back or buttocks, in other words, parts of the body covered by Rassfeld's dressing gown, which he must have pulled on in a hurry when he heard the commotion coming from Bruck's room.

Gingerly, Caspar closed the medical director's eyelids. Not out of respect but because he instinctively wanted to check for signs of rigor mortis.

How do I know this? How do I know that post-mortem discoloration becomes visible after thirty minutes, whereas signs of rigor mortis generally take between one and two hours to manifest themselves – in the eyelids first of all?

He couldn't answer those questions. He became painfully aware of only one thing at the very instant when Yasmin angrily kicked the instrument cabinet behind him and Bachmann clasped his hands behind his head in consternation. Part of him welcomed the horrific scene around him. Yes, he was almost thankful because it was a distraction. Frightful though it was, it ensured that he didn't have to cope with a far more terrible monster: himself.

'I'll be back soon, sweetheart, then everything will be all right – everything'll be the way it used to be. Don't worry, darling, okay? I made a mistake but I'll get you out of there, and then...'

His stomach rumbled. He wondered if it really was nausea, or if the vital spirits of his true self were angrily trying to make themselves heard.

'Do you mind?' Bachmann said beside him. It sounded as if he'd already asked that question more than once.

Caspar stepped aside. He tried to concentrate on what was being said around him, but in vain. He stared at Rassfeld's corpse, his thoughts becoming more and more confused.

Perhaps I'm just a harbinger, a Trojan horse laden with something lethal that's only waiting for the right moment to burst forth?

To Caspar, the inexplicable cause of the amnesia that must have brought him to the gates of this snowed-in mental hospital and the fact that he had several times seen the Soul Breaker's face in his dreams seemed suddenly like two parameters in an equation containing three unknowns – one he couldn't solve because his traumatised brain kept shunting his thoughts onto a disused siding that led to his daughter.

What did I do?

'He suffocated,' Schadeck said judicially.

Caspar seemed to hear his voice through a dense curtain. He nodded. The paramedic was right. Decomposition gases couldn't be responsible for the bloating of the face; Rassfeld had been in too cool an environment. Everything indicated that the professor had been unconscious when the Soul Breaker slid him into the airtight compartment.

Caspar was about to check the rigor mortis again when he heard a gurgling sound behind him. He turned very slowly, convinced that they'd fallen into a trap. It sounded like the juicy breathing of their pursuer, the effect of the self-inflicted wound in his throat. To his relief, however, Jonathan Bruck hadn't crept up behind them. The source of the sound was Sophia, who was convulsing in her wheelchair at that moment.

'Oh hell,' groaned Yasmin, taking a step backwards.

'What's the matter with her?' asked Greta. She showed more presence of mind than anyone else by going over to Sophia and dabbing the saliva from the corner of her mouth with a handkerchief.

'She probably choked, that's all,' Caspar lied, deliberately suppressing the medical dictionary definition which he could, for some inexplicable reason, have recited verbatim:

Death rattle. Colloquial expression applied mainly by hospital staff to the respiratory sounds that introduce the start of the dying process once patients lose control over their swallowing reflex. They last on average for fifty-seven hours and are generally so unpleasant and unsettling for fellow patients that the moribund are usually isolated in separate rooms.

I must be a doctor, he thought, not for the first time, simultaneously wondering why he found the idea so unpleasant it gave him gooseflesh.

What would be so bad about it?

It would account for his medical knowledge, likewise for his memory of the recording machine into which he had probably dictated a patient's report at his desk.

That was why terms like 'catatonic rigidity', 'waking coma' and 'locked-in syndrome' flashed through his mind whenever he looked at Sophia.

So what would be so bad about it?

'I think she's trying to tell us something,' he said, uncertain whether he was saying this merely to disrupt his train of thought. He was now standing beside the wheelchair with Greta, whereas Schadeck and Bachmann had remained with Rassfeld's body. He glanced over at them.

The porter, his forehead beaded with sweat and a look of disgust on his face, was engaged in lifting the medical director's corpse so that Schadeck could look for something beneath it.

Another slip of paper.

Caspar turned away, but the sight that met his eyes was no less distressing. Sophia was opening and closing her mouth like a stranded fish. Her parted lips blew a little bubble of saliva. Then her tongue darted out and burst the delicate film.

'Sopor…' she muttered, rolling her eyes.

'You poor girl,' the old lady whispered. 'You poor, poor girl.'

'Find anything?' Caspar called tensely, without turning round.

'A riddle, you mean?'

'Yes.'

'No luck,' Schadeck replied. 'He wasn't holding anything in his hands and there's nothing in the pockets of his pyjamas or dressing gown. Nothing lying on top of his body, either.'

'I see.' Caspar stepped back, his eyes still fixed on Sophia's parted lips. Her tongue was now flickering uncontrollably back and forth between them. Revolted by the question though he was, he had to ask it:

'Did you look in his mouth as well?'

They had hesitated at first, uncertain which of them should be assigned the grisly task. In the end it was Caspar himself who removed a pair of surgical gloves from their carton and pulled them on before forcing the stiff jaws apart with his numb fingers. Everything went very quickly after that. The twice-folded slip of paper had been lying on top of the tongue like a Communion wafer, readily visible. When Caspar removed it, a greyish skein of saliva trailed after it.

He deposited it on the dissecting table in the harsh glare of the mirrored halogen spotlights. It occurred to him, as he looked at the spittle-smeared tips of his latex-sheathed fingers, that he still had no shoes on. He hardly felt the cold, strangely enough, probably because his entire body had taken on the temperature of the flagstones beneath his bare feet.

'Well, what's on it?' Greta asked, prompting him with a nod. She seemed to assume that the finder was entitled to the first look.

He unfolded the little slip of paper, which the Soul Breaker had torn off a prescription pad as before.

'"You go in through one entrance and come out through three,"' he read out.

'What?'

Caspar read it out again. 'I don't get it,' he said.

'I've never come across it before either...'

'All right, let's go, chop chop!' Schadeck clapped his hands and pointed to the exit.

'But I know...' Greta started to say.

'You know the answer?' Schadeck demanded brusquely.

'No, not yet, but I might discover it if you didn't keep interrupting me,' she retorted, her chin jutting defiantly. 'May I have my say?'

'Oh sure, we've all the time in the world.'

She gave the cynical paramedic a pitying smile and addressed herself to Caspar. 'I know what type of riddle this is. Once you've discovered that, the rest isn't so difficult. This, for instance, is what they call a metaphorical riddle.'

'Meaning what?' Schadeck demanded impatiently.

'Meaning that the words in the riddle can have several meanings,' she said without looking at him. 'You only have to spot the ones that matter.'

Bachmann cleared his throat and took a step towards her. 'I don't quite understand, Frau Kaminsky.'

'Then I'll give you an example. The only metaphorical riddle I know is this one: "You buy it, only to throw it away at once."'

Caspar heard Schadeck muttering 'I don't *believe* this!' in the background as Greta continued her introduction to the modern riddle undeterred.

'The verb "to throw away" can mean a lot of things. The first thing one thinks of, especially in conjunction with "buy", is rubbish. But you won't get at the answer that way.'

'Why not? A rubbish bag would fit, wouldn't it?' asked Yasmin.

'No, not at all. You buy a rubbish bag to put something in it first, not *throw it away at once.*'

'I see,' said Caspar, 'so it isn't a condom or a handkerchief either. But what's the answer?'

Greta gave him a mischievous smile. 'It's the "throw" that matters, not the "away". What sort of object is designed solely to be thrown?'

'A frisbee.'

'Bingo! Or a rubber ball. There several possible solutions, you see?'

'Who told you that one?' Schadeck thrust Caspar aside and planted himself in front of Greta. They were so close, she couldn't ignore him any longer.

'What business is it of yours?'

'I don't know you, lady. You're only here because *he* wanted it.'

Caspar blinked involuntarily as Schadeck aimed a forefinger at him. He caught another momentary glimpse of the swastika-shaped scar on the inside of the paramedic's wrist.

'Mr Blackout,' Schadeck pursued, 'who claims he can't remember who he is and happened to be admitted here just when the Soul Breaker was taking a break.

And now you stand here fraternising with this nameless person and solving one riddle after another.'

Greta shook her head. 'I think you're a very rude and impertinent young man.'

'And I think we all deserve an explanation, seeing our lives are in danger. Well, who did you hear that riddle from?'

'Professor Rassfeld.'

'Of course, I'd have picked him too. What a shame he isn't in a position to confirm your statement.'

Bachmann cleared his throat and intervened with uncharacteristic vehemence. 'Take it easy, Tom. Frau Kaminsky has been a patient here for years. There's no reason to doubt what she says. I believe her.'

'Really?' The veins in Schadeck's throat were bulging.

'Yes. Rassfeld examined the Soul Breaker's previous victims at Westend Hospital, so he probably tackled the riddles that came with them. They may even have worked out the answers together, but too late.'

'Oh yeah, and perhaps that's just a guy out there with hiccups, and he can only get rid of them by killing people. Come off it!'

Schadeck took hold of Yasmin's arm. He wanted to have at least one person on his side, given that the others seemed to have ganged up on him, but she shook off his hand and turned to Greta.

'Can you solve the other riddle? Rassfeld's, I mean?'

Yasmin glanced briefly at the refrigerated locker containing his corpse, which Caspar had already closed.

'Most certainly. I already have.'

'Really?' Yasmin's eyes widened.

'Of course,' Greta said triumphantly. 'As I told you, once you've cracked a metaphorical riddle the others aren't so difficult.'

Caspar went over to the dissecting table and picked up the slip of paper found in Rassfeld's mouth. '"You go in through one entrance and come out through three,"' he read out.

'A maze? A rabbit warren, maybe?' Bachmann suggested.

Schadeck snorted impatiently. He put an imaginary pistol to his head and pulled the trigger.

'Impossible,' said Greta. 'How can you emerge from three exits at the same time?'

'So what is it?' Caspar was also losing patience. It was nearly half past two in the morning, a blizzard was shaking the clinic's foundations, and an even more violent storm was raging within its walls, unleashed by a psychopath who tortured his victims into a coma, murdered them, or simply made them disappear. However one viewed the situation, this certainly wasn't the moment for a guessing game in a morgue.

'The answer's quite simple.' Greta looked round expectantly. Tom Schadeck was the only one she avoided eye contact with. 'It's a T-shirt.'

'A T-shirt?'

'Yes. You could have thought of that yourself.'

As soon as her meaning dawned on him, Caspar became conscious of the cold to which the scalding tide of adrenalin in his bloodstream had desensitised him until now.

Of course. You go in at the bottom and your head and arms emerge from three holes at the top.

'What is it?' he asked in the sudden silence that had descended. Schadeck, in particular, was eyeing him suspiciously.

Looking round at the others – at Greta's and Yasmin's blouses, Schadeck's rollneck sweater, Bachmann's overall – he became unpleasantly aware that he was the only person present wearing a T-shirt.

2:26 a.m.

'Take it off.'

'Don't be daft.'

'I mean it. Take off that goddamned T-shirt. At once!'

'Are you out of your mind?' Bachmann demanded, coming to Caspar's assistance, but Schadeck wouldn't let matters rest.

'Do you really think it's pure chance, all that's been happening here? This psycho knows something! He could be in league with the Soul Breaker!'

Yasmin shivered and hugged herself, but no one paid her any attention.

'Why should Bruck leave us a riddle that casts suspicion on his confederate?' Greta demanded indignantly, pointing to the slip of paper on the dissecting table.

'Besides,' said Bachmann, 'it would mean that you're in it too. After all, you brought him here...' He stepped back instinctively as Schadeck's hand shot out, but he wasn't its objective.

Caspar had also seen the hand coming and might even have deflected it if his subconscious hadn't reapplied the emergency brake. A quick turn, and Schadeck might not have managed to grab his T-shirt and yank it down. He heard the cheap cotton rip. Paradoxically, the sound of the snapping fibres seemed to harmonise with the screeching in his ears. The memory train had returned, filling his nostrils with dense smoke.

'What the hell?' he heard Schadeck exclaim just before Caspar felt himself topple over backwards and plunge into the void. His tongue was paralysed after that. Incapable of explaining the origin of the burns the paramedic had just discovered on his chest, he lacked the strength to concentrate on anything other than the memory clips that were showing on his mental screen.

Flashback

'It's time. She's ready for you.'

He was once more seated at his desk with the woman's voice issuing from the intercom.

'We've got everything ready, Dr Haberland.'

He laid the dictation machine aside.

Haberland? Is that my name?

Imprisoned in his three-dimensional flashback, he got slowly to his feet, walked across the office past the medical diplomas on the wall, and opened a padded white door.

Then the director of his memory film fast-forwarded, and all he saw were fleeting, feverish clips: the little girl's weary smile, which exposed her brace. Her curly fair hair, her head subsiding sleepily onto the treatment couch.

And then the tremors. The spastic convulsions of that frail little body, writhing like someone undergoing exorcism as a pair of strong hands tried vainly to force it back on the table. His hands.

Caspar heard a crack and his cheek began to sting, but he only blinked. Then everything went dark. The memory train had entered a tunnel or was traversing uninhabited territory – a forest, perhaps – in the middle of the night. He saw nothing more for quite a while until the train gave a sudden, violent lurch as if it had left the rails.

His body was shaken. There was another crack, louder this time, and from one moment to the next he was in entirely different surroundings. They reminded him of the dream from which Linus had roused him a few hours earlier.

He wasn't in a train any longer, he was in a car – his car. Torrential rain was deluging the windscreen – descending on it far faster even than the trees were flying past his window.

Why am I driving so fast through such a storm?

He turned on the windscreen wipers, but they failed to clear the misty film of moisture even at maximum speed.

I'm weeping! Why? And why aren't I concentrating on the road – why am I groping for something... on the passenger seat?

He picked up the folder and flicked through it. The photos were roughly in the middle.

There were two of them. The larger, the one of Jonathan Bruck, fell out onto the passenger seat beside a half-emptied bottle of whisky.

But that didn't matter. The little passport photo was far more important.

Why am I taking my daughter's picture out of the medical record and staring at it? Why aren't I looking at the road ahead, the rain-flooded roadway which my eyes, blinded by tears, can barely see in any case?

The two airbags exploded and the seat belt bit into his chest, but his car's built-in safety systems were powerless against the flames that darted from the dashboard moments later. He tried to move his legs, crumpled his daughter's passport photo in his hand as he strove, in pain, to turn and open the door, but he was paralysed. Or wedged.

Hell, I'm stuck. I can't get out, I must... wake up... I must...

2:31 a.m.

'...wake up!' He heard another slap, louder this time. His left cheek stung.

'That's enough, not so hard,' said a voice overhead.

'He's shamming,' said Schadeck.

Just as Caspar opened his eyes a car came racing towards him, headlights blazing. He flung up his arms, which were promptly grabbed by two strong hands. Then he blinked and the headlights merged into a halogen spotlight. He must have passed out again, and they'd laid him down on the dissecting table. He coughed, tasting blood in his mouth.

'Are you all right?' Bachmann asked anxiously. Schadeck's boyish face swam into view beside the porter's bullet head.

'What did you remember?' he demanded sharply.

'I had an accident,' said Caspar.

'Yes, you fell over backwards and cracked your head,' Bachmann told him.

'No, I don't mean that.' Caspar shook his head, although that accounted for the throbbing pain in his skull, which was growing worse. He propped himself on one elbow and coughed again.

'The accident must have occurred some time ago.'

'What exactly happened?'

He wondered whether to suppress some of the truth in the same way as he had so far said nothing about his fragmentary recollections of the Soul Breaker.

'I skidded off the road in a rainstorm,' he conceded at length. 'My car burst into flames and I was nearly burned to death. Hence the scars.'

'So it's that simple?'

No, it isn't, thought Caspar. He could understand why Schadeck didn't believe him.

'That's a load of crap.'

'Why should he make it up?' Greta asked wearily. She was holding onto the handles of Sophia's wheelchair.

'To distract attention from the psychopath and those

sinister riddles of his.' Schadeck aimed a menacing forefinger at Caspar. 'Strange, isn't it? The answer to the last riddle led us to Caspar's T-shirt and what he was hiding beneath it: scars that look like he'd stuck his chest in a microwave.'

Greta feebly shook her grey head. 'I could have been wrong. A sweater would fill the bill too, and you're wearing one.'

'Yes, but I don't have any burns. His chest looks as if it was disfigured in the course of some perverted ritual, not the innocent accident he's trying to sell us.'

'It wasn't innocent, I was drunk.' Mustering all his strength, Caspar sat up and swung his legs over the edge of the dissecting table.

'Oh yeah?' Schadeck laughed derisively. 'I offered you a swig earlier on, but you refused. I thought you didn't drink?'

'I had a reason then.'

'Like what?'

Caspar sighed. 'I'm still not quite sure, but there really are a lot of indications that I'm a doctor. I had a young patient, a girl. I think she was my daughter. I was treating her, anyway, and I suspect I made a mistake of some kind.'

'A professional blunder, you mean? You gave your daughter the wrong treatment?'

'Probably. I fear so.'

He tried to banish the image of her spastic

convulsions. Instead, with the violence of a medicine ball held under water and released, his memory of Katja Adesi, her schoolteacher and the second victim, shot to the surface.

'At all events, immediately after treating her I drowned my despair in half a bottle of whisky, got behind the wheel of my car and crashed into a tree.'

Putting his hand beneath the remains of his torn T-shirt, Caspar ran his thumb over the biggest of his scars, which snaked down his chest to just above the navel. He looked down at himself. In artificial light the hairless scar tissue resembled a stream of pink lava erupting from a seismic fissure.

All at once his fear evaporated, to be replaced by a more intense emotion: sorrow. He knew the true meaning of his scars: they signified that he had made some appalling mistake and would never be able to keep his promise.

I'll be back soon, sweetheart, then everything will be all right – everything will be the way it used to be.

'I'm not sure... I think... I suspect that...' said Schadeck, mimicking Caspar's attempts to explain himself. 'So you're totally uninvolved, are you? How, pray, did the Soul Breaker know about your scars? Eh, eh?'

'I don't have to take this shit from you!' Angrily, Caspar jumped off the table and clenched his fists. 'You've got a nerve, trying to pin something on me.

Where were *you* when Rassfeld disappeared? Who produced that second riddle from the bag? Eh, eh?' he sneered, imitating Schadeck in his turn. 'You see? Two can play at that game.'

'Stop squabbling, the pair of you,' Greta interjected, and Schadeck actually seemed to subside a little.

'All right,' he said, 'let's assume you aren't involved. What else could the riddle mean?'

'I've no idea.'

'I may have one.'

They all swung round, surprised by Yasmin's unexpected interruption.

'What is it?'

'Well, I...' She cleared her throat nervously and started twisting her thumb ring again. 'I thought of it when I was sitting in front of the fireplace with Sophia.'

'Thought of what?' Schadeck, who was standing next to her, solicitously brushed a strand of red hair off her forehead.

'Fire,' she replied. 'The shutters shouldn't be lowered at all, you said so yourself. Because of the fire risk and so on.'

'Well?'

'Perhaps these crazy riddles are the Soul Breaker's way of giving us clues. It's like a sick paper chase, and Caspar's burn scars are just another pointer.'

'To an emergency exit, you mean?' Caspar looked at her enquiringly.

'Yes. The thing is…' Yasmin hesitated once more before putting her plan into words. 'Why don't we start a fire? The shutters would be bound to go up when the smoke alarms went off.'

'Not a bad idea,' Caspar started to say, but the words were drowned by Bachmann's agitated voice.

'What if they didn't? No, no, no, it's far too risky. I don't know the system well enough. We've never put it into operation.'

'He's right.' Schadeck made a dismissive gesture. 'If it didn't work we'd be roasted to death in here.'

'Not necessarily,' said Caspar. He paused until he had the others' full attention, then outlined his plan.

2:36 a.m.

It was a mistake, of course. They shouldn't have abandoned their original intention and split up. Caspar guessed that his idea would end in disaster as soon as he suggested it. However, this was the only way it would work if it worked at all.

Greta, who was alone in being attracted to his suggestion, volunteered to join him on his trip to the scanner room. That was completely out of the question, naturally. Apart from Sophia, she was the weakest link in the chain. They would find it hard enough to get to safety when the time came, and he couldn't afford to run for it accompanied by a seventy-nine-year-old widow with hip problems. In the end it was Bachmann who went with him, though only under protest. The others, after a short but heated argument, had gone back upstairs and locked themselves into the library.

'This is an even bigger mistake than my marriage,' the porter muttered, but he took the plastic container Caspar had found in one of the built-in cupboards in the outer room: CLINIX-CLEAN, an alcoholic cleaning fluid laced with ammonia. Stuck to the front of the container was a black and yellow warning triangle with a leaping flame on it.

'What can go wrong? It's got fireproof doors and its own ventilation system, hasn't it?' Caspar nodded in the direction of the leaded glass partition that separated the outer room from the scanner room like the window in a recording studio. 'The scanner room was your own suggestion.'

'Yes, but as a place to hide in. Not to torch it.'

Caspar removed a second container and shut the cupboard door. He hoped Bachmann wouldn't detect from his resolutely confident tone that he, Caspar, shared his doubts.

'If we're lucky the shutters will go up as soon as the smoke alarms go off. Then the others can escape from the library into the grounds.'

Caspar realised that his hurriedly concocted plan hadn't been thought through sufficiently. For instance, he had no idea how they would push Sophia down the hill without getting her wheelchair stuck in a snowdrift. Like the other members of the party, however, he could only think one step at a time. He hoped something would occur to him once they'd succeeded in escaping from the clinic's imprisoning walls.

'The worst that can happen is the shutters stay down,' he went on. 'But since we're setting the fire in the scanner room, the fire doors will at least prevent us from destroying the whole building. Besides...' He pointed to an extinguisher on the wall beside the door to the passage. 'Got a lighter?'

'Matches.' Bachmann patted the breast pocket of his overalls.

'Okay, let's...' Caspar stopped short and looked up at the ceiling.

'What's the matter?'

'Can't you hear it?'

'What?'

'That noise.'

Bachmann was about to shake his head when he froze with the container in his hand. The throbbing sound was barely audible at upper basement level, but it was perceptible nonetheless, like the subliminal bass of a cinema subwoofer. Strangely enough, it occurred to Caspar that the weird sound would have made a good acoustic background for the memory sequence of his last car journey.

'Sounds like a helicopter landing,' said Bachmann, expressing what Caspar was hoping. His pulse quickened, and for the first time for hours he felt faintly hopeful.

Perhaps Linus summoned help? It's possible.

Of course. Didn't Yasmin say there was someone outside on the balcony?

Frowning, Bachmann put his ear to the wall with the fire extinguisher on it.

Yes, of course, Linus left after Bruck. The shutters locked him out. He must have gone off and informed the police.

Caspar's hopes rose still further as the throbbing sound increased in volume. Then Bachmann extinguished them with a shake of the head.

'It's just the storm,' he said regretfully. 'It's pressing against the shutters from outside. That one up on the third floor is wedged open with a metal bar, don't forget. The wind is probably whistling through it and causing a partial vacuum. The building's hermetically sealed, after all.'

Vacuum? Hermetically sealed?

Caspar wondered if he was getting more and more paranoid. To his ears, this sounded like a far too professional explanation for a porter. On the other hand, Bachmann couldn't be accounted a conventional hospital porter. He was on close terms with Rassfeld and furthered his education by reading books on public speaking. *All the same...* There was that other matter that had aroused his suspicions a few hours before.

'What was that business with the snowmobile?' he asked, taking a thick pad of paper from the computer table in front of the glass partition.

'Huh?'

'I mean, after you'd picked up Schadeck and Bruck from the overturned ambulance in the driveway and brought them up here. Linus showed it to me. Someone had pulled out the fuel hose.'

'Really?'

Bachmann was looking puzzled, and Caspar felt annoyed with himself for having raised the subject at all. What did he hope to elicit by asking stupid questions? A confession? *Yes, I'm sorry. I didn't want anyone leaving the clinic.*

'Must have been Schadeck. I've always thought there was something fishy about him.'

'Yes,' was all Caspar said. He clamped three medical textbooks under his arm. 'Anyway, it doesn't matter now.'

They went next door together.

The room was dominated by the futuristic-looking MRI scanner, which the art director of a sci-fi film might well have used as the gateway to another world. Caspar stationed himself beside it and looked up.

'Is that thing with the flashing light what I think it is?'

'Yes.'

'Then this is the place to do it.'

Taking two towels from the scanner's sliding couch, Caspar bundled them up and dropped them on the floor beneath the smoke alarm. Then he tore several pages from one of the books and propped up the others like billets of firewood.

'Just tip that stuff over it,' he told Bachmann. The porter unscrewed the cap of the canister, looking as if he couldn't believe what he was doing.

'You realise this machine cost several million euros?'

Caspar grinned feebly. 'Sorry to say so, but we're hardly going to get into trouble with the boss, are we?' He gave Bachmann a nod. 'So get on with it before we end up like him.'

The cleaning fluid slopped over their makeshift bonfire, glug-glugging almost obscenely. Bachmann produced a box of matches from his breast pocket and was about to strike one when the communicating door behind them shut with a faint click.

'What the devil...?'

Caspar swung round just in time to see a dark figure flit across the control room beyond the glass partition. Then the scanner began to flash. At the same time, there issued from the depths of the tube a sound like an axe hammering an empty metal drum. All this happened within the fraction of a heartbeat, just as Bachmann, startled, dropped the burning match.

2:39 a.m.

Two columns of flame leaped ceilingwards simultaneously, but only one of them was real. The other proved to be a reflection in the glass partition. Caspar thought at first that the face behind it was also an optical illusion. Then the half-naked man pounded on the glass with his fist and he recognised the rage-contorted features. There was no doubt about it. Jonathan Bruck was still wearing the green hospital gown, but the front of it was now spattered with rust-coloured stains and a large quantity of blood seemed to have seeped through the bandage around his throat, which had slipped.

Caspar started to sweat. Turning round, he felt the heat on his face and stated the obvious. 'We must get out of here!' he told Bachmann, who had also seen the Soul Breaker and was retreating towards the door with his back to the wall. The fire was producing more and more smoke.

'It's no use,' Caspar shouted, more loudly than necessary, in a break between two bursts of scanner noise. He rattled the knob of the communicating door in demonstration of this fact. For safety reasons the automatic time lock could only be opened once the scanner had completed its programme, and Bruck had only just activated it. If it was set to a virtopsy programme, that would take hours!

'Let us out!' Caspar yelled, hammering on the glass

himself now. The big pane barely vibrated under his fists. Bruck had no intention of releasing them. As if to intensify his captives' horror, which was already extreme, he bent down for a moment. When he straightened up he was holding a pair of scissors. His lips moved, mouthing some unintelligible words, and then...

Oh, my God...

...he drove the scissors into the palm of his left hand.

What's he doing? Caspar wondered. The answer came at once. Bruck spat on the pane and pressed his gashed palm against its smooth surface. Caspar thought he could hear the high-pitched squeak of lacerated flesh on glass as the Soul Breaker's hand slid slowly down the pane, leaving a long smear of blood behind it.

He's trying to tell us something! It's a sign like the knife in his throat.

Caspar was simultaneously horrified and fascinated. Meanwhile, his nose had begun to run as thickening smoke stung the mucous membranes. It was a while before his streaming eyes could make out what Bruck had written on the glass in mirror writing. His first thought was a snake, then an SOS sign. Eventually, even though the Soul Breaker's blood ran out before he could write the final vowel, he came to the obvious conclusion: *Sophi...*

Of course. The madman was out to get the psychiatrist and complete his work on her. That was why they hadn't expected Bruck to attack them down here in neuroradiology when his true quarry was awaiting him upstairs in the library. But now he'd checkmated them. They were imprisoned in an inferno of their own making. Even if the shutters went up at once, it would do them no good down here: they would die of smoke inhalation unless they thought of some way of putting out the fire in double-quick time.

But how? The goddamned fire extinguisher is outside.

Caspar peered at the flames and the Soul Breaker in turn.

I left it out there deliberately, so we could prevent the fire from spreading.

He hadn't considered the possibility that they might be locked in *after* lighting the fire. What was more, he had forgotten about the second canister of cleaning fluid, which chose that moment to explode.

2:43 a.m.

The sudden, fiery blast propelled him backwards like a gust of wind. He even thought he felt it shrivel the fine hairs on his bare skin.

'Help me!' shouted Bachmann, whose right trouser leg had caught fire. Caspar tore off the tattered remains of his T-shirt and beat out the flames with short, sharp, well-directed blows.

What now?

His T-shirt had barely sufficed to extinguish the porter's trousers. How could they tackle the blaze, which was already licking at the scanner room's wood-panelled ceiling?

Caspar turned on the spot, desperately hoping to discover a second fire extinguisher somewhere on the wall. As he did so, he caught another glimpse of Bruck. Still staring through the glass with foam on his lips and madness in his eyes, he was almost apologetically shaking his head as if to say: '*Sorry, but I'm afraid you're collateral damage.*' Caspar felt like a captive beast in a zoo being watched by an insane visitor who has set fire to its cage and is blocking its only means of escape. He went down on his knees, hoping that the smoke would be thinner there, and saw to his horror that the flames had already spread to the cloth seat of the revolving chair beside the scanner.

Without a moment's hesitation, he grabbed the chair by its hot metal legs and, heedless of the pain, hurled the blazing object at the window. The glass vibrated somewhat more violently this time, and a fine crack appeared at the point of impact, but they were still shut in.

He wanted to grab the legs of the chair again but could hardly see a thing. The smoke was even thicker than it had been in his car crash nightmares, and he had to knuckle his smarting eyes. Shaken by a paroxysm of coughing, he thought his lungs were about to burst when a current of air on his face told him that Bachmann must have picked up the chair and sent it hurtling through the glass partition.

Screwing up his eyes, he saw the porter kick out the rest of the shattered pane with his boots and then, like a drowning man summoning up his last reserves of energy, clamber over the edge of the frame and into the comparative safety of the outer room.

'Get the fire extinguisher!' Caspar yelled. The flames behind him were now feeding on fresh oxygen. Unscathed so far, the scanner continued to transmit its bursts of rhythmical magnetic impulses at full and brutal volume.

'Hello?' Caspar called. Receiving no answer, he decided to liberate himself. He couldn't remain in this inferno, even though climbing through the shattered window would be far more painful for him than for Bachmann. His feet were bare, after all.

Like Bruck's.

Caspar supported himself with both hands on the jagged window frame, lacerating his palms. He cried out in pain as he transferred his entire weight to them while launching himself sideways into the outer room. He rolled off the frame and fell to the floor. A fresh wave of agony surged through him before the first could subside, because he'd driven a spatula-sized splinter of glass into his shoulder on landing. Another fragment dug into his bare heel like a bottle cap and broke off deep in the flesh at the very first step he took.

He hobbled over to the wall and grabbed the fire extinguisher, only to overestimate his remaining strength and almost drop it, but he finally managed to hump the heavy steel cylinder over to the desk, operate the lever and play the jet of white foam over the blaze until every flame in the scanner room had been extinguished.

Exhausted, he leant against the widescreen monitor on the desk, inwardly preparing himself for the next attack. Bruck had to be somewhere, after all.

He knew he'd only disposed of the least significant of the dangers that threatened him, so it came as all the more of a relief when a familiar face appeared in the doorway leading to the passage.

'Schadeck?' he said, laying the fire extinguisher aside. 'Did it work? Have the shutters gone up?'

Schadeck shook his head and came in. Either the fire hadn't burned for long enough or the scanner room's smoke alarm wasn't linked to the overall security system.

'So why are you here? Did Bachmann send you?'

'No,' said Schadeck, coming a step closer. Then he drew a pistol and fired straight at Caspar's chest.

TODAY

Very much later, many years after The Fear

1:32 p.m.

The gust made the building tremble as if an underground train were passing beneath it. The professor looked up, but his students were far too engrossed in their reading matter to be distracted by the sound of the wind. It was darker now, and they'd turned on the little reading lamp he'd taken the precaution of placing on the table between them.

Seen from the other end of the table, they looked like a pair of schoolkids cramming for an examination.

Patrick was reading with his head propped on his hands, whereas Lydia traced the course of every line with her pencil, mouthing the words and making occasional notes on a pad to the right of her copy.

The professor stood up and arched his back. In spite of the pain it caused him, he followed his orthopaedist's advice and rotated his shoulder joints every two hours.

In his eyes, the doctor's advice was as ineffectual as that of the friend who had persuaded him to go to Lydia's strip club.

She made another note, and he resolved to peek at her pad sometime. He walked past the empty shelves from which all the books had been removed, probably for sale on the internet or in some flea market. Only one volume had failed to find a home elsewhere. Covered in dust, it languished behind the cracked glass of a bookcase. Although the spine was scratched and stained with mouse droppings, it looked as if it had been put there that morning, especially for the benefit of the building's unusual visitors.

The professor walked on, for one thing because he couldn't bear to see his own guilty, hollow-cheeked face reflected in the bookcase. For another, because he didn't want to know which volume of the medical dictionary was involved. He had also avoided looking at the fireplace hitherto, but now his eye was caught by a squashed plastic cannula protruding like a spillikin from an assortment of rubbish: a bent television aerial, snippets of electric wiring, a ripped-up carpet tile.

Don't do it!

An inner voice commanded him to leave the thing where it was.

It shouldn't have shouted so loudly. He'd had no intention of extracting the cannula and, quite possibly, collapsing his mental house of cards.

He cleared his throat softly so as to warn the students of his approach, but they were far away in a world of their own. *Proof of the existence of telepathy*, Stephen King had written once. An author implants his thoughts in the minds of his readers. Often at a distance of thousands of kilometres, he makes them see, feel, sense and discover places they've never been to before.

But what if those thoughts are evil?

Still unnoticed by his students, the professor avoided casting a shadow on Lydia's pad as he stole up behind her. Her girlish handwriting conformed to all the usual gender clichés: neat, tidy, rounded.

Caspar? she'd written at the head of the grey, recycled sheet. Beneath it, in parentheses, was the information she'd so far gleaned from the text: (Doctor / father of a daughter? / Hamburg? / professional blunder?)

Lydia had devoted the next column to the Soul Breaker. The professor smiled sadly as he read the last word, which she'd adorned with three question marks and underlined twice.

Soul Breaker = Jonathan Bruck (doctor, colleague, self-mutilation, <u>Motive???</u>)

She evidently considered the latter question worthy of a slightly indented paragraph of its own: MOTIVE

Torture Sophia? Prevent her from divulging her knowledge? Of Caspar? Of Caspar's daughter?

He couldn't be absolutely certain of what came

next because Lydia's elbow was obscuring some of the words. He thought they read:

Caspar's admission to the clinic = fortuitous? (How does Schadeck come into it? What connection with the other victims?)

The final words were clearly visible and in capitals:
THE SOUL BREAKER'S REVENGE?

Wind buffeted the rain-streaked window panes. Patrick looked up for the first time, but only briefly and in order to reach for the bottle of water in front of him. He hadn't noticed that the man in charge of the psychiatric experiment had left his place and was standing immediately behind him.

Surprising, thought the professor as he turned away from Lydia and her notes. *Really surprising how, in spite of drawing the wrong conclusions, one can arrive at the correct and all-important question.*

As though attracted to it by an invisible magnet, his gaze returned to the fireplace. From where he was standing it looked as if its mouth had been stopped with rubbish to prevent the fire from ever divulging another secret.

Paper cracked like a knuckle as Lydia turned to page 196 of the medical record.

Patrick, who read somewhat more slowly, followed her into the dream-world of Caspar's memories a few minutes later.

Flashback

In his dream, the sorrow Caspar felt was like a living creature. It consisted of innumerable tick-like parasites that had taken root in his psyche and were sucking all the joy out of him.

Whenever he opened his mouth to apologise to the eleven-year-old daughter whom he had left defenceless, a fresh swarm of ticks crawled into his mouth, thirsty and famished, ready to burrow into the mucous membranes of his windpipe and gullet, there to drink their fill of his vital spirits. He knew he could never be happy again. Not after that mistake.

So he put the bottle to his lips again and took another swig although he could hardly see a thing. In this rain. And driving so fast along a country road on the run from himself.

He hadn't believed it could happen. His method of treatment had never gone wrong before, and now it had. It had failed the most important patient in his life.

He reached one-handed for his briefcase, took out the photo and kissed it, then raised the bottle again.

Oh God, what did I do to you?

He was groping for the windscreen wiper knob with the hand that held the photo, meaning to turn it to maximum, when he saw the tree. He braked, shielding his face with his arms. 'What on earth did I do?' he cried again.

Then it was light. He was still asleep, of course. He could hear his own laboured breathing – the breathing of someone asleep or ill – but he couldn't wake up. He was still imprisoned in his nightmare, even though his surroundings had suddenly changed. No longer in his car, he was sitting on the edge of a hard bed. His bare legs were dangling over the side and he was wearing a plastic wristband with a number on it.

'You didn't do a thing,' said a voice. Although he had never heard it before in his nightmares, it sounded familiar. Friendly, but with a sinister undertone, it belonged to someone who was either a heavy smoker or a patient with a throat complaint. Or both.

'Yes, I did. I killed my daughter.'

'No,' said the voice, 'you didn't.'

Caspar saw a door open – a door that hadn't been there a moment ago – and a man came in. Tall and rather overweight, his build went with the voice. A dark shadow was lying across his face.

'If it wasn't me, who was it?'

'That's the wrong question,' said the voice, and the shadow lifted a little.

'What went on at my practice?'

'That's better. That question is far more to the point. I answered it in my letter to you.'

'Letter? What letter? I don't know what you mean. I know nothing of any letter. I can't even remember my daughter's name.'

'Yes, you can,' said the voice, and for one brief instant it materialised before his eyes into an all too familiar face.

He screamed when he recognised Jonathan Bruck. And he screamed even louder when the Soul Breaker underwent another transformation.

Forty minutes before The Fear

'Who are you?'

The swollen veins in Schadeck's neck told Caspar that the paramedic had just been shouting at him. All he himself felt was a slight pressure on his eardrums. He had also, since recovering consciousness, heard a steady hum. He was shivering with cold but sweating at the same time.

'I don't know.'

His tongue felt like a prune. He could scarcely move it, but that was, without doubt, his least urgent problem at the moment.

What happened? Where am I?

He tried to raise his arms and legs, but he could move them only a few millimetres.

I'm tied down.

He strained at the rubber straps that were pinning

him down on the dissecting table. Instantly, a shooting pain travelled from the small of his left arm, via his shoulder, to his temples. He felt sick. The pain became quite unbearable as his head fell back onto the table's cold metal surface.

Oh God, Schadeck must have got the anaesthetic pistol from the dispensary, shot me with it and dragged me into the path lab.

Caspar shut his eyes because the halogen lights were dazzling him and he thought he was about to vomit at any moment. From fear. And because of the poison in his system.

'What have you done to me?' he croaked, unsure if his voice was intelligible. The humming, drumming sound had also increased in volume.

'Pull yourself together, the anaesthetic only lasts ten minutes and time's up, so come on, out with it! Who are you? What are you doing in this place?'

A current of air blew the hair off Caspar's sweaty forehead. It was created by something Schadeck was waving like a fan. When a sheet of paper fell out of it, Caspar recognised it as a patient's medical record. *His* record.

'Wondering where I got it from?' said Schadeck. 'It was in the library, lying open on the table. Your friend Jonathan left it there for us.'

'He's no friend of mine,' said Caspar. He wondered why there was a needle sticking in his arm. At the same time, he realised that the drumming in his ears was coming from the room next door. The MRI scanner! The virtopsy programme was still running! The fire couldn't have damaged the expensive machine.

Schadeck uttered a sarcastic laugh. 'Afraid it's pointless to deny it.'

Caspar blinked hard, several times, to dispel the grey film that seemed to be blurring his vision like ground mist.

'Well, now do you remember?'

Schadeck slapped him on the forehead with a soot-stained envelope, then extracted the sheet inside it, which was badly scorched. A whiff of burned paper filled his nostrils.

'Recognise the handwriting?'

For N. H., Caspar read. He couldn't help nodding, but not because the handwriting rang a bell. He had recognised the initial letter of his surname, which had occurred to him for the first time only a couple of minutes earlier: *Haberland*.

This, he supposed, was another piece of the jigsaw puzzle with which Rassfeld and Sophia had meant to familiarise him by degrees, certainly not in circumstances like the present. Schadeck turned the envelope over, and the sender's initials on the back – J. B. – were like a mute accusation.

Jonathan Bruck.

Caspar wondered why the letter had been more badly scorched than its outer covering.

'I think your pal took a lot of trouble with his choice of words. To the extent that I can decipher them, at least.' Schadeck adopted a theatrical tone of voice, substituting dramatic pauses for those paragraphs and phrases that had been rendered illegible by fire.

Dear Colleague...
...a tragic occurrence, but one for which, to the best of my knowledge, you bear no blame, because...

At this point an entire paragraph had been obliterated.

...you should consequently stick to the plan we discussed. It would be better for you to go to the Teufelsberg Clinic before Christmas... and...

Schadeck replaced the sheet of paper in the folder containing his medical record, then swiped Caspar across the face with it, jerking his head sideways.

'"Dear Colleague"? "Our plan"? What does that mean, eh? What's it doing in your file?'

'I don't know.'

'Stop playing games, Caspar, or Mr N. H., or whatever your name is.'

Schadeck lashed out again with the folder, catching Caspar's forehead with the sharp edge.

'The fact is, *you* know the Soul Breaker. *You'd* seen

him before, and he advised *you* to come here. As a *colleague*.'

'No.'

'Very well... let's try something different.'

Schadeck aimed a furious kick at an instrument trolley, sending several objects clattering to the floor. Bending down, he reappeared with a coarse-toothed bone saw in his hand.

'Then I'll have to get the truth out of you some other way.'

3:01 a.m.

The worst feature of the whole situation was his inability to deny everything.

Schadeck was quite right about one thing and had even supplied irrefutable proof of it: he knew Bruck. He was at least as well acquainted with him as he was with the second victim, Katja Adesi, his daughter's primary school teacher. He knew he'd seen them both before – in the real life of which he had only fragmentary recollections. But, if there really was a plan to assemble them all in this psychiatric institution on Christmas Eve, it must have been devised by a madman. Possibly by himself.

What on earth did I do?

Caspar saw the individual pieces of the puzzle in front of him. Although he could surmise, from their shape and colouring, how they might combine to form a picture, the picture itself eluded him.

The mistaken treatment, the disastrous drive through the night that had left its mark on him for ever.

How do they all fit together?

And how come Bachmann had found him lying unconscious in a ditch if he'd apparently tried to sneak into the clinic hours earlier, accompanied by his dog?

'Where are the others?' he asked to gain time.

Schadeck was standing behind his head now. This only intensified his fears, because he could no longer see what the paramedic was up to. To judge by the hissing sound, he was spraying the saw blade with disinfectant.

'Don't worry about the women, I've locked them up in the library.'

Another hiss.

'And Bachmann?'

'Who are you kidding? *You* were with him last.'

Caspar's head was abruptly yanked backwards. He half expected to be scalped at any moment, Schadeck was tugging at his hair so hard. Contorted with rage, the paramedic's upside-down face was hovering only a few centimetres above his own. A thread of saliva detached itself from Schadeck's lips and narrowly missed his eye.

'Right, so much for the warm-up. Now let's get the show on the road.'

The blade, shiny with moisture, strayed into Caspar's field of vision. He gave an involuntary gulp and felt his Adam's apple impinge painfully on his straining throat.

'No, don't. Please...' He was pleading for his life now. He wrenched at the straps, arched his bare chest and yelled as hard as his hoarse voice would allow.

'That won't do you any good,' said the face above his. 'All that can save you now is the truth.'

'But I don't know anything!'

'Know why I don't believe you?'

Caspar shook his head vigorously, choking down the bile that had risen into his throat.

'Because you remind me too damned much of myself.'

Schadeck held up his scarred hand. 'I told you about my father,' he said. 'The night my mother didn't put enough salt in the mashed potato, he hit on the amusing idea of sticking my hand in a waffle iron.' The hand disappeared again. 'After he broke my mother's jaw he went to the pub. By the time he staggered home she'd gone to the hospital, but this time she'd left him for good and taken my brother and sister with her. I'd stayed behind on my own to settle matters with the old man once and for all, but I underestimated him. He might have drunk the pub dry, but he was still as strong as an ox.'

Schadeck came round the side of the dissecting table.

'He clamped my hand in the waffle iron and demanded to know where the others had gone. I screamed and struggled and begged him to stop, but he only laughed. Know what I learned that night?' Schadeck asked softly, ominously, before answering his own question: 'Brute force will get you nowhere.'

He tossed the bone saw onto the side table. Caspar uttered a groan of relief.

'The pain was unbearable, but I didn't give them away. Dad didn't stop until the stench of burned flesh made even him feel sick. He thought I honestly didn't know where they'd gone, the drunken idiot. If he'd looked in a medical dictionary for once in his life, he'd have been able to get the truth out of me far more easily.'

'What do you mean?' asked Caspar, his relief giving way to vague apprehension.

Schadeck laughed. 'I'll show you. You're a doctor, after all. Does sodium thiopental mean anything to you?'

'It's a barbiturate,' Caspar said automatically. *Highly effective, induces total unconsciousness within a few seconds. Commonly used in the induction phase of general anaesthesia.*

'Correct,' said Schadeck. 'A big dose will send you into the world hereafter. In lower doses it acts as a depressant, rendering a person relaxed and irrepressibly talkative. That's why secret services are so fond of using it for interrogation purposes. Well, what do you think? Isn't it great how well stocked the clinic's dispensary is?'

He pointed to the drip needle in Caspar's arm.

'Keep nice and still or I'll squirt the thiopental into your eye instead of the vein.'

3:03 a.m.

The truth serum legend occupies a prominent place in the realm of modern myths. Most people believe in the existence of a chemical substance with which a torturer can break the will of his victims; a substance which, once it has entered their bloodstream, will extract any secret from them, however closely guarded.

But the reality in which Caspar was imprisoned at this moment was of a different nature. Worse. Hopeless.

For the anaesthetic that was being injected into him lifts the biochemical carpet beneath which a person has swept his most intimate secrets. A phenomenon familiar to all anaesthetists, it transforms them into father confessors when patients involuntarily confess their direst sins in the last few seconds before surgery. Women, in particular, tend to reveal their sexual predilections in a drastic manner. So thiopental weakens the brain's control centre. But it releases only thoughts that are deliberately suppressed, not those unconsciously buried in the ruins of the soul.

'Stop, don't, wait…' Caspar implored, mainly to gain time. Something cold was numbing his left arm from the inside. He couldn't see how much of the hypodermic syringe's contents Schadeck was injecting into his veins, but it felt like half a litre of coolant.

'Don't worry, I know how to give injections. My father got the first one I ever gave while he was sleeping it off, but that was a bigger dose, if you know what I mean.' Schadeck uttered a bark of laughter. 'How about you, though? What have you got to confess?'

The paramedic's voice sounded strange, like that of someone speaking in an empty church. It mingled with the pulsating thuds of the scanner, but they had grown fainter, as if someone had closed a hitherto open soundproof door.

'I've... I've just thought of something,' Caspar lied. The idea he'd had a moment ago had disappeared into the ground mist of his consciousness. The narcotic was befuddling him.

'I'm listening,' said Schadeck.

The icy sensation was steadily spreading. It had travelled up his shoulder and was nearing his heart.

'You... you said something just now...' Caspar smiled despite himself. This was absurd. Schadeck wasn't a qualified anaesthetist. If the paramedic had got his body weight wrong and miscalculated the dose by only a few millilitres, he would go out like a light within seconds, but until then the narcotic was numbing his fears. Instead, a multitude of ideas seemed to be trying to make themselves heard simultaneously, and he sensed how much of an effort it would be to prevent his mouth from running away with him.

'What did you call the stuff?' Staring at the needle in his arm, he wished someone would keep him conscious by splashing cold water in his face.

'Thiopental?' Schadeck's voice seemed to come from far away although he was standing right beside him.

'No, no…'

He blinked, then opened both eyes wide and strove with all his might to keep them from closing.

Of course, that's it.

He raised his head as far as he could, to the extent that his dizziness and nausea permitted, and that accelerated the process. The more he strained his neck, the more the points in his head switched over, enabling the memory train to head for its first important intermediate station.

'A hypnotic,' he said, and his cervical vertebrae cracked as he nodded vigorously. 'You said it was a hypnotic. Release me, that's the answer!'

3:06 a.m.

The pressure diminished but the cold persisted. At the same time, Caspar felt unpleasantly intoxicated. His heart jumped like a defective CD. Now and then it beat normally. At other times it fluttered up and down beneath his ribcage in a syncopated rhythm, frequently skipping a beat.

It hurt a lot. The pain took his breath away, but at least he could still speak even though his voice sounded more and more like a drunk's.

'That's the answer,' he repeated.

'What do you mean?' Schadeck had to repeat his question twice before he hoisted it in.

'The riddle Sophia was holding in her hand,' he said haltingly.

'It's the truth, although the name is a lie?'

'Yes.'

'Well?'

'The answer…' Caspar swallowed hard. His throat was sore and his tongue seemed to have doubled in size. 'The answer is "hypnosis".'

'Why?'

'The word comes from the Greek. *Hypnos*, the god of sleep.'

Caspar had the unreal sensation that he was listening to himself speaking, but only after a long delay, like someone conducting a transatlantic phone call in the old days. Still, at least he'd formulated an entire sentence.

'What the hell are you getting at?' demanded Schadeck.

Caspar concentrated on his breathing. Before replying he drew a deep breath and then exhaled, counting up to three as he did so. 'It used to be thought that hypnosis was a sleep-like condition. That's wrong.'

He shut his eyes again and talked louder, partly to prevent himself from being lulled to sleep by his own voice.

'On the contrary, the subject is awake. Only his controlled consciousness is restricted, as in the victims' case. As with Sophia. The Soul Breaker hypnotised them. That's the truth, although the name is a lie.'

'Hogwash!' Schadeck bellowed the word, and his voice drew a metallic echo from the aluminium doors of the path lab's refrigerated lockers.

Caspar opened first one eye, then the other. A shaft of concentrated agony pierced his retina and seemed to stab him in the brain.

'Why?' he shouted back. At least, he thought he'd raised his voice but he wasn't sure. 'I don't have the strength to explain it all now. Listen to me.'

He struggled against his restraints, but he couldn't move the arm with the needle in it because Schadeck was now pinning him down on the dissecting table with both hands.

'You need me conscious.'

'Why?'

'Sopor,' Caspar said hoarsely. He coughed. Already raw from the smoke, his throat had been lacerated still further by the few words he'd uttered. He felt incredibly thirsty, and part of him wished Schadeck would dispose of his headache by finally injecting the rest of the anaesthetic. But he couldn't afford to lose consciousness if he wanted to get out of there alive.

'Sophia herself supplied the clue,' he went on, catching Schadeck's eye. 'The Soul Breaker puts his victims into a deathlike sleep under hypnosis – into that agonising spiral between waking and sleeping from which they can't escape.'

'Hypnosis?' Schadeck repeated incredulously.

'Yes.'

Distraction, shock, surprise, doubt, confusion, dissociation.

Caspar was acquainted with the factors which, either separately or cumulatively, create a condition in which a person's thoughts and actions can be externally manipulated.

'Okay, that's enough!' yelled Schadeck. 'Everyone knows it's impossible to hypnotise a person against their will.'

'You're wrong!' Caspar said feebly. He made the mistake of thrusting out his chin. A split second later, being no longer in control of his movements, he banged his head on the dissecting table. Another dazzling flash transfixed his closed eyes. For one brief, terrible moment it lit up an image from the past which he would sooner have obliterated: the memory of a fair-haired little girl shaking her head to indicate that she didn't want him to treat her.

Oh no, I did it. I did it against her will...

'Hollywood myths,' he heard Schadeck say angrily. 'Innocent citizens brainwashed into becoming terrorists and planting bombs to order, eh? People committing suicide because someone utters the magic words, eh? What else are you going to tell me to save your skin, eh? It's all nonsense.'

'No, it isn't,' said Caspar. 'I can prove it to you. Release me.'

'Dream on.' Schadeck picked up the syringe again.

'Stop, stop, stop.' The rising tide of thoughts in Caspar's head had passed the danger mark. The flood barrier that guaranteed his ability to communicate was about to give way. Classical medicine did indeed assume than no one could be put into a trance against their will. But what if a victim was unaware that hypnosis was in progress? What if their determination to resist had previously been weakened by shocks, traumata or drugs?

He wanted to tell Schadeck about a CIA project dating from the Cold War – one that had explored militarily useful brainwashing techniques and produced some startling results. For some inexplicable reason, he found he knew this 'Artichoke Memorandum' by heart:

Under the guise of taking a blood pressure reading, the subject may be coaxed into relaxation. Or a blood test may be used to administer a drug. Or an eye examination to cause the subject to follow the movements of a tiny light or to stare into a flashlight while verbal instructions are given.

He wanted to tell Schadeck about the 'vitamin' injections administered to human guinea pigs without their knowledge, which really contained sodium amytal, and about the mysterious Alzner Protocols, the very reading of which was mind-altering. He also wanted to quote from the Ethics Commission's final report:

After the inflicting of intense physical pain and mental torture, in particular the occasioning of extreme, traumatising states of shock, the administering of mind-altering drugs renders it possible to put suggestible persons into a hypnotic trance against their will, and to dominate their consciousness.

All this and much more was on the tip of his tongue, but he lacked the strength to say it. Meantime, his vocal cords had fallen prey to a sort of feverish fatigue, with the result that all he could do was mumble incoherently.

'You too, you could…'

'Well?'

'…do that too.'

'What?'

'Hypnotise me.'

Caspar clenched his fist, deliberately driving a splinter of glass into the flesh. The pain distracted him.

'It all depends on circumstances. Look at me. I'm at your mercy. The more poison you inject, the more easily you can break me.' He coughed again, this time because he'd choked on his own saliva.

'But not for several weeks, surely?' Schadeck kicked the table angrily. 'And certainly not to death, like the first victim. I'm beginning to think you aren't a doctor after all, or you'd know that every defective hypnosis sooner or later develops into natural sleep. All the victims would have woken up of their own accord. They certainly wouldn't have died.'

Yes, I am a doctor. Caspar was sure of this now, the memories were returning ever quicker. If they'd been in Rassfeld's office he could have proved it to Schadeck – shown him the psychiatrists' directory, a complete list of registered practitioners. He could see his own entry: *Dr Niclas Haberland, specialising in neuropsychiatry and ultra-depth hypnosis.*

'You're right,' he said, trying to pacify Schadeck before he pumped more thiopental into him. 'Medical hypnosis is normally harmless. Loss of rapport is the worst that can happen...' Caspar was surprised how familiar he found the technical terms. 'In other words, when the hypnotist can't communicate with his patient and the latter ceases to respond to him. Yes, you're right in that respect. All you have to do is wait – everyone wakes up in the end. Unintentional injuries caused by negligence are one thing – as, for instance, when a woman from a television audience crawls around on all fours like a dog and falls into the orchestra pit. But no one has ever conducted research into whether it's possible to harm someone deliberately, don't you see?'

Caspar was only whispering now and couldn't be sure if he'd just said all those things aloud. His powers of perception were close to zero. He'd lost control over himself – ironically enough, just when he needed to lecture on hypnotic techniques.

'If someone really has developed a method of hypnosis with which people can be deliberately sent into a waking coma – a method which can ultimately have fatal side effects – we'll never read about it in any medical journal because that would be a prohibited human experiment. But that, I'm afraid, is what is happening here. Here in this clinic, and we're taking part in it!'

Caspar could tell that some of what he'd said had not entirely missed the mark. When Schadeck clasped his hands behind his head and stared at him irresolutely, he added: 'Undo me, please. I think I know how to release Sophia from her death-sleep and get us all out of here.'

Schadeck pursed his lips dubiously and ran his fingers through his hair. He sighed, and a moment later Caspar felt the pressure on his arm diminish. The drip needle had been removed and was lying among the autopsy instruments on the side table.

'One false move and I'll finish you off.'

The paramedic was just undoing the strap around

Caspar's left wrist when the impossible happened. Somewhere in the building a telephone rang.

3:09 a.m.

'Stop, don't...' he shouted, but Schadeck had already dashed out into the passage without a backward glance.

It's a trap, he wanted to yell, but his voice failed him.

Supporting himself on his left hand, which was now free, he turned on his side and proceeded to undo the other straps with trembling fingers. The colours around him had changed, as had the sounds. The MRI scanner was still thudding away like a psychedelic techno disc in the room next door. The hammer blows sped up, drowning the sound of the telephone that shouldn't have been ringing. For one thing because the lines were down; for another because it sounded far too loud. It shouldn't have been audible down here in the basement.

Unless...

Caspar tried to stand up, missed his footing and landed with a crash on the hard stone floor. He heard something crack in his left shoulder and uttered a yell. His senses might be numb, but not his pain centre.

The instrument table fell over when he tried to pull himself up by it. On impulse he picked up a scalpel that had landed right beside his knee. Then he exchanged it for the syringe. If he had to defend himself, a well-aimed injection would act quicker even though the syringe had already lost a good proportion of its contents.

He gave another yell when he accidentally put his weight on the wrong foot and rammed the splinter still deeper into his heel. Laboriously, he hobbled the length of the dissecting table and made for the exit. It was only a few steps away, but everything swam before his eyes. At first he even got the impression that the distance between himself and the open door was steadily increasing.

He lost his balance again and had to put his weight on his injured foot, but at least the pain prevented him from passing out. An insoluble contradiction was raging inside him. On the one hand, he wanted to escape before the Soul Breaker got to him; on the other, he yearned to sleep for evermore.

Sleep, he thought, and suddenly the smell of smoke was back in his nostrils, although this might have been because he was now in the passage, only a few metres from the scanner room in which he himself had started a fire. *Why doesn't Sophia simply fall into a deep sleep?*

By now he had somehow made it to the lift and pressed the button. Climbing the stairs was out of the question. At present, every step would have been an insurmountable obstacle.

He rested his forehead against the lift door and tried to think, feeling the vibrations of the scanner and of

Schadeck's heavy boots on the ground floor above him. The phone had stopped ringing.

Schadeck is right. Why don't the victims simply wake up, and why are they all holding a slip of paper bearing a riddle?

The lift cable gave an arthritic creak as another thought occurred to him.

One moment...

The answer was so obvious, he couldn't believe it at first.

Sopor. Deathlike sleep. Of course.

We were so blind.

It had happened before their very eyes. Sophia was displaying all the symptoms of a patient manipulated by an unscrupulous hypnotist.

Bruck must have taken her back to some trauma in her past – to her greatest fear, her most intensely traumatic experience. *Perhaps to the moment when her ex-partner took her daughter away from her?* The Soul Breaker had then deliberately severed the connection between himself and his victim, as he had with the other victims.

He had deliberately brought about a loss of rapport and ensured that Sophia no longer responded to external stimuli, so no one but himself could get through to her.

However, Linus's unexpected appearance had disturbed Bruck before he could take the decisive final step, with the result that Sophia did what normally happens in the case of defective hypnosis: she woke up again and again.

Caspar remembered her fluttering eyelids, her groans, and the few moments when she displayed a reaction and tried to speak, only to relapse into a trance.

And we could have freed her.

They could have broken the cycle and revoked the posthypnotic command to which the Soul Breaker had subjected his victims: that they should relapse into a hypnotic state as soon as they opened their eyes; as soon as their pupils were exposed to light.

Oh, my God.

Caspar hammered on the door as if that would speed the lift's descent, but the electronic indicator above his head registered no change.

So it's the stairs after all.

He staggered sideways, avoided another fall by clinging to the banisters at the last moment, and hauled himself painfully up the stairs with one leg trailing.

It was so simple. The solution to the riddle was the solution to the riddle.

3:11 a.m.

He clasped his chest with his injured hand as a form of counterpressure to his heart, which was beating faster every step he took.

'Schadeck?' he shouted. He was eager to tell the paramedic of his conjectures and hoped they made sense.

If he was right, all they had to do was wait until the next time Sophia opened her eyes and then utter the keyword. If her psyche had not been too badly damaged, she would regain control over her consciousness. Either that, or subside into a merciful sleep.

'Schadeck?'

Still no response, even though he had shouted at the top of his voice.

He reached the top of the stairs at last, and his bloody feet left their first imprints on the reception area's thick, cream-coloured carpet. The lift doors were clicking away behind him. They weren't fully closed and kept toing and froing by a few centimetres. He wondered whether to remove the wooden chock that was preventing them from closing, but was deterred by the fact that no light was escaping from the interior. What if the Soul Breaker chose this moment to leap at him out of the darkened cabin?

He needed assistance, he decided.

Where has Schadeck got to?

Loath to confront the unknown danger armed only with a hypodermic syringe, he peered in search of help along the gloomy passage leading to the library.

And why is the door ajar?

What puzzled Caspar even more was the shiny object

a few metres ahead of him. It seemed to be rotating, and it reflected the flickering light of the library's open fire.

Drawing nearer, he saw what was lying overturned and abandoned in the middle of the passage: Sophia's wheelchair, whose slowly revolving wheel had almost come to a stop.

3:12 a.m.

I am Niclas Haberland.

Eyes narrowed, he braked the rubber tyre to a halt with his forefinger.

'Sophia?' he whispered, pushing open the library's heavy door with his bare foot.

I'm Niclas Haberland, neuropsychiatrist.

His lips moved like those of a child silently reading a schoolbook.

He repeated the same words again and again like an incantation designed to ward off the evil he expected to find inside the library.

I'm Niclas Haberland, a neuropsychiatrist specialising in the field of medical hypnosis.

His fingers tightened on the hypodermic in his hand. Then he went in. Saw the figure in front of the fireplace. And shut his eyes.

I'm Niclas Haberland, a neuropsychiatrist specialising in the field of medical hypnosis. And I made a mistake.

She was still there when he opened his eyes again: seated on one of the dining room chairs near the smoking fire. Her skin had taken on the deathly pallor of the ashes on the hearth.

Greta Kaminsky's chin was resting on her chest. Her right hand dangled limply, her left hand reposed on her lap. She looked as stiff and motionless as a doll that might keel over sideways in the slightest draught.

For a moment Caspar imagined he saw the old lady slip off her chair, hit her head on the floor and crumble away to dust.

He whispered her name and took a cautious step towards her, uncertain whether her chest was rising and falling, or whether this was just an illusion created by the fitful glow of the fire behind her.

Schadeck, Yasmin, where are you? he wondered as he looked for some sign of life. A throbbing carotid, a quiver of the violet lips. Anything.

Within arm's length of Greta now, he knelt down. Depositing the hypodermic syringe on the carpet beside her feet for fear of hurting her, he called her name aloud. Everything happened far too quickly after that.

He couldn't have said which he heard first, the cry of mortal agony or the metallic click. He didn't even know how he managed to run back along the passage so fast – back in the direction of the lift from which the sounds of a struggle were coming. The doors were somewhat wider open and light was issuing from the cabin: the thin, tremulous beam of a small flashlight playing over Bachmann's office near the entrance. Caspar came to a halt. The passage was too narrow and the lift still too far away for him to see inside. All he definitely saw was that the doors were no longer obstructed by a wooden chock. Only her legs and feet were still protruding. The Soul Breaker had already dragged the rest of Sophia's body into the darkened cabin.

Outside the clinic

The gale had become more intermittent. Although it still hurled itself with elemental fury at roof tiles, shutters, overhead cables and any other unsecured objects unwise enough to get in its way, it took an occasional breather as if preparing to snap television aerials or uproot trees with new-found strength. Faithfully accompanying the gale on its trail of devastation was the snow, an accomplice that concealed the worst of the damage beneath a white cloak of invisibility and hurled itself into the face of anyone who endeavoured to watch the storm at its destructive work.

Although the wind had dropped one point on the Beaufort scale, no one would have left the shelter of their home at this hour. Unless, of course, they were compelled to. Like Mike Haffner.

'The cushiest job in the world? Like hell it is!' Haffner

snarled. Being alone in the snowplough's cab, he was talking to himself. He thumped the plastic steering wheel with both hands.

He might have known it. He should never have listened to Schwacke. That pothead could hardly tell the difference between a spliff and a tin whistle, let alone organise a nice little earner for a friend. 'Two thousand euros, old buddy,' Schwacke had rhapsodised. 'Two thousand guaranteed, even if it doesn't snow, and we all read the papers, don't we?' He pulled his lower lid down with his middle finger and winked conspiratorially. 'Global warming, CO_2, greenhouse effect. If we get another snowy winter, old buddy, I'll join Anabolics Anonymous.'

Haffner fished out his mobile phone with a view to calling his former schoolfriend and wishing him cancer of the balls. No, preferably something infectious – ebola, for instance. It was Schwacke who had talked him into quitting his secure job at the videotheque and starting work with F. A. Worms & Co., the private snow-clearing business.

'Worms turn out in storms,' claimed the slogan on the back of the snowplough, and Haffner had discovered, when the phone rang twenty minutes earlier, that the lousy firm took it literally. 'As long as the bus stays upright, you can drive it!' the operations manager had told him brusquely. And now he was supposed to clear a route to some fat cat's garage in this posh outer suburb.

No signal!

Haffner tossed his mobile into the footwell and turned on the radio, which was also fading in and out. The DJ must have thought himself humorous in the extreme, because he was playing 'Sunshine Reggae'. Either that, or the music editor was as nuts as Schwacke. He left it on all the same. You could hardly hear anything anyway, what with the bronchitic roar of the diesel inside the cab and the howling of the wind outside. Speeding up, he skidded blindly round a bend in the road. He ought to have been driving more slowly in this blizzard, but that would have reduced the engine noise. If *he* had to work, why should these fat cats enjoy a good night's sleep? He floored the gas pedal.

Damn you, Schwacke, I'll have your guts for garters, he thought briefly, just before a figure loomed up in his headlights.

Must be seeing things, he said to himself. *No one would be daft enough to go for a walk in this lot.*

He was wrong. Pulling up just in time, he lowered the window and stuck his head out. 'Shit, what the hell are you doing out here?' he yelled. The half-naked man was waving his arms around in a panic-stricken way. His hands were dark blue with cold, his features

drawn and exhausted. Haffner couldn't tell whether he
was trembling with fear as well as cold, nor could he
understand what he was shouting.

'Phosia! Phosiapatikil!'

It sounded like gibberish. To Haffner, at least.

Inside the clinic

Caspar still didn't understand the underlying plan, but he recognised its sinister objective.

The Soul Breaker had got them to leave the path lab. They had done him that favour and split up, and he had made it unobserved into the lift he needed to transport his doomed victim to his lair in the lower basement: the laboratory accessible only with the aid of Rassfeld's special key, which Bruck had doubtless taken from the murdered medical director and must at this moment be inserting in the slot beside the brass button marked '-2'.

One hesitant step at a time, like a child loath to tread on the cracks in a pavement, Caspar slowly neared the lift to check the accuracy of his terrible suspicion. His pyjama legs rustled every time he moved. He paused briefly, hugging the wall and still unable to see into the lift whose doors kept opening and shutting on Sophia's lower thigh. He heard a whistling, bubbling intake of breath. Then her feet twitched, her toes turned up, and a little more of her disappeared into the cabin.

Heedless of his lacerated feet, Caspar broke into a run. He couldn't afford to wait any longer. If he wanted to save her, he had to act.

Without thinking, he made a dash for the lift, pressed the call button and suppressed his fear by shouting for Schadeck.

He continued to shout as the door slid open and his brain refused to accept the scene that met his eyes.

Bruck was kneeling on the floor of the cabin clasping Sophia's head with both arms. He might have been trying to apply a chiropractic grip.

Or to break her neck.

The torch clamped beneath his left arm had slipped in the course of his attempt to drag her inside. Its beam now illuminated the upper part of his body, almost as if he wanted to advertise its horrific appearance. Draped around his neck like a blood-encrusted scarf, the torn bandage exposed the wound below his Adam's apple, which had burst open, emphasising it in a macabre way.

The Soul Breaker looks a broken man himself, was Caspar's first thought as he stuck his bare foot in the door. *Punch-drunk and incapable of dragging any-one anywhere, let alone of killing them.* Bruck's most animated feature was his eyes, which reflected the light of the torch in a ghostly manner.

Before Caspar could weigh up his chances, he obeyed an instinctive impulse and leaped blindly into the lift. The mirrored cabin swayed beneath his feet as he hurled his full weight at Bruck. In so doing he smothered the cry on the Soul Breaker's lips, which sounded like the name of his fourth victim.

Sophiiiiii...

He was initially surprised by the relative feebleness of Bruck's resistance. For the first few seconds it felt like a fight between well-matched opponents – between two injured men who were lashing out at random in the hope of keeping their adversary at bay. Then blood spurted from Caspar's nose. The torch had fallen to the floor long ago and was slithering around between their bare feet, so he hadn't seen the elbow coming at him out of the gloom.

Infuriated, Caspar felt for Bruck's face and clamped his hand over the psychopath's mouth despite the knee that kept ramming itself into his stomach. Then his thumb slid down and embedded itself in the throat wound. He exerted pressure, and Bruck's unintelligible howls rose to a scream. Caspar's thumb was now deep in his windpipe, thumbnail and all.

Bruck's resistance was lessening, but then Caspar felt a sudden, unbearable pain in the pit of the stomach – one that took possession of his entire body. He tried to turn away before Bruck could kick him in the crotch again, but too late. He jacknifed, hit his forehead on

Sophia's head, and lay doubled up on the floor beside her. In expectation of another blow he shielded his face as best he could, but Bruck had fallen to his knees and was retching in agony.

Caspar backed away, feeling for Sophia's legs, and brushed against the torch. As he grabbed it and picked it up, intending to shine it in the Soul Breaker's eyes and dazzle him, its beam picked out a woman's trainer.

A shoe?

He saw only now that they weren't alone. In addition to himself, Bruck and Sophia, someone else lay slumped in the far corner of the big hospital lift.

Yasmin.

She was bleeding. That, at least, was the only logical reason he could find for the discoloration of her pale blouse just where a black rubber handle was protruding from her chest.

No time for that.

Caspar spat out the blood that had accumulated in his mouth and wrapped his arms round Sophia's knees. Then he scrambled to his feet and backed out of the lift at a crouch, dragging her along like a roll of carpet. In so doing he tore out a big hank of the hair on which Bruck had been kneeling, still clutching his throat with both hands. Blood was coming from his mouth too.

Sophia was almost outside when her legs slipped through Caspar's bloody fingers. Ignoring the pain in the hand he'd cut in the scanner room, he wiped off the blood on his scarred chest, folded her hips in a desperate embrace and threw himself backwards.

Bruck had also got to his feet, but he swayed like a boxer taking a standing count and seemed to lack the strength to launch another attack. He just stood there with his mouth open, a bubble of saliva forming on his lips. He stretched out his arms, but Sophia was beyond his reach.

Caspar had done it. Sophia's head bumped across the threshold of the lift as he dragged her clear. The Soul Breaker seemed to shout her name once more before the lift doors slid shut, muffling the sound of his agonised voice.

The last thing Caspar saw was the bent leg of the nurse for whom he could have done nothing.

Breathing heavily, he flopped over sideways without letting go of Sophia's ice-cold foot. He ran his thumb across the sole, saw her toes curl under its pressure, and had an urge to be content with this sign of life – to go to sleep right there beside the stairs, on the carpet of the Teufelsberg Clinic's reception area. He knew that it was a mistake – that he ought to remain awake – but he had almost dozed off when he coughed himself awake again. He had to sit up or he would have choked.

He spat, and a sprinkling of blood and saliva landed on the black boots that had suddenly appeared beside him.

He looked up.

'Where have you been?' he asked Schadeck in a faint voice.

'I went looking for the phone. That wanker rigged it up to ring itself and replaced it in front of the mike, so we'd hear it down in the basement over the public address system.'

Caspar nodded. He'd suspected as much.

'And did that take so long?'

'No.' Schadeck laughed and came a step closer. 'I spent the rest of the time watching you.' For the second time in half an hour he drew the anaesthetic pistol. This time, however, he only used the grip – to hit Caspar on the head as hard as he could.

Flashback

'Hey, don't tug like that, Tarzan. It's icy.'

It was only a half-hearted attempt to restrain his dog, which was tugging hard at the lead. What was the matter? Had something startled him?

Or was Tarzan annoyed because he'd left him tied up for so long, out here in the cold? He probably thought he was going to be abandoned again, the way his previous owner had left him and the rest of the litter to die in that derelict car after poking out his eye with a stick.

'Yes, yes,' he called to the young dog, 'I want to get away from here as much as you do.'

The mongrel must have picked up a scent. A fox or a wild boar, perhaps. Scents sometimes lingered in the air for hours after animals had passed a particular spot, but there was nothing to be smelled out here in the driveway save woodsmoke, which wasn't surprising in view of all the chimneys jutting from the building behind him.

'Wait, can't you…' He wondered whether to let go of the lead. The going was getting harder the further down the slope he went. Fresh snow had covered the patches of ice on the asphalt and the porter couldn't have salted it yet. He'd made a special point of waiting for him to leave, but it had been futile.

He felt inside his overcoat, but there was nothing in the breast pocket. It had just been burned before his very eyes.

The profound, melancholy pain of grief reared up in front of him like an insurmountable wall. All in vain, all to no avail. He had made a final attempt and failed as expected. And now he was standing here in the driveway, incapable of moving, unable to break through the barrier of depression that was preventing his return to a normal life.

His arm jerked as Tarzan gave it another tug but his body remained where it was, rooted to the spot and as cold as the fir trees beside the road whose branches threatened to snap beneath their burden of fresh snow. And then... he heard a bubbling sound. As he fell, the surrounding air began to seethe like a saucepan of milk boiling over. That sound became mingled with a whisper and the world around him revolved. He heard branches snap, caught a sudden glimpse of trees from another angle, felt the lead around his wrist draw tighter. Then came a crack, although none of the trees had lost a branch. At the same time the bubbling and whispering sounds grew louder, though the whisper had really ceased to be a whisper and now resembled

*a high-pitched, slightly distorted voice that was steadily
receding into the distance.*

*Then he heard something snap – a piece of wood
or a bone – and realised that it had to happen the
instant his head hit the ground. Just before the flames
appeared right in front of him. They came not from the
dashboard, as they had on the day it all began, but from
the fireplace in which branches were crackling and the
blazing fire was being sucked up the chimney by an icy
wind. And then he heard the voice as well. Metallically
unfamiliar but loud and clear.*

'You can have her,' it said. 'Come and get her.'

3:20 a.m.

Caspar tried to open his eyes and escape the dream,
but in vain: he was awake already. The fire in front of
him – the fire into which he'd been staring for quite a
while – was as real as the words he could hear over the
in-house public address system.

'Come and get her!' Schadeck's harsh voice was
issuing from the loudspeaker above his head.

Schadeck? What the hell's he playing at?

Caspar's attempt to rise from his library chair failed
for several reasons. Mainly because he was mentally
and physically incapable of the simplest actions after
the extremes of pain and violence he'd endured in the

last few hours. He had almost died of smoke inhalation and been anaesthetised against his will. In addition to lacerating his hands and feet, he had probably acquired a broken nose from Bruck and owed the icy waves of nausea he was experiencing to concussion sustained at Schadeck's hands. He didn't have the strength to stand up, so the dressing gown cord with which the paramedic had lashed his wrists to the back of the chair was quite superfluous.

'You can have her, Bruck. I've pushed her out into the entrance hall.'

The microphone produced a momentary squawk of feedback before Schadeck released the talk button.

Oh, my God. He means to sacrifice her.

As if Schadeck's words were extinguishing his last glimmer of hope, the flames on the hearth suddenly dipped and a dense cloud of smoke poured into the library.

Caspar shut his streaming eyes and prayed that the blizzard which was forcing its way down the chimney would subside.

'You want her, Bruck? You can have her, she's your Christmas present. Take her and do what you like to her, but then push off. That's the deal, okay?'

Caspar made another attempt to rise. He almost fell over backwards into the fire, but that was all. He started sweating.

'You can have the others as well. They're in the

library, where you stabbed Yasmin. The old girl's still alive.'

Turning to look, Caspar detected a slight change in Greta's posture. Her mouth was shut now.

'And the psycho is tied up, so he's easy meat. Help yourself to them both or just Sophia, I don't care. The main thing...'

Schadeck broke off but kept the button depressed.

'Shit, no! What the...'

Two seconds later there was a crash. Cut short, the scream reverberated around the clinic's empty rooms and rang in Caspar's ears.

You're a fool, Schadeck! You're such a fool...

What had Bachmann said? There were only two mikes hooked up to the public address system, and the paramedic had made a target of himself beside one of them. All that remained in doubt was whether Bruck had eliminated him before or after going to get Sophia.

There's only one certainty...

Caspar tugged desperately at his bonds with one eye on the door to the passage, which was ajar. Schadeck had removed the key.

... Bruck is on his way here!

It wasn't long before the sound of footsteps shuffling down the passage confirmed this.

Fire.

Smoke.

Books.

Greta.

Searching around for some way of escaping from the inevitable, Caspar's brain had gone into energy-saving mode. He was capable only of one-word thoughts as his eyes roamed the library.

Riddles.

Bruck.

Greta.

Books.

While he registered the fact, on one level of consciousness, that the shuffling footsteps in the passage had paused for several seconds, his instinct for self-preservation was draining the very last of his adrenalin. He stared into the fire, thinking of the car in which he had almost burned to death, and wondered if that would have been a more merciful end. Then he shut his eyes, unable to banish the image of an imaginary clock on a blazing dashboard ticking away the seconds of life that still remained to him. The circling hand was already in the red zone.

Red as fire.

That was it. The final possibility.

Fireplace.

Smoke.

Fire!

He abandoned his futile attempts to spread his shoulders and snap the cord. Instead, he threw his whole weight forwards and humped the chair nearer the hearth.

The fire. I must get closer...

He flung himself sideways. Once, twice, until at last he overbalanced. Then gravity took over and he fell to the floor. The impact was a painful reminder that he'd already half-dislocated his shoulder when falling off the dissecting table. His head landed somewhat more gently on a mound of cold ash.

I must get at the fire, he told himself again and again, repeating the words in his head like a mantra.

Still lashed to the chair, he was lying at angle to the hearth and much too far from the flames, but at least he had a better view of the door, which still hadn't budged a millimetre. All was not yet lost. He drew up his legs, knocking over the fire irons as he did so, but he could tell from the increased heat on his back that he must be nearer his objective.

Next, he threw his weight against the groaning chair back. And then, without warning, the heat became unbearably painful. Only once before in his life had he yelled as loudly, and that was when he had almost burned to death in his car. The flames seemed to scent a chance to complete the process, but they didn't scorch his chest this time; they seared his upper arms like red-hot razor blades, which told him he was almost in the right position.

Almost. Another couple of centimetres, and the incandescent log would not only scorch his wrists but burn through the cord around them.

Caspar gritted his teeth to stifle the scream that rose to his lips. In addition to the sweetish stench of scorched flesh, he thought he could at last smell smouldering cotton fibres.

Sure enough, the cord was starting to give a little.

Or is it only my imagination? Is the pain driving me completely insane?

He strained at the cord so as to expose as much of it as possible to the flames.

Is it giving? I think...

Yes.
No.
Yes.
No.
Too late.

He withdrew his arms from the fire and looked at the door. It was open wide now – far wider than it had been seconds earlier. A cold draught came whistling across the floor and into his fear-dilated eyes. He couldn't tear them away from the Soul Breaker, who was just entering the room.

3:25 a.m.

Caspar shrank away from the unbearable heat and bowed his head. His wrists were definitely looser now, but what good was that?

He wasn't up to another fight.

Groping around in the ash behind his back, his fingers closed on a glowing ember. In agony, he dropped it at once. It was pointless.

In his position, with his wrists still bound behind his back, he couldn't have hurled anything into Bruck's face. And, even if he had, what would it have achieved?

We should have climbed out up the chimney... Ironic that such an idea should occur to him now, when all their opportunities had been squandered and all their escape routes blocked. Anyway, they would have been bound to find the flue obstructed by a grille. Entertaining such thoughts was futile now that the Soul Breaker was only five limping footsteps away from his pinioned quarry.

Bruck's laboured breathing whistled through the wound in his throat as he took another dragging step. He switched a shiny object from his right hand to his left.

Another four paces.

A knife? A pair of scissors?

The firelight was too faint and fitful for Caspar to identify it without his contact lenses. Bruck had probably obtained a scalpel from the dispensary. Perhaps he'd already used it to dispose of Schadeck.

Three more paces.

Caspar wriggled around on the floor like a spider condemned to keep turning on the spot because a child has torn off one of its legs. He hoped for a miracle, prayed that Greta would recover her senses and brain the Soul Breaker with the poker, but he saw out of the corner of his eye that her legs were still dangling limply over the edge of the chair at least three metres away. He might as well have expected her to run a marathon.

He felt an urge to cry for help. Paradoxically, the smoke in his lungs reminded him that someone had once advised him always to shout 'Fire!' if danger threatened, not 'Help!', because most passers-by will respond to the latter cry by looking the other way. He might almost have laughed at the thought, had death not been so close.

Two more paces.

And then, just as Caspar saw that the object held like a pencil in Bruck's long fingers was indeed a scalpel, and just as his sensitivity to pain was completely overwhelmed by a last great surge of panic – at that very moment, the Soul Breaker broke into a dance.

It was a horrific ballet performed by a dishevelled maniac who appeared to have lost all control over his limbs. To Caspar he seemed to be doing a dance of death in slow motion. In reality, the whole performance lasted only a few seconds.

It began when Bruck's mouth opened – slowly, like a tadpole's. His left leg trembled convulsively. He raised his foot and flailed both arms at the same time, seemingly in a vain attempt to keep his balance.

Then he doubled up as if someone had punched him in the stomach. One circling arm froze in mid movement, the other hand reached for his foot.

Bruck pirouetted as if giving Caspar an opportunity to inspect the sparse hair on his legs, and that was how he came to see it.

No! Oh, my God...

The syringe.

Of course. I put it down on the floor before taking a look at Greta.

He couldn't believe his luck. A few minutes ago Schadeck had tried to torture him with it. Now, only one short pace from him, the Soul Breaker had trodden on the plastic cylinder and driven the needle into his bare foot, right into the instep. If he hadn't been shuffling that way – if he had been dragging one foot after the other – the needle would probably have hit a bone and snapped off. As it was, it had buried itself in soft tissue and Bruck's own weight had depressed the plunger.

Hence the dance. Hence the trembling.

By the time Bruck tried to pull the needle out of his foot it was too late. Thiopental was one of the fastest-acting barbiturates in existence, and in his weakened state anaesthesia would result within seconds.

His eyes widened in surprise, rolling upwards until only the whites were visible. Then the psychopath toppled over, right on top of Caspar, and buried him beneath his body.

His ribs cracked first, then the back of the chair. Caspar couldn't breathe, and his fear of death acquired a claustrophobic dimension.

What now? What shall I do?

The syringe had been half empty, so Bruck would recover consciousness in a few minutes. Caspar was doubly hampered by his bonds and the psychopath's weight, which seemed to become heavier with every painful breath he drew.

The scalpel, which had fallen from Bruck's hand, was far too near the fire for him to reach.

Besides, I'm no escape artist. I'm Niclas Haberland, a neuropsychiatrist specialising in the field of medical hypnosis. And I've made a mistake.

Holding his breath, he drew up both legs as far as the weight on top of him allowed and tried to find a fulcrum that would enable him to lever the unconscious man's body off him.

Crack.

The source of the sound this time was neither a burning log nor a fractured rib; it was the chair, which simply hadn't been designed to take the weight of two men's bodies.

Although Caspar's wrists were still bound, the back of the dining room chair had been poorly glued and came away from the seat.

He drew up his legs again until his knees were in the pit of Bruck's stomach, supporting him like a partner in a two-man gymnastic exercise. Then, gritting his teeth, he rolled aside. It worked first time – fortunately, because he wouldn't have had the energy for another attempt and might have expired in Bruck's lethal embrace.

Unencumbered by his inert burden, Caspar braced his feet against the floor and thrust himself backwards parallel to the hearth. When that failed to have the desired result he launched a final, desperate attempt to free himself: he turned on his side, once more putting his weight on his injured shoulder, and rolled away from the fireplace. That was all it took to splinter the back of the chair and detach it from the seat entirely. Although his hands were still tied behind him, he was free in other respects. He could move – could have got to his feet and shaken off the cumbersome chair back – but all he wanted at that moment was to close his eyes and go to sleep. To exchange horrific reality for a dream. Like Bruck, who was curled up in a foetal position, breathing stertorously.

But for how much longer? Ten minutes? Five?

Caspar shut his eyes and listened to his own bronchitic breathing, which was vainly trying to clear the mixture of blood, saliva and smoke particles from his mouth. Its rhythm was spasmodic like that of the MRI scanner down in the basement where Sophia doubtless was at this moment. Alone and at death's door.

Her image took shape in his mind's eye – the image of the psychiatrist who had ministered to him so kindly when he needed her help to rediscover himself and the daughter he'd abandoned *in extremis*. Now that he had reassembled a few fragmentary memories, Sophia was far more lost than he had ever been. Imprisoned inside herself, incarcerated in the dungeon of her own body. *Who knows, perhaps I'll be able to repay you sometime*, he'd told her once, when she was doing her best to alleviate his mental anguish, which had been nothing compared to what they'd all had to undergo in the course of this terrible night.

Yasmin, Sibylle, Bachmann, Mr Ed, Linus, Rassfeld...
Sophia.

He clamped his eyelids together in an effort to retain the image of that young, vulnerable woman who now had only one slim chance of survival: Caspar himself.

Certain that he was already embarking on a lost

cause, Caspar opened his eyes and rolled over onto his knees. Two minutes later he had freed his hands and got to his feet in the hope of saving Sophia and, thus, himself.

3:29 a.m.

People are supposed to discover their true selves in extreme situations – at moments when circumstances render it impossible for them to act in accordance with the values instilled in them by years of conditioning at the hands of parents, schoolteachers, friends, and other influential persons. A crisis is said to resemble a sharp fruit knife. It removes the peel and exposes the core: the amorphous, largely instinct-governed primordial state in which morality is dominated by self-preservation.

If that theory was correct, Caspar made a surprising discovery: that in the innermost depths of his soul he was a weak person. Why? Because he simply couldn't do it. He couldn't, even though it seemed right – indeed, crucial to his survival – and even though it was doubtful if he would ever be presented with a better opportunity to kill Bruck.

He stared in turn at the unconscious man at his feet and the scalpel in his hand, trying to persuade himself to cut the psychopath's throat or at least his wrists. But he couldn't. With the best will in the world, he couldn't.

Turning away, he limped over to Greta. He tried to tell himself it was only that he lacked the physical strength to take the Soul Breaker's life, but he knew that was untrue. He'd never killed anyone before. He'd never deliberately harmed anyone before, though he sometimes took decisions that amounted to the same thing.

I'm Niclas Haberland, and I made a mistake.

Greta was breathing shallowly through her half-open mouth. Her eyelids were flickering, her bent fingers drumming on her lap in time to some tune she was hearing in her artificial dreams. A white felt cloth was draped over her chest like an undersized bib. Caspar didn't have to sniff it to know what it had been soaked in.

But why? Why didn't Bruck stick to his usual behaviour pattern? Why kill Rassfeld but merely chloroform Greta? And why should he want to put Sophia, of all people, into a condition that permanently imprisons her in the no man's land between life and death?

Greta grunted indignantly and her head lolled sideways at a precarious angle when he tipped her chair back, but she didn't topple off – fortunately, or he would never have succeeded in getting her out of the danger zone. Although she was as light as a feather, the chair legs left little furrows in the old parquet floor as he dragged her backwards out of the library.

Where to now?

It was far harder to drag the chair along the passage,

which was thickly carpeted, and he had to take a rest. Bathed in sweat, he leant against the wall behind which must lie the storeroom where Sibylle Patzwalk had had her fateful encounter with Bruck. Out here in the passage the wind-boosted roar of the fire sounded fainter, but he could once more hear the scanner hammering away in the basement one floor down.

Crrrack. Crrrack. Crrrack.

Like pistol shots fired at regular intervals, the sound of the magnetic impulses came echoing up the stairwell. To Caspar, their clockwork regularity seemed an urgent reminder that time was going by.

Half a syringe of dilute thiopental. How much longer?

He took hold of Greta under the arms and lifted her. Her silk dressing gown made it easier to drag her along the carpeted passage and into the storeroom that way.

Thank God.

In contrast to the library, the key was still in the storeroom door. Caspar removed it and locked the door from the outside. He was trembling all over – trembling uncontrollably – he noticed that only now. The sole difference between his own condition and Sophia's was an ability to take conscious decisions. At the moment he couldn't even have shouted for help. To that extent he'd been right to expend the last of his strength on getting Greta to a place of safety. Bruck was simply too heavy. He would have collapsed halfway there.

I must go on.

He removed the storeroom key and tried it in the library door. It didn't fit, of course. He had used up his quota of luck the instant the Soul Breaker drove the needle into his foot.

Crrrack. Crrrack.

Where to?

He was feeling like a dehydrated marathon runner in the final straight, except that the longed-for tape he had to breast at the end of a final, merciless sprint kept receding. But he made his way along the passage until he was standing in the semi-darkness of the entrance hall. He looked round but could see nothing. Neither tyre tracks in the carpet nor a wheelchair, let alone Sophia herself. If Schadeck had left her here as a sacrifice, Bruck had already collected her.

But where is she now?

Crrrack. Crrrack. Crrrack.

He looked straight ahead, drew his eyebrows back with both forefingers to alter the focus of his pupils, but he couldn't have made out what was at the far end of the passage even with contact lenses. His weary eyes were misted over with tears and smoke. He thought he could see a beam of light just beyond the water cooler. The door of Rassfeld's office was ajar. He wondered if he had the energy to drag himself that far.

But why? To find Schadeck's blood-drained corpse? To discover what medical instruments of torture Bruck had armed himself with before carrying Sophia off and coming to get them in the library? One of them, the scalpel, Caspar was clutching in his hand.

Crrrack. Crrrack.

He swung round and stared into the lift. His first impulse was to flee from the figure that had clearly been lying in wait for him in the darkness. A figure that seemed strangely familiar.

His limited powers of perception were such that he didn't realise, until he raised the hand holding the scalpel, that the man who resembled him so much was his own likeness.

Crrrack.

He stepped towards his reflection, tripped over his own feet, and stumbled headlong into the dark lift. Something splintered – from the throbbing pain in his big toe, the remains of a shattered light bulb.

Crrrack.

He looked at the indicator board. Rassfeld's shiny silver bunch of keys was hanging from one of the keyholes. Tears came to his eyes when he saw what the Soul Breaker had added to it. Sophia's necklace was dangling before his eyes like a hypnotist's pendulum.

Her amulet. He's used it as a trophy. No…

Caspar corrected himself.

Not as a trophy. As a clue, instead of a riddle.

He reached for the mother-of-pearl pendant. It felt damp, but that might have been because his hands were sweating.

Very well. There's no going back anyway.

He put out his hand and pressed the '-2' button. The darkness that enveloped him the moment the doors closed was darker than he had ever known.

3:31 a.m.

Caspar couldn't recall, on his journey to the source of fear, whether he was an atheist or a believer. He suspected he had once enjoyed going to church, but it must have been long ago, because he couldn't think of any prayer whose words would have reassured him now.

He exerted pressure on his eyeballs to stimulate a reaction from his optic nerves. This normally caused kaleidoscopic, rainbow-coloured flashes of light to dance in front of the retinas, but even that phenomenon failed to materialise. He was afflicted instead with another form of illusion, because the lift began to rotate and his circulation went completely mad. His sense of balance had lost its last point of anchorage in the darkness. Without moving so much as a millimetre, he was inwardly revolving around himself.

Half a syringe, highly diluted...

He couldn't help reflecting, dizzily, that Bruck might even now be regaining consciousness. It surprised him how calmly he accepted the idea that the Soul Breaker might, at that very moment, be gripping the legs of the dining table and hauling himself erect.

As long as I'm inside the lift, I'm safe.

Caspar was briefly but firmly convinced that he would never be able to leave it again. Every passing second augmented his certainty that the lift would never come to a stop but continue to glide for ever down an endless shaft in which the warmth and darkness steadily increased.

He was all the more astonished to be dazzled by a blinding glare. The doors had opened.

-2.

He was where he had never wanted to be.

Blinking, he emerged into the light.

Tock. Crrrack. Tock. Tock.

The brightly lit laboratory level had to be connected to the floor above by ventilation ducts. At all events, the scanner sounded considerably louder down here than it had on the ground floor. Even so, to Caspar the thuds emanating from the MRI room seemed to be muffled by an acoustic filter.

He shielded his eyes from the harsh glare of the halogen ceiling lights that illuminated the bare concrete walls, which were institutional green in colour.

Tock. Crrrack. Tock. Tock.

Caspar's ears had become inured to the scanner's ominous, intermittent knocking sounds in the same way as the nose of someone in a windowless room can accustom itself to a bad smell which a newcomer would find intolerable. His diminished powers of perception had succeeded in banishing the hypnotic sounds to a remote region of his consciousness. He did not, however, succeed in doing the same to the muffled, almost animal cries that greeted him in the laboratory's anteroom.

3:32 a.m.

Caspar was almost rent asunder by the struggle going on inside him. Two elemental forces had decided to fight a last, decisive duel inside his body. He could feel one pulling him back – urging him to run for it – while the other strove to send him to Sophia's rescue. Utterly devoid of willpower and a plaything of his own conflicting instincts, he observed the scene his brain refused to accept with the detachment of an uninvolved third party.

Only a few metres away, Sophia was apathetically seated in her wheelchair in front of the glass door that separated the little anteroom from the laboratory beyond.

She's bait, it flashed through Caspar's head. First the amulet, now her. *Bruck is luring me to my death.*

The pane of fluted, frosted glass behind her must have been toughened, because the feet and fists that were raining such desperate blows on it sounded from outside like someone politely tapping on the door.

Caspar took a shuffling step in Sophia's direction, quite unaware that his instinct for self-preservation was losing the battle.

Sophia. He yearned to rescue her, if only to atone for a mistake he could scarcely remember making.

Her eyes were closed and her head was lolling sideways against the poker still inserted in one of the holes designed to accommodate the head rest. The infusion bag once attached to it must have been torn off when Bruck attacked her, and the empty plastic tube was dangling down beside the spoked wheels as limply as her arms. There was no doubt about it: she was in another world – a happier one, Caspar hoped. At all events, she seemed quite unconscious of the drama going on behind her.

They want me to let them out. What on earth has Bruck been doing to them in there?

Caspar saw a hand flatten itself against the inside of the pane. He wasn't sure, but it looked big and coarse, like...

Bachmann's?

Next he noticed something dark imprint itself on the glass roughly at knee level. It looked like... He brushed a damp lock of hair out of his eyes.

...like a tongue?

No. A nose.

Mr Ed and Bachmann! My God, they're alive...

At that moment, as if mocking that conjecture, the shadowy figures behind the glass door disappeared. The knocking stopped too.

What does Bruck plan to do with them? Why did he take them to the laboratory and lock them in?

Another thought flashed through his mind.

A mistake. I made a mistake. Not only then but tonight. Just now. It's something I...

He took another step, only to shrink back in alarm an instant later.

The frosted glass door shuddered. Once, then again. Someone, presumably Bachmann himself, was using his full weight as a battering ram. To no effect. The reinforced metal hinges were even more resistant than the toughened glass.

...something I overlooked.

Caspar was now standing in front of the door. He depressed the grey handle. In vain.

Bruck had locked them in, but there was no keyhole to be seen in the doorplate beneath the chunky handle.

Of course not.

Rassfeld had devised a more intelligent means of preventing unauthorised persons from entering his laboratory. It was protected by a magnetic card which the Soul Breaker must have taken from him. Secured to the wall beside the door was a black metal box, a coded electronic device resembling the input unit of a cash dispenser.

The code. Of course.

If Sophia knew the code that would raise the shutters, she might also know the code that would open this door – they might even be identical. He had to discover the code and release the others before Bruck came back for them.

But for that I need to...

He swung Sophia around to face him, alarmed by the little drops of blood escaping from her nose, and raised her left eyelid with his thumb. Her eyeballs twitched, which was a good sign in the circumstances. It might mean she was in the process of emerging from the death-sleep cycle. In other words, nearing the moment when he could rouse her from her hypnotic state by revoking the command which the madman had implanted in his fourth victim's psyche.

'Can you hear me, Sophia?' He took her cold hands in his and chafed her wrists.

'You must wake up, understand? You must concentrate on me. You're the key.'

The key! Oh, no!

Her limp wrists slipped from his grasp.

Caspar turned round and started walking – painfully slowly, like someone having to struggle against the current of a river in spate. Back to the lift, where he'd made a disastrous mistake.

As long as I'm in the lift, I'm safe.

Quite so. A few moments ago, when he'd left the goddamned key in the keyhole without turning it back and engaging the lock.

That was what I overlooked.

When he finally reached the lift, he found himself staring into his own eyes. Except that this time his reflection wasn't looking back at him from inside the cabin. It was mirrored in the aluminium doors, which were closed. The Soul Breaker had already summoned the lift.

3:34 a.m.

The tremors began the instant the lift cables went taut. Sophia's body gave a series of epileptic jerks, making the entire wheelchair rattle. Caspar had lost his sense of time. He hadn't noticed how long the lift actually took to travel down the shaft between the few floors, but he realised that Bruck would reach the bottom in fewer than twenty desperate heartbeats. He held his breath as if that alone could cause time to expand and delay the inevitable.

Boom.

The hostages behind the frosted glass door pressed their fists and mouths against it and shouted at the top of their voices, not that Caspar could hear much through the toughened glass. Meanwhile, Sophia reared up ever more violently in her wheelchair. She jerked her head back, arched her body and clung to the wheelchair's plastic arms like a drowning woman. Streaked with dust and sodden with sweat, blood and saline, her hospital gown slipped off one shoulder. Then her head hit the japanned metal handle of the poker with a sound like two billiard balls colliding. Caspar hurried over, took hold of her head and cushioned the next collision with the back of his hand. To save her from further injury he pulled the poker out. It resisted his efforts at first, but as he wrenched it out of its mounting he realised that the thing in his hand might be his last remaining hope.

The lift! The door!

He didn't squander the rest of their precious time by trying to smash the unbreakable frosted glass; he hobbled back to the lift as fast as he could and looked up at the indicator.

Upper basement level. Only a few more metres.

It's got to work. Dear God, please let it work.

The poker was about the length of a tennis racket and displayed signs of use. As luck would have it, the end was somewhat flattened like the blade of a screwdriver. Using it as a crowbar, Caspar rammed it into the crack between the doors.

If the lift has an automatic safety system…

He bit his lip as he managed to lever the doors a few centimetres apart.

...it'll stop as soon as – oh no! Shit!

The poker slipped out of his hands and the doors snapped shut again. They'd been open just long enough to show him how close to death he already was. The underside of the cabin was just above his head.

All right, one last try...

Again he drove the poker into the crack, again he threw his weight against it, and again the doors opened a few centimetres. He felt a blast of stale air and smelled the lubricating oil that scented the dusty breeze from the lift shaft. The MRI scanner suddenly sounded far louder than before, either because his senses were working at full stretch, or – more probably – because the open doors were enabling its washing-machine clatter to penetrate the lower basement level more easily.

Oh, no...

He thought he would fail again – thought he would lose his grip on the poker a second time – but he managed to widen the gap sufficiently to be able to jam his bare foot in it before the doors could close. There was a loud click, and he thought for one moment that his toes had been crushed. The truth was, his prayers had been answered: the lift had come to stop because its safety system's digital brain had registered that the doors had been improperly opened.

Done it!

Not a moment too soon, either: the bottom of the cabin was now at eye-level. Craning his neck and peering through the narrow gap, Caspar found himself looking straight at the Soul Breaker's bloody feet.

He averted his gaze in disgust, then wedged the poker between the aluminium doors so that the L used for raking embers jammed them apart. That done, he mopped the sweat off his forehead, swallowed twice to equalise the pressure that had built up in his ears in the course of his exertions, and returned to Sophia.

Thank God.

She was looking calmer. The terrible tremors had subsided and were now confined to her eyelids, which was a good sign. She was waking up.

Or was she?

Caspar hobbled over and kneeled at her feet.

'Sophia? Can you hear me?' he asked.

He wondered whether to restrain her twitching eyelids with his fingertips. For the moment he limited himself to brushing the encrusted secretions from her long eyelashes to make it easier for her to open her eyes.

He also chafed her wrists, noticed with mounting delight that her clammy hands were faintly returning his pressure, and thought involuntarily of the cryptic slip of paper they'd been holding.

It's the truth, although the name is a lie.

'Hypnosis!' He whispered the answer with his lips close to her ear. He had to get through to her – had to catch the moment when her subconscious opened a window and enabled him to revoke the posthypnotic command, but he had no idea how long that window would remain open.

Something uttered a groan behind him, possibly the lift, possibly the Soul Breaker, whose unintelligible yells mingled with the pounding of the scanner and the muffled cries for help coming from behind the frosted glass door.

Ignoring all these noises, Caspar focused his attention on Sophia, the woman with whom he had now swapped roles. At this moment, he was the doctor and she the patient to be released from her mental prison, her deathlike sleep.

He brushed the hair back behind her slightly protruding ears, the way she herself had always done, gently massaged her neck in the hope of eliciting a positive response, and repeated the answer to the riddle.

'Hypnosis.'

Again and again he whispered it in her ear while the din around them steadily increased in volume.

'Hypnosis, hypnosis, hypnosis...'

His subterranean surroundings had dissolved. He was deaf to the creaks and groans, the whimpering and banging – deaf even to his own words.

Hypnosis, hypnosis, hypnosis...

His lips brushed her earlobe like a lover's, and then, just before he uttered the last syllable, she responded at last.

Her eyelids flickered and opened.

A tsunami of endorphins surged through his blood-stream as he gazed into her lucid, expressive eyes.

He had attained his goal and got through to her, touched her inwardly as well as outwardly.

Tears sprang to his eyes. He wanted to clasp her to him, hold her close and kiss her, never let her go again. And then, an instant later, he wanted to scream.

But he couldn't. He opened his mouth but no sound emerged.

Sophia's expression had undergone a horrific trans-formation.

She was smiling.

'You've solved the riddle, Niclas,' she said. Rising effortlessly from the wheelchair, she drove a hypodermic needle into his arm.

One minute before The Fear

'Now, where had we got to in our last session when that stupid dog started barking?' Sophia said softly. 'Ah yes, that's right, darling. Your eye drops.' And she took a small plastic bottle from the pocket of her gown.

He tried to resist, tried to turn his head aside, but every available nerve pathway seemed to have been blocked by whatever she'd injected him with.

What was more, she was kneeling on his upper arms and sitting astride his rumbling stomach. Under normal circumstances he could easily have disencumbered himself of someone twice her weight but now he was paralysed. Far more effectively paralysed than she had pretended to be the whole time.

Why?

He stared into her eyes in the hope of finding some explanation, some look of hesitation, but that was a mistake. She seized the opportunity to release a big drop of highly concentrated scopolamine onto his cornea.

It stung like mad, and he reacted at once to the alkaloid which oculists normally use to dilate the pupils before a sight test. By the time Sophia had repeated the procedure and dilated the other pupil, he was already feeling the effects.

'Why?' he muttered, feeling strangely soothed. The drops were numbing his parasympathetic nervous system, depressing his already weakened condition and dispelling his nausea. His tense muscles relaxed. He hadn't felt as carefree for a long time, even though danger was hovering immediately overhead.

Sophia smiled and brushed her hair behind her ears.

'Marie,' was all she said. A simple name, but it was enough to render the terrible truth comprehensible to him.

So that was it. Of course. He remembered now. *That's her name: Marie!*

The fair-haired angel whose treatment had gone wrong in some way. His first professional blunder. But Marie wasn't just his, she was...

'Our daughter,' Sophia said calmly.

Of course. That was why he'd always felt so attracted to her. That was why she'd always seemed so familiar. Because he knew her. But from way back. Years ago.

'You took her away from me.'

No, I didn't, he wanted to say. *You left me when*

Marie was three years old and moved to Berlin. To be with your new boyfriend.

'But now I'm going to avenge her.'

I'm going to fight him. I've got an important date in court soon. Cross your fingers for me.

So that was what she'd meant.

It was paradoxical. The more he fought against the poison that was depressing his nervous system, the more clearly he remembered their terrible past together.

He had scarcely seen Marie for eight long years. Then came that worried phone call. From Katja Adesi, her teacher at primary school.

That was why he'd gone to Berlin and taken Maria back to Hamburg. To his practice.

It's time. Your daughter is ready for you. All the preparations are complete, Dr Haberland.

He had hypnotised her. Without Sophia's knowledge. Because he wanted to discover if his daughter had been abused.

And now Sophia was sitting in judgement on him because Marie had suffered a stroke while being hypnotised by him. Paralysed ever after, she vegetated in a kind of waking coma from which she would never emerge.

Imprisoned inside herself. Like someone in a sleep of death. Like the Soul Breaker's victims.

But that was impossible. The worst that could happen after negligent treatment was loss of rapport. Marie's condition couldn't possibly have been a side effect of his medical hypnosis.

The convulsions. The uncontrolled movements of her limbs. The permanently restricted reflexes.

That was why there were no bars over the windows. No one had carried off his daughter by force.

I'm scared, Daddy. You won't be long, will you?

The prison from which he'd wanted to release Marie was her own body. She was buried alive inside herself.

'You're wrong...' he vainly tried to say, but his tongue was as immovable as all the other muscles in his body. However, Sophia appeared to answer him despite this. She addressed him in a firm, level voice, evidently explaining something. He couldn't filter it out of the background noises, but he guessed what she was trying to convey: that she was now his judge. She was trying him for an act he'd only remembered at this instant. The clinic was her chosen courtroom and the trial had begun a few hours ago, not that he'd realised he was in the dock. All that now remained was to pass sentence, here in the laboratory's anteroom.

'Stop, please don't, you're making a big mistake,' he tried to say, simultaneously reflecting how stupid they all had been. And how blind.

So that was it. The answer to the riddle.

It had all been just play-acting, just an appalling charade. Sophia had been confronting them all the time with a horrific distorting mirror that displayed the merciless truth, clearly visible to all but in reverse: the Soul Breaker was a woman, the victim was the perpetrator, her defenders were her quarry. They had blindly joined forces against the only person who knew the truth and had tried to save them: Bruck.

It was Sophia, not Bruck, who had murdered Rassfeld and dragged him into the path lab. It was she who had wanted to split them up and isolate her final victim: Caspar himself. That was why she had planted the riddles – in her own hand, in Rassfeld's mouth, in Sibylle Patzwalk's bag.

Of course. We never looked at Sophia for very long; the sight of her was simply too distressing. Anyway, why should we have?

She had probably prepared the first two riddles in advance, but later she'd had to improvise. Yasmin had dressed her in her medical gown, the pocket of which contained a ballpoint and a prescription pad. The last riddle had been almost illegible because she'd had to write it blind – beneath the bedspread Yasmin had draped over her.

Caspar's memories of the events of the last few hours shattered into a thousand bloody fragments and instantly rearranged themselves into a terrible new mosaic.

So that accounted for all their various courses of action. It also explained why Bruck had put up so little resistance in the lift. He had never meant to kill Sophia, only to isolate her, and had come back with the scalpel to free Caspar. Bruck had intended to cut him loose, not cut his throat, thereby wasting valuable time which Sophia had used to kill Schadeck, take the lift down to the basement, and stage-manage her appearance outside the laboratory itself.

Caspar tried again. 'No, please don't. I know you think I'm to blame for our daughter's stroke, but it wasn't like that. Her teacher suspected she was being abused. Marie was drawing strange pictures, that's why she called me – you know that. I only hypnotised her to discover if it was true, and – yes, something went wrong, but...'

I'm Niclas Haberland, a neuropsychiatrist special-ising in the field of medical hypnosis, and I made a mistake.

'...but hypnosis wasn't responsible. That's why I came here, to explain things.'

That was why he had wanted to visit her at the clinic ten days earlier. To have it out with her at last – to hand her the expert opinion which confirmed that the stroke Marie had sustained could not have been caused by defective hypnosis.

The letter from J. B., Jonathan Bruck. A colleague of Rassfeld's and an expert on strokes.

This was what he wanted to tell his ex-partner while she rested one hand on his forehead and used the other to wipe the blood from her nose, which she must have hurt while struggling with Bruck. Or with Yasmin, whose stab wound was obviously her handiwork as well.

It was incomprehensible. He had ventured into this spider's web of his own free will. He had even put his only would-be saviour out of action in the lift by using an implement to which Sophia had needed to draw his attention.

Now that his amnesia was evaporating, Caspar yearned for another merciful loss of memory. Why couldn't everything remain as inexplicable as the question of why Bruck was here in the clinic? Why had he driven that knife into his neck, and why had Sophia had to torture all those other women?

Why did he remain in the dark about those questions when he was now haunted by the appalling realisation that Bruck had never meant to harm them at all? On the contrary, unable to communicate because of the injury to his throat, Bruck had made several attempts to shout Sophia's name aloud and had even tried to write it in his own blood on the window of the scanner room. But they'd misinterpreted all his signs and resisted his efforts to remove them from the danger zone to the self-contained safety of the laboratory, as far away from Sophia as possible. The man hammering on the glass door wasn't a hostage but a refugee, nor had he been shouting for help but trying to warn Caspar against Sophia before it was too late.

I was so stupid. So blind. So unwitting.

Caspar opened his parched lips. His eyes were watering, their artificially dilated pupils defencelessly exposed to the glare of the overhead lights. They smarted because he couldn't distribute the cleansing lachrymal fluid with his eyelids. As if passing through a prism, the light dispersed by the tips of his gummed-up lashes enclosed Sophia's lovely face in a fuzzy, rainbow-hued vignette.

And then he could hear again.

The acoustic barrier collapsed, but only for one little moment. The whistling in his ears, which he'd noticed only when it stopped, was replaced by Sophia's low, sympathetic voice.

'The harder you fight it, the further you'll fall,' she said softly, gazing into his staring eyes.

What does she mean? One last riddle, is that it? My last chance?

'The harder you fight it, the further you'll fall,' she repeated. Then someone pulled him away from her.

His immediate reaction was to rejoice. He thought of Bruck, who must somehow have managed to dislodge the poker, or of Linus, who had surely summoned help from outside. But then it occurred to him that he was physically incapable of movement. He was falling – falling through the floor, which had suddenly dissolved beneath him. The concrete mutated into a morass from which an icy hand shot up and dragged him into the depths. Only now did he fully grasp his predicament.

And now he did put up a fight. Against Sophia's hypnotic gaze. Against her quietly insidious voice. Against the mixture of thiopental and scopolamine that had broken his determination to resist.

Hollywood myths! Schadeck's voice from the past reverberated in his head. *It's impossible to hypnotise a person against their will.*

It all depends on circumstances, he'd replied in the path lab.

After the inflicting of intense physical pain and mental torture, in particular the occasioning of extreme, traumatising states of shock, the administering of mind-altering drugs renders it possible to put suggestible persons into a hypnotic trance against their will and dominate their consciousness.

Caspar thought of the cuts he'd sustained, of the injury to his shoulder, of his torture at Schadeck's hands, of his scorched wrists and the fear he'd been exposed to in the last few hours. Conscious of the barbiturates that were immersing him in apathy, he heard, by way of the ventilation system, the psychedelic thudding of the scanner: appropriate background music for the introduction of a hypnosis he couldn't now resist because Sophia had already built up a connection with him and implanted in his mind a treacherous command he could no longer revoke of his own volition.

The harder you fight it, the further you'll fall.

And so he stopped fighting, inwardly closed his wide-open eyes, and ceased to resist his plunge into the void.

He plummeted down a cold, dark shaft in which no light had ever shone before. Into the dungeon of his soul.

One hour and thirty-five minutes since the onset of The Fear

5:13 a.m.

The smoke was a living creature, a swarm of microscopically small cells that permeated his skin and corroded him from within.

The particles concentrated their attack on his lungs, finding their way down his windpipe and into his bronchial tubes. Far worse than that, however, were the flames erupting from the dashboard. Their red tongues licked his shirt and seared the skin that was already, like plastic melting in the flame of a cigarette lighter, forming blisters below his heart.

He looked down at himself, then used a strength born of unbearable pain to floor the gas pedal. Not to set the car in motion again, but to push the seat back. He wanted to put as much distance as possible between himself and the blaze.

He spat a gob of blood and smoke-stained mucus into

the flames and recapitulated the events that had landed him in this hopeless situation. He had treated Marie without her mother's permission in the firm belief that hypnosis could have no side effects.

And then the girl had had a stroke. During the session. Marie would never recover, never laugh again. Her brainstem was so badly damaged, they could count themselves lucky if she regained her swallowing reflex.

How on earth could it have happened?

He heard the bottle in the footwell shatter. The bottle with which he'd anaesthetised himself after that fateful session and before driving off.

And now he was sitting here, wedged into a wrecked car and holding a photo of his daughter, who would never lead a normal life again. He was burning up, inwardly and outwardly at the same time.

He put out his hands to the flames as if he could ward off the death whose incandescent arms were embracing him. And then, just when he thought he could stand the smell of seared flesh no longer – just as he was about to try to rip that smarting flesh from his chest with his bare hands – everything went transparent. The wrecked car, which had skidded off the wet road and crashed into a tree while he was fumbling for Marie's photo in the folder, disappeared. The smoke and flames – yes, even the pain – dissolved into black nothingness.

Thank God, he thought, *only a dream*. He opened his eyes. And was mystified.

The nightmare in which he'd just been imprisoned had merely undergone a change, not lost its shape.

Where am I?

At first sight, in an underground passage. Two masked men were standing over him, both with guns at the ready. Their black combat suits bore the word POLICE in phosphorescent capitals.

'Can you hear me?' asked one of the men, raising his vizor. He had a jagged scar immediately above his left eye.

'Yes,' Haberland replied.

Why am I semi-naked? Why, dressed only in a pair of filthy pyjama trousers, am I sitting in a wheelchair, staring at a green concrete wall?

'Hey, Otto, look at his eyes.'

The other policeman came closer. He lowered his machine pistol and raised his vizor likewise.

'He's drugged.'

'Maybe that's why he can't speak,' said the man with the scar.

'But I can,' said Haberland. He tried to grasp his burning throat but failed.

'We've got a ten-thirteen here,' Haberland heard Otto say into his radio. 'He's alive but unresponsive. We need a doctor urgently.'

'What's your name?' asked the first policeman, who was now kneeling in front of him. He pulled off his ski mask to reveal an ill-trimmed beard.

'Casp…' he tried to reply, then corrected himself. 'I'm Niclas Haberland.'

I'm Niclas Haberland, a neuropsychiatrist specialising in the field of medical hypnosis. And I made a mistake.

He repeated it, but the policeman from the tactical support unit merely shook his head regretfully.

'Any more of them down there?' hissed the radio.

'Yeah, reckon so. There's a glass door leading to a laboratory or something. Toughened glass, from the look of it. Movement visible inside.'

'Backup's on the way.'

'Check.'

Otto turned off his radio. A few seconds later some lift doors opened on his right. At least two more men came clumping along the passage in their combat boots, safety catches off.

'Bloody hell. What the devil went on here, Jack?' demanded a new voice. The question was clearly directed at the man with the scar, who was now standing behind Haberland's wheelchair. 'No idea,' he replied. 'This guy is completely unresponsive.'

What is this? Why won't you listen to me?

Haberland felt himself being tipped backwards into a recumbent position. He was now looking straight up at the dazzling overhead lights.

'What about the one you freed from the lift? Has he said anything?' Jack asked the newcomers.

'No, he's in shock. He's also had a tracheotomy – whistling like a tea kettle.'

Haberland's wheelchair was trundled forwards.

'How are things looking upstairs?'

'Pretty nasty. Bloodstains and signs of violence everywhere. There seems to have been a fire in the scanner room. Two dead so far. One had his throat cut, the other was lying in a refrigerator in the path lab.'

'IDs?'

'Positive. Thomas Schadeck and Samuel Rassfeld. Schadeck was in charge of that overturned ambulance beside the entrance, Rassfeld seems to have been the medical director.'

Schadeck? Rassfeld? Of course...

Haberland saw his own reflection. He registered the bloodstains on the floor of the lift into which they were wheeling him.

'I can explain everything – I know what happened!' he cried.

'Did you hear that?' asked Otto. Jack pressed the ground floor button and turned round. The doors closed. Both policemen switched on their torches.

'What?'

'For a moment I thought he said something.'

Jack shrugged. 'It was probably the doors squeaking,' he said with a grin, but he shone his torch in Haberland's face again, just in case.

'Look!'

'What?'

'His hand. There's something in it.'

Haberland felt two black-gloved fingers cautiously prise his own apart.

'You're right.'

'What is it?'

The beam of the torch left his face.

'A piece of paper,' said Otto.

Oh, my God.

Panic-stricken, Haberland racked his brains for some way of attracting their attention.

'That's weird.'

'What is?'

'This guy was holding a piece of paper with a riddle on it.'

'Shit, you mean…?'

'Yes, yes, yes!' yelled Haberland, but he saw to his horror that the lips of his reflection in the mirror at the back of the lift hadn't moved a millimetre. *'That was the Soul Breaker, Sophia Dorn!'*

'"Drop me when you need me,"' Otto read out. '"Retrieve me when you need me no longer."'

'Huh?'

'It's got to be a joke in poor taste. Or a copycat.'

'What do you mean?'

'Think. The Soul Breaker only targets women.'

'NO!' Haberland yelled. Aghast, he tried to shut his

eyes, but even that was beyond him. *'Please, this isn't a joke. You've got to get me out of here. Not out of this building, out of myself! Don't you understand?'*

No, of course they didn't.

He knew he could neither speak nor write nor read at that moment. Sophia had deprived him of every possible means of communication. The upper basement level button on the brass plate had just lit up. They would soon be reaching the ground floor.

Sophia did this. She hypnotised me – she took me back to the scene of my worst trauma: the burning car. Now and then I emerge from my nightmare and return to reality. Then my eyes open and you have a chance to revoke my loss of rapport by saying the word that will release me. Don't you understand? If you miss the crucial moment, I slip back into my nightmare. Then the death-sleep cycle begins all over again. Please, you've got to help me!

'Any idea what it means?' asked Jack.

'What? "Drop me when you need me; retrieve me when you need me no longer."? Not a clue,' he heard the other policeman say, but his voice faded into the far distance, nor was Haberland aware of the doors opening at the ground floor or conscious of being handed over to a paramedic.

An invisible force had already stretched out its icy hand and started to haul him back. Back to the place he never wanted to see again for as long as he lived – the place he'd left only minutes before: the inferno in the wrecked car.

He had tried to signal to the policemen that they must go in search of Sophia, the ex-partner whom he had secretly visited two weeks ago in the hope of clearing the air. He had meant to solicit her understanding and give her the letter from the doctor who'd treated him after the car crash. In Dr Jonathan Bruck's expert opinion, hypnosis had played no part in their daughter's stroke, which would have occurred in any case.

But Sophia had refused to listen. She'd thrown the letter into the fire and sent him packing. He'd had no choice but to go off and retrieve his dog, which he'd left tied up outside the clinic. He could remember Tarzan – or Mr Ed, as everyone here called him – tugging at the lead because he'd picked up a scent, and then he'd fallen and hit his head.

But he was incapable of conveying all this to the policemen and paramedics whose figures were slowly dissolving before his eyes as he relapsed into his hypnotic nightmare.

He was back in the burning car once more – back in the sea of flames which Sophia had ordained to be his everlasting punishment.

TODAY

Very much later, many years after The Fear

2:56 p.m.

Lydia finished reading first. Her boyfriend, who needed more time, didn't turn over the last page until twenty minutes later.

'What now?' he asked, staring incredulously at the back of the folder. 'Is that all there is to it?'

The professor removed his reading glasses and nodded gently. He had been closely observing his students' demeanour for the last few minutes – noting how they silently mouthed certain words or instinctively scratched their heads before their eyes moved on to the next paragraph.

Lydia had taken to pulling down her lower lip while reading the last few pages, whereas Patrick had continued to prop his head on his hands. He now had red patches on his cheeks.

'I said you didn't concentrate hard enough at first, didn't I, Patrick?'

'Yes, but how could we be expected to guess the ending?' Wearily, Patrick arched his back and stretched.

'It's quite simple. The clue was on page 21. Remember the answer to the first riddle Greta asked Caspar?'

'The surgeon was a woman.' Lydia smote her brow. 'Well, I'm damned!'

'Okay, okay, so I didn't get it, but how does the story go on?' Patrick demanded impatiently. He hugged his chest and shivered. Lydia looked around for her anorak.

It had grown still colder as the light started to fade, but they hadn't noticed this while reading.

The professor pulled his notepad towards him and jotted something down.

'All in good time. First I'd like to hear your off-the-cuff reactions. What did you think when you'd read the last sentence?' He nodded to Lydia.

'Me?' she said, tapping her chest with an air of enquiry. 'Well, I...' She cleared her throat and reached for the bottle of water. 'I kept wondering whether it all really happened that way.'

She took a swallow. The professor laid his ballpoint aside and picked up the original text.

'Good question. This medical record is written almost exclusively from one individual's subjective viewpoint, so there are bound to be lacunae. There's also sufficient scope for varying interpretations. However, what is certain is that Niclas Haberland was an expert in the field of medical hypnosis and had specialised in the therapeutic treatment of children. Years earlier he'd had a passionate affair with a female colleague who gave birth to a daughter named Marie. Their relationship very soon disintegrated. Sophia Dorn was awarded custody and moved to Berlin.'

The professor stretched his legs beneath the table.

'One day, Haberland received a worried phone call from Berlin. Marie had been painting some disturbing pictures in art class. Her form mistress, Katja Adesi, wasn't sure of her ground and didn't want to involve the authorities prematurely, so she consulted the girl's biological father first. Haberland came to Berlin determined to get to the bottom of the matter.'

'He hypnotised Marie?' said Lydia.

'Hamburg is only ninety minutes from Berlin by train. He took her back to his practice, intending to return her to her mother that night. But it never came to that. The session ended in disaster. His daughter suffered a brainstem infarction, or stroke.'

'Bloody hell.' Patrick looked as if he had toothache. 'So the plug had been pulled.'

'What do you mean?' asked Lydia, turning to him. The physical distance between her and her boyfriend was appreciably greater than it had been at the start of the experiment, almost as if their reading matter had driven an invisible wedge between them. The professor made another note.

'Well,' he said, looking up, 'your friend was using a metaphor for what we call locked-in syndrome. A condition in which the brain still functions but can no longer establish any connection with the outside world. Just imagine: you can't see, hear, taste, smell, breathe or feel. Only think.'

'Good God.'

'Such a severe side effect of faulty hypnosis had never been observed before.'

Lydia cleared her throat again. 'Did the girl die?'

'Worse than that. Marie spent the rest of her life a physical and mental ruin. Her mother was also shattered, but inwardly and without showing it. Her boyfriend left her soon after this stroke of misfortune. He insists to this day that he never laid a finger on Marie.'

A pebble clattered against the big French windows. As yet, the freshening wind was laden only with debris and rubbish, not snow. The weeping willow bowed its head before the gale as the professor went on speaking.

'To begin with, Sophia sought satisfaction by legal means. She instructed a solicitor, Doreen Brandt, but Brandt eventually declined to file a suit against Niclas Haberland because she thought it would be very hard to prove that he'd blundered. She advised Sophia to settle out of court.'

The professor rose and, like Patrick, loosened up by flexing his shoulder muscles. Despite all the exercises he did, his aching joints would be bound to remind him, tomorrow if not sooner, that he'd spent too long sitting down today.

'Sophia grew more and more desperate,' he went on, going over to the oil radiator that was softly gurgling near the fireplace. 'Whatever enquiries she made, she always got the same answer: hypnosis couldn't do such severe damage. Her sorrow escalated into a perverse and obsessive urge to avenge Marie. She wanted to prove to everyone that it was indeed possible to break someone's psyche under hypnosis. Worse still, she wanted to punish those whom she considered guilty by putting them into the same state as Marie.'

'Locked in. Imprisoned in a deathlike sleep.'

'Quite so.' The professor acknowledged Patrick's interjection with an approving nod. 'Sophia had taken an interest in hypnosis as a medical student, but she'd always rejected its use for therapeutic purposes. Now, with insane desperation, she practised the technique for use as a weapon. The method she devised was really quite simple. She began by taking her victims back in time, under hypnosis, to the worst moment of their worst nightmare. Then she induced an artificial loss of rapport.'

Patrick shook his head in horror. 'You mean she sent them to hell and locked the door on them?'

'Figuratively speaking, yes. She quite deliberately relinquished control over her victims and left them in an ungovernable condition. But, since every defective hypnosis inevitably develops into normal sleep, from which the subject sooner or later awakens, she ended by issuing them with a posthypnotic command: as soon as they surfaced, they were to submerge once more.'

'How she did do that?'

'Have you ever seen a stage hypnotist at work, Lydia?'

'Only on TV. He put a man into a trance. Then he told him he was a dog. He would remember nothing when he woke up, but whenever the audience called out "Walkies!" he was to bark three times.'

'Which he duly did, I suppose.'

'Yes.'

'That's a crude but apt example of the sort of post-hypnotic command Sophia implanted in her victims' minds, except that no one had to call out "Walkies!". It was enough for them to open their eyes and expose them to light. That was the trigger. The brighter the light, the quicker their inevitable return to a hypnotic state.'

'Horrible.' Lydia shivered and zipped up her anorak.

'But it worked. That's how Sophia managed to lock her victims into a cyclical deathlike sleep which could be ended only if someone uttered the right keyword during their waking phase: the answer to the riddle on the relevant slip of paper.'

The professor rested his hands on the ribs of the electric radiator. Although they nearly blistered his fingertips, the warmth didn't extend beyond his wrists.

Patrick's next question gave him gooseflesh. It almost hurt.

'What happened to Haberland?'

TODAY

3:07 p.m.

'Haberland?' the professor repeated quietly. He went over to the French windows. 'Before I tell you something about his subsequent life, I think we should devote a little more time to his past.'

He was now speaking with his back to them.

'Marie's stroke was, of course, the worst trauma he ever experienced. Unable to grasp what he'd done to his own daughter, he got drunk. As a result, he had a terrible car crash that almost cost him his life. After his external injuries had healed he was treated by Dr Jonathan Bruck. In the course of therapy they talked about Marie. Bruck had obtained her medical records from the clinic where Haberland's daughter was in intensive care.'

'So much for professional confidentiality,' he heard Patrick mutter.

'After evaluating Marie's blood values, the doctors

had become convinced that her stroke had occurred *during* hypnosis but not as a *result* of it. Sophia was so incensed by this diagnosis, she had her daughter brought back to Berlin.'

He turned to face his students.

'But the Hamburg doctors were right. As I already said, according to our present state of orthodox medical knowledge, it really is impossible to inflict such damage as a result of negligence.'

'Page 216 of the record,' said Lydia, leafing back through her copy.

'Correct. Bruck urged Haberland to discuss these findings with the mother of his child and have it out with her. Although in two minds at first, Haberland set off for Berlin just before Christmas, accompanied by his dog.'

'Tarzan, alias Mr Ed.'

The professor ignored Lydia's comment with a good-natured smile.

'He took a train to Berlin with the expert opinion in his briefcase. His courage initially failed him when he reached the gates of the Teufelsberg Clinic. How would Sophia react, given that she had hitherto rejected all contact and branded him a murderer since the tragedy? What would she do if he turned up unannounced despite her express prohibition? After much hesitation he pulled himself together and walked up the drive to find out.'

'Well,' said Lydia, 'whatever he was afraid would happen, it certainly wasn't half as bad as what actually did.'

The professor laughed drily. 'True. Sophia had already tried out her Soul Breaker method on three women by this time. Not everyone is susceptible to hypnosis, as you probably know, certainly not against their will. Vanessa Strassmann was. She was entirely innocent. It was simply her bad luck to have attended a high-school course in amateur dramatics with Sophia. Her extremely suggestible personality made her an ideal first subject for Sophia to practise on. No wonder Haberland couldn't remember her when he saw that newspaper picture of her. She'd never had any personal contact with him or Marie.'

Patrick looked at the professor enquiringly and turned back to the beginning of the document like Lydia. The professor gave him an encouraging nod.

'Vanessa Strassmann was the first of the series. Sophia lured her to a hotel room on some pretext or other. She had evidently been raped in the past, and Sophia confronted her with her abuser again and again – under hypnosis.'

'I felt like giving up at that point,' Patrick muttered.

'Spurred on by her success, Sophia proceeded to try out her technique on the woman she regarded as initially responsible: Katja Adesi, the schoolteacher whose suspicions of abuse had set the ball rolling.'

'And the third victim?' asked Lydia. 'Doreen Brandt?'

'...was the lawyer who'd declined to file a suit against Haberland. Since she had never accepted the brief, it was a long time before any connection could be established between her, Sophia and the other victims. Besides, the police were looking for a man.'

'Okay,' Patrick said impatiently, 'but we were really talking about Caspar – Haberland, I mean.'

'Oh yes, I'm sorry. Well, he was always Sophia's real objective – her masterstroke. Page 214 describes the various techniques that can be employed to enforce hypnosis, but they all have one thing in common: they're based on the surprise effect.'

'But Haberland's unheralded visit pre-empted that.'

'Quite so. You can imagine how startled Sophia was when Haberland suddenly confronted her. It was he who had taken *her* by surprise, and he made yet another attempt – as she saw it – to lie his way out of responsibility for Marie's condition. He even presented her with a letter from a reputable psychiatrist, Jonathan Bruck, which purported to certify his innocence!'

The professor slapped the table with the flat of his hand.

'And this when she had already proved, three times over, that it was indeed possible to endanger someone's life by means of hypnosis.'

'So she chucked Bruck's letter in the fire and pumped him full of anaesthetic?'

Patrick had also stood up to stretch his legs. Lydia, who didn't budge, was nervously twisting a lock of hair.

'Not exactly,' said the professor. 'She threw the letter in the fire and told him to go to hell. He set off, collecting Tarzan on the way – he'd left the dog tied up outside. Later, Sophia must have changed her mind, because she retrieved the half-charred remains of Bruck's letter from the fire.'

'And Haberland's amnesia?' Excitedly, Lydia put the strand of hair in her mouth. 'Was simply occasioned by a fall.'

Patrick's uncertain frown told the professor that he would have to be more explicit.

'Haberland was mentally punch-drunk, you see. He'd undergone a traumatic experience, one he wanted to forget at all costs. Bruck had even tried to treat him for the effects of what he thought he'd done to his daughter. And now his first attempt to over-come that trauma by talking to Sophia in person had come to nothing. He was hurt and bewildered, angry and depressed. His brain was crying out to forget what he'd been through with Marie, so it seized the first available opportunity to escape from a sense of guilt.'

'The fall?' said Lydia.

'Yes. Tarzan tugged at the lead and Haberland lost his balance on the icy slope. He hit his head on the road and knocked himself out. He was suffering from hypothermia by the time Bachmann ferried him back to the clinic hours later.'

'Back to that demented woman.'

The professor nodded. 'Sophia made the most of her unexpected opportunity. The advantage of surprise was now back in her court, thanks to Haberland's amnesia. When conducting a preliminary examination of her "patient"' – the professor mimed some quotation marks in the air with his fingers – 'she stripped him of anything that might have pointed to his true identity and implied that he'd been mugged. She never notified anyone in the police, of course. What additionally lent themselves to her vindictive scheme were Rassfeld's delaying tactics and his aversion to outside interference.'

'But why didn't she hypnotise Caspar right away?' Lydia asked.

'Good question. In fact, she was in two minds. On the one hand she wanted to punish Haberland and consign him to hell; on the other, hell would lose some of its sting if he couldn't remember Marie and, thus, his alleged guilt. That was why she wanted first to dispel his merciful amnesia and then to break his soul. The events of that night presented her with a chance to do both.'

'But how did Bruck get involved?' asked Patrick.

Lydia got in first. 'That was only logical,' she said. 'Sophia was taking it out on anyone who tried to tell her that hypnosis can't be harmful. By handing her Bruck's expert opinion, Haberland had supplied her with another victim free of charge, so to speak.'

'Good thinking,' the professor said approvingly.

'Really?' Lydia smiled.

'That was precisely what happened. Sophia was wholly unacquainted with Bruck before Haberland came to see her. Now that he was on her personal blacklist, she marked him down as her fourth victim.'

'But how?' asked Patrick.

'In an utterly unscrupulous manner. She simply phoned Bruck and asked for his professional advice about an amnesia patient who had just been admitted to the clinic. Bruck offered to help and made a special trip from Hamburg, particularly as he suspected that the amnesiac might be Haberland, who hadn't been in touch for a day or two. Sophia booked him a room at the Teufelssee Motel, not far from the clinic, where they met.'

'And where she put him under enforced hypnosis.'

'More or less.'

'What does "more or less" mean?' Patrick's cheeks were still red, but not from the pressure of his hands. Although the temperature was steadily dropping, he seemed to be getting more flushed by the minute. The professor made another mental note without knowing whether such reactions were relevant to the end result. Then he answered the question.

'Well, she didn't entirely succeed. She trickled scopolamine into Bruck's eyes and put him into a trance. After that she doused him in liquor from the minibar to make him seem drunk when he was found. But this time it didn't work properly. Perhaps they were disturbed, perhaps she made a mistake. Besides, as I already said, not everyone is hypnotisable. Bruck was a difficult subject in any case, but Sophia did manage to put his communication centre out of action. That, for instance, was why he couldn't leave Caspar any written message, though his ability to communicate steadily improved. You'll recall how he tried to write Sophia's name on the window in his own blood.'

The two students nodded.

'Although she left him severely affected, she didn't succeed in implanting the posthypnotic command. When Schadeck collected Bruck from the motel, he managed to extricate himself from his deathlike sleep by his own efforts.'

'How?'

'By stabbing himself in the throat.'

'What?!' Lydia registered stark horror, whereas Patrick's face remained quite expressionless.

'Yes. What prompted his action isn't entirely clear, but enquiries have elicited that Bruck swallowed a wasp as a child and almost died when it stung him in the throat. I suspect that Sophia reactivated that trauma – that nightmare – under hypnosis.'

'And that was why he punctured his own windpipe?' Lydia grasped her throat and gulped involuntarily.

'Yes. He must have entered the waking phase while lying in the ambulance and thought he was choking to death. At the same time, he knew that hypnosis can be terminated by a powerful stimulus – acute pain, for instance. And, as I've already said, he hadn't been hypnotised as successfully as the previous victims. Being a doctor, he also knew that a tracheotomy isn't necessarily life-threatening but requires prompt treatment. Furthermore, he realised that they must be in the vicinity of the Teufelsberg Clinic, the location not only of the perpetrator but also of her next victim: his patient Niclas Haberland. And here we enter the realm of speculation, because the information Bruck gave the police was extremely sketchy, thanks to the traumatic experiences he'd undergone that night, and not all of it is available to me. Perhaps chance took a hand, or perhaps he wanted to kill two birds with one stone. At all events, he achieved the desired result, albeit in a very drastic manner. Schadeck lost control over his vehicle and came to a stop, and Bruck was admitted to the clinic.'

'And that's when it all began.'

'Not quite.'

'How do you mean?'

Not for the first time, the professor scanned his test subjects' enquiring faces.

'Well, you're forgetting Linus.'

TODAY

3:13 p.m.

Patrick glanced at his watch, but his brief look at the dial was more a displacement activity than anything else. Although today was 23 December, the day before Christmas Eve, the professor knew that time was the least of his guinea pigs' concerns.

'Linus. Yes, you're right. What happened to him?'

Phosiapatikil...

The professor blinked before resuming his account.

'Sophia tampered with the snowmobile's fuel hose so as to keep Bruck pinned down at the clinic overnight.'

'Why?'

'In order to kill him, Lydia. He was the strongest potential witness for the prosecution. Moreover, she had at all costs to prevent an encounter between Bruck and Haberland, whom she had destined to be her final victim and crowning achievement. She stole into Bruck's room after midnight, probably intending to smother him with a pillow, which would have been an unsuspicious cause of death in view of the injury to his windpipe. However, she was spotted by Linus, who was a poor sleeper and often roamed the passages at night.'

'And Linus woke Haberland and told him what had happened: *Phosiapatikil*. Sophia's trying to kill the patient!'

'So *that's* when it all began.' Shivering, Patrick removed his hands from the pockets of his jacket and reached for the bottle of water, but he didn't put it to his lips.

'Exactly. Sophia couldn't complete the job because Linus had interrupted her. Bruck escaped through the window, leaving her in a quandary. How could she account for her presence in Bruck's room – after midnight and clad only in her nightdress? How could she neutralise Linus, who was no idiot despite his inability to communicate? Panic-stricken, she decided to go for broke. She scribbled a brief riddle on a slip of paper, got undressed and lay down in the bathtub. When Haberland came in and found the riddle in her hand he was bound to assume that she was the Soul Breaker's fourth victim. In reality, her object was to gain time, divert attention and sow confusion. She'd been presented with an unexpected opportunity. With a little skill and improvisation, she could break Haberland's psyche and, at the same time, pin all her crimes on Jonathan Bruck. She would even be able to produce numerous witnesses who could testify to his atrocities. But for that the shutters must come down and stay down.'

'And that was why she murdered Rassfeld?'

'The only person apart from herself who knew the code. Precisely. When Yasmin went to fetch the earplugs and the shutters were lowered, she hit Rassfeld over the head with a chair – hence the blood on the floor of the scanner room. Then she dragged him into the path lab and stowed his unconscious body in one of the lower refrigerated lockers.'

'And the riddle? How could she have known at this stage that Rassfeld would be found later on?'

'She couldn't. That was pure chance, and the riddle itself had no direct significance. Unfortunately, Yasmin had been kind enough to fetch Sophia's medical gown from her room, and the riddle she'd really intended for Caspar was already in the pocket. She stuffed this into Rassfeld's mouth, sneaked back to the scanner and crawled inside. Yasmin returned, found the medical director gone, and went off to fetch help. Meantime, Sophia proceeded to strap herself down.'

'Hence the loose strap on page 87?'

The professor acknowledged Patrick's interjection with a raised forefinger.

'Correct. And then she started screaming to divert all suspicion from herself.'

'Diabolical,' said Lydia, nervously plucking at her

lower lip. 'She persuaded everyone to suspect the good guy and protect the enemy.'

'But what exactly happened in the scanner room?' Patrick was sounding dubious again. 'I mean, when Caspar and Bachmann started the fire? Why did Bruck lock them in?'

'Because they were safe from Sophia in there,' said the professor. 'But only, of course, if they didn't suffocate themselves with smoke inhalation. That was why he activated the scanner, to alert them before they started the fire. But it was too late, they'd already done so and he himself had no key to the door, so he couldn't open it again.'

'Okay, I get it. The noises they heard in the scanner room – was that Linus going for the police?'

'No, not yet. That was just the blizzard. All the same, it was Linus they owed their lives to that night. Before the shutters were lowered he escaped onto the balcony, where he startled Yasmin when she came to lock the room. He broke his ankle jumping to the ground, but he made it as far as the road and the residential area where Mike Haffner nearly ran him over hours later.'

'And Haffner summoned the police?'

The professor nodded. 'It took them some time to interpret Linus's gibberish. Fortunately, though, Bruck had managed to thwart Sophia's efforts and save the lives of most of her potential victims. Dirk Bachmann,

Sibylle Patzwalk, Greta Kaminsky and Mr Ed all survived. Even Yasmin was released from the laboratory and her knife wound attended to in the nick of time.' He sighed. 'For Haberland, alas, the police arrived too late.'

'Too late? What happened to him? And where's Sophia?'

Patrick raised his head and looked at the professor, screwing up his eyes as if dazzled by something.

The professor turned back to the window and gazed out into the fading light.

'Well,' he said in a low voice, 'that's why we're here today.'

'What do you mean?' he heard Lydia ask behind him.

'It's part of the experiment. That's just why you should study the patient's record so closely.'

'Why?'

He slowly turned to face his students.

'To check the truth of this story. To discover what really happened in the end.'

TODAY

The gurgling of the oil radiator had grown louder, but the temperature in the library seemed to go on falling the longer he talked.

'All I can tell you is that Sophia disappeared that night – for good.' The professor seemed suddenly to have aged several years. 'Marie has been in a high-dependency ward at Westend Hospital ever since. She's no longer on a ventilator and can communicate by blinking her right eyelid. Apart from that, the doctors have reported no significant improvement in her condition.'

'Just a minute,' said Patrick. 'You mean Sophia simply abandoned her daughter – after all that?'

'It seemed so at first.'

The radiator creaked. It sounded almost like a log smouldering on the hearth, and the professor was half tempted to turn and look. At the same time, he wondered if his listeners had detected the growing tremor in his voice.

'But then, a year later, the nurses found a little present lying on Marie's bedside table.'

'What sort of present?' Patrick and Lydia asked almost simultaneously.

'It was in a lilac-coloured jeweller's box, and it contained a necklace with a charm pendant. You can guess who it belonged to.'

Lydia frowned and raised her hand like a schoolkid in class. 'Didn't anyone see this mysterious visitor?'

'A high-dependency ward isn't a high-security wing. Besides, lots of visitors wear surgical masks. No, nobody saw anyone come or go.'

'Never?'

'The necklace wasn't the only gift Marie received. Others turned up every Christmas. Sometimes it was a little bottle of scent – Marie's forehead would smell of it when the nurses came to check on her – or sometimes a musical box or a rare coin. And accompanying each present was a little slip of paper folded in half.'

Lydia's intake of breath was clearly audible. 'What was on them?'

'Nothing. They were blank.'

The professor opened his hands like a conjurer who has just made a pocket handkerchief vanish into thin air.

'And these presents have been Sophia's only sign of life?' Patrick demanded suspiciously.

'Not quite. She's rumoured to have been treated years later by a well-known psychiatrist. Under a false name, of course. She apparently called herself Anna Spiegel.'

This time, both students started at the mention of the name. Patrick's lips parted slowly.

'And the psychiatrist's name was…?'

'Viktor Larenz. We spoke of him at the beginning of this experiment. He can no longer be questioned about this case, unfortunately. The document you've been reading came to light when his practice was dissolved, and experts are still in dispute over who wrote it, Larenz himself or his sinister patient. However, it's said that his involvement with the case made him ill, and that Sophia Dorn, alias Anna Spiegel, was the true subject of a hallucination which Larenz reactivated later, during a bout of schizophrenia. But that's another story – one that hasn't been definitely substantiated and doesn't belong here.'

'Oh yes, I think it does. After all, you gave us this crap to read.' Patrick tapped the folder with his forefinger. 'Who do you think wrote it?'

'Well…' The professor hesitated. 'To be honest, you'll find a clue in the text itself. On page 214, line 18.'

'The Alzner Protocols?' Lydia read out slowly.

The professor exhaled a deep breath. 'Which could be an anagram of Larenz,' he said.

'But why should Larenz incorporate a play on words in his own document?' asked Patrick.

'The professor's just trying to tell us.' Lydia glanced at her boyfriend irritably. 'Sophia wrote it.'

'Hang on!' Patrick gave an incredulous laugh. 'How do you make that out? It's written almost entirely from Caspar's perspective. How would Sophia have known what he was going through, what he was thinking and feeling, unless…' He broke off.

'Unless she'd been inside his head. Exactly.' The professor's hand trembled as he ran his fingers through his thinning hair. 'An hour and a half elapsed between Haberland's hypnosis and the arrival of the police. Time enough for Sophia to learn everything at first hand. She held the key to his consciousness, after all. Any facts Haberland didn't tell her she could have learned from the press later on. For instance, how Linus was nearly run over by Mike Haffner's snowplough.'

Patrick could sit still no longer. He sprang to his feet angrily. 'You mean we've spent all this time absorbing a document written by a psychotic murderess? A document that drove a psychiatrist insane?'

'Whoa, whoa, whoa!' The professor made a soothing gesture. 'That's only a rumour; it isn't necessarily the case. Besides, you're both under medical supervision. If either of you notices anything odd in the next few days, please contact me at once.'

He put his briefcase on the table and took out a little pad of yellow Post-its.

'Why? What are we *likely* to notice?' Patrick demanded. The professor picked up a ballpoint.

'As we all know, Sophia Dorn was obsessed with the idea of hypnotising people against their will. The expert consensus is that she must have improved and developed her methods during her years on the run.'

'Kindly get to the point.' Patrick's tone was now devoid of all respect, not that the professor took this amiss in view of the circumstances.

'Psychiatrists have long debated whether it's possible to hypnotise a person simply by getting them to read something.'

'Like what, pray?'

'They wonder whether these Alzner Protocols mentioned on page 214 really exist. You may be holding a copy in your hands at this moment – a document with an invisible subtext which only the subconscious can read.'

'Are you serious?' There was a hint of panic in Patrick's voice. 'Have we both been hypnotised simply by ploughing our way through this madwoman's effusions?'

The professor shrugged. 'It's possible. The purpose of this experiment is to find out. Forgive me, I couldn't enlighten you in advance or it wouldn't have worked.

Personally, however, I don't believe it. I think it's a latter-day legend, a scientific myth which we'll disprove between us.'

'What if we don't? What'll happen to us?'

'I don't know. But, as I say, please call me if you experience anything untoward.'

Lydia's eyelids quivered. 'Can you get us out? Out of this trance, I mean? If we're in one.'

'*If* you are, yes. Certainly. I know the keyword.'

'The keyword?'

'The answer to the last riddle: "Discard me if you need me; retrieve me if you need me no longer." If there's a subliminal message – a concealed subtext, in other words – we believe that this keyword can revoke its posthypnotic effect.'

'You *believe* so. How reassuring. What *is* this keyword? Come on, out with it.' Patrick levelled a menacing forefinger at the professor, who merely shook his head.

'The experiment would have failed if I told you now. Just wait and see if a change occurs in some aspect of your life. Make notes, but please don't be concerned. You can reach me any time of the day or night. Nothing's going to happen to you.'

'I'm not leaving here until I know the goddamned keyword!' Patrick almost shouted the words. The door behind him creaked open and an elderly man put his head in.

'It's all right, everything's fine,' said the professor.

The man raised his eyebrows but withdrew, shutting the door behind him.

'No, everything *isn't* fine. Tell us the answer to that last riddle right now, or...'

The professor nipped Patrick's outburst in the bud. 'All right, all right,' he said.

He was ready for this, having anticipated it. He went over to the pair, picked up their folders, and inserted a yellow Post-it in each.

Lydia and Patrick looked at him enquiringly.

'That's my email address. If you're really worried, email me and I'll send you the information you've just requested by return. That means it'll be up to you whether or not to cut the experiment short. But please don't do so unless there's absolutely no alternative. I ask you this in the name of science. Do we have a deal?'

The professor returned to his place. He gathered his papers together and proceeded to stow them in his scuffed old briefcase.

Lydia stood up.

'But it was solved, wasn't it?' she said hesitantly. 'The Haberland riddle, I mean? He survived the affair in the end, didn't he?'

The professor, who was just putting away the original document, stopped short.

'No,' he said quietly, and his eyes misted over again. Lydia nodded to him as if that simple gesture of encouragement was required to elicit the most painful of all truths. Once upon a time, in that dimly-lit strip club with its over-loud music and under-strength beer, she had seemed far less naked and vulnerable to him than he now did to her. He wondered whether she realised that.

'I'm sorry,' he said. 'I'm afraid Niclas Haberland was past saving.'

TODAY

3:42 p.m.

The rusty gate slammed shut.

'Really brave of you,' grunted the elderly caretaker, extracting the heavy bunch of keys. He stuck it in the pocket of his donkey jacket and pulled his gloves on. 'I never thought you'd come back.'

'It was just a one-time thing to do with my students.' The professor chuckled. 'You're still here, though.'

'Worse luck,' the caretaker growled derisively as they walked off. 'I look in once a month to see if everything's okay. I need to top up my pension, since my wife doesn't contribute.'

'Hasn't anyone ever tried to buy the old place?'

Bachmann sniffed. His eyes roamed over the former clinic's frosted, ivy-clad facade. 'Oh, sure. It was shut down after Rassfeld's death, of course. Nothing definite appeared in the papers, but there were plenty of rumours. Hardly surprising, because little was said officially. Bruck returned to Hamburg – he refused all invitations to write a book about that night. Sibylle Patzwalk went to work in a hotel and Yasmin chucked her job. I heard she made a record with Linus – quite a hit, apparently. Typical of that scatty girl.'

Bachmann looked up as a flock of crows soared over their heads.

'Greta Kaminsky was the only one who ever gave an interview to the press. She seriously thought that night had cured her anxiety psychosis, so she'd be able to celebrate Christmas on her own in future. Can you believe it?'

The flock scattered, only to reassemble moments later. Bachmann lost interest in the birds and looked back at the professor. His eyes were dim, and he definitely needed stronger glasses.

'To this day, people think the clinic was a lunatic asylum whose patients slaughtered one another. That's why so many of them believe the site is haunted. Silly, really, but it seems to have put investors off. There've been lots of plans. Luxury housing development, a restaurant, even a hotel. Nothing ever came of them.'

'Do people ever mention Sophia?'

The old caretaker gave an almost imperceptible start at the sound of her name. He scratched his grizzled sideburns.

'Children say she's a witch and still lives here. Up in the attic with her disabled daughter. Stuff like that.'

He laughed with an effort. The professor had never seen a grown man look sadder.

'No offence, but I'm going to take a turn around the building, Cas—' Bachmann stopped short. 'Sorry.'

'That's all right.' Haberland put out his hand. 'Happy Christmas. It was good to see you again. And thanks for opening up.'

'Don't mention it. Just as long as it doesn't become a habit.'

They exchanged a final nod and went their separate ways, two men who had been through so much together in a single night that there simply wasn't room in this life for any more shared experiences. Not even for a brief conversation.

Haberland faced into the wind and turned up the collar of his baggy overcoat. Gingerly, he set off along the footpath that wound down the hillside to the road. Sleet and a sudden freeze-up had been forecast for today, so he'd put on his heavy winter boots. Back then he'd turned up in the shoes that had ultimately proved his undoing.

Back then. In another life.

Now he was another person. He hadn't been lying when he'd told Lydia that Niclas Haberland was no more. A man of that name lay, for ever broken, at the bottom of his own soul. Although Bruck had solved the riddle and released him after two days, even that brief spell in his personal prison had been too long. He had returned to reality, thanks to Bruck, but had never found his way back to himself.

Discard me if you need me; retrieve me if you need me no longer...

He'd often wondered why Sophia had left those riddles behind. After all, she'd given her victims a potential means of escape that was denied to Marie. He'd construed it at first as a vestige of compassion and later as an expression of an irrational hope that their daughter, too, might be extricated from her labyrinth of suffering by a single word. Today, after years of torment, he knew better. The riddles were a material part of his punishment: proof of her omnipotence. Sophia had locked him up inside the gates of hell and left the key on the outside because she didn't care if someone came along and opened them. Why not? Because she possessed the power to lock him up again at any time.

Retrieve me...

Ever since that night he'd been haunted by an un-reasoning fear that Sophia had never reappeared only because she'd hidden inside him. Not physically, of course, but metaphorically. If she'd seen to it that he could be roused from his deathlike sleep by a single word, why shouldn't she have taken it into her head to implant another posthypnotic command of which he was unaware? After all, she'd had him under her control for long enough to drain his mind of all the information she needed to write that patient's record.

That was why he jumped whenever the phone rang, whenever he heard a strange voice or an unfamiliar word on the lips of a newsreader: because he had been prepared for the worst ever since escaping from his spiritual purgatory. And that was also the purpose of this experiment. He had to discover how powerful Sophia really was and whether she had found a way, years after her disappearance, of implanting herself in the human psyche.

Haberland swallowed, wondering if the tickle in his throat was the beginning of a cold. His scars were tingling a little, as they usually did when snow was on the way. The ones on his chest were the first to make themselves felt, but the dead tissue on his wrists was also becoming more weather-sensitive as the years went by.

Something cold and wet abruptly thrust itself into his palm. He looked down.

'Ah, there you are,' he said to the tail-wagging dog. Tarzan had gone off into the woods while he was talking to Bachmann. He never stayed away for long. His right hind leg had grown increasingly lame in recent times and his right eye, too, had lost much of its sight. The days when he'd had to be kept on a lead were long past.

'We must be careful not to take a tumble, mustn't we? We've still got to look in on Marie.'

He fondled the old dog's head and turned for the last time. The former clinic stood silhouetted against the wintry sky like a dark monolith. The ground floor windows had been boarded up. On the upper floors the last estate agent had contented himself with drawing the tattered curtains. There wasn't a light on anywhere, discounting the little builder's lamp over the entrance.

Haberland's eyes narrowed. For a moment he thought he'd glimpsed movement behind one of the faded curtains in an attic room on the fourth floor. But the light was already fading fast, and besides, experience had taught him that it was hard to distinguish between reality and illusion in this place, even in broad daylight.

It could have been pure imagination. Or a rat. Or maybe a draught from a broken window pane. Haberland hitched up one of his sleeves and scratched his wrist.

The Met Office was right, he thought, *it's going to snow*. He turned to Tarzan, who was looking up at him expectantly.

'Well, what do you think? Are we going to have a white Christmas this year?'

Delightedly, Tarzan limped off with Haberland following in his wake. Rather too quickly. He swayed and raised his left arm in alarm, almost losing his balance. Then his boots found a purchase and he followed the tracks they'd left in the frozen slush on the way up. Cautiously, step by step, he trudged down the drive and away from the old building on the Teufelsberg that had once harboured the source of his direst fears, and which now, bloodless and deserted, was waiting behind him for a miracle to occur: for someone to come and brush the dust of the past off its furniture, kindle a warm fire on the hearth, and put a bright light in every window to keep dark memories at bay and banish evil spirits to the cellar of oblivion.

So that all would once more be as it used to be.

Amplifications, Acknowledgements and Apologies

I don't know about you, but I'm one of those people who always read the acknowledgements before they embark on the opening chapter. This has often spoilt my enjoyment of a novel because the author has used its closing pages to provide his readers with hints on further reading, thereby giving away the book's central theme and, thus, its whole point.

Recently, for instance, I read a historical thriller in which the murderer had multiple personalities. You weren't supposed to discover that until the end, but I – thanks to the acknowledgements – knew it from page one onwards.

So why am I writing this here? Because I myself would very much like to furnish you with some hints on how to reimmerse yourselves in the medical topics addressed by this psychothriller. Even though many of them may seem to defy belief, most are (once more) under discussion.

But how to demonstrate this without giving too much away? Fortunately, there exists a textbook bearing the innocuous title *Unsichtbare Ketten* [*Invisible Chains*], whose author is the psychologist Dr Hans Ulrich Gresch. Although Caspar doesn't remember it at the time, he quotes almost word for word from this work. Also referred to in the text is the fascinating standard work by Bryan Kolb and Ian Q. Whishaw, *Fundamentals of Human Neuropsychology*, which Caspar discovers in the library. The page number quoted is correct.

The Teufelsberg Clinic, on the other hand, is as fictitious as the whole plot. Like every good lie, however, it contains a grain of truth because I've been presumptuous enough to transfer an existing private clinic of similar design to the authentic Teufelsberg in Berlin, a man-made hill consisting of rubble salvaged from the German capital's post-war ruins. What's more, in a fit of authorial megalomania, I've located the Teufelsberg a bit deeper in the Grunewald Forest than it actually is.

Incidentally, the song Caspar likes so much is 'In Between Days' by The Cure, but I'm sure you spotted that immediately. If you still haven't solved the last of the Soul Breaker's riddles, here's a little clue: the solution is hidden in the following acknowledgements. Isn't it, Gerlinde?

★ ★ ★

My thanks go first, as usual, to my readers. If you didn't read my books I'd have to do things I find far less fun than writing – like work, for instance. Many thanks, too, for your numerous hints, comments and suggested improvements, for your criticism and encouragement and everything else that reaches me mainly via my email address, fitzek@sebastianfitzek.de or my visitors' book at www.sebastianfitzek.de.

I sometimes feel like a singer who only has to bring his microphone to a concert while an army of roadies behind him does the real, tough construction work. For instance:

Roman Hocke, the only person who can be told, again and again, that he's the world's best literary agent without it going to his head.

Manuela Raschke, without whose managerial skills I would long ago have been lost, neglected, and probably arrested.

Gerlinde. Coming from the world's greatest fan of horror films, your suggested improvements were once more indispensable to this book, too. Thanks for being the anchor in the crazy maelstrom of our lives.

Sabine and Clemens Fitzek. You enabled me to flaunt your medical knowledge, for instance by familiarising me with the fundamentals of virtopsy. I shall repay you by laying all the blame for my mistakes at your door. Deal?

Christian Meyer. It's cool that everyone thinks you're my bodyguard merely because you look the part. I now take you on all my reading tours, and will continue to pester you with questions about firearms.

Sabrina Rabow. Work with few people, so the saying goes, but make sure they're the best. That's only one of the reasons why I'm glad our paths crossed years ago and you've looked after my PR ever since.

The many people whose ability, knowledge and creativity I admire, and for whose inspiration I'm infinitely grateful: Zsolt Bács, Oliver Kalkofe, Christoph Menardi, Jochen Trus, Andreas Frutiger, Arno Müller, Thomas Koschwitz, Simon Jäger, Thomas Zorbach, Jens Desens, Patrick Hocke, Peter Prange, and, of course, my father, Freimut Fitzek!

Now for the people who couldn't possibly be omitted from any list of acknowledgements because the author wouldn't exist without them:

Carolin Graehl. What makes your meticulous but sympathetic copyediting so perfect is – among other things – your pointed questions about the manuscript. You turn a collection of ideas into a readable, exciting book.

Regine Weisbrod. It's incredible. Now I know why so

many authors rave about you. If you don't take on the editing of my next book as well, I'm afraid I'll have to kill you. (I'm not joking. I'll simply attach your name to a corpse!)

Dr Andrea Müller. You discovered me and turned me into an author. It's lucky we were able to work on the outline together before the competition shamelessly snaffled you for being so successful.

Beate Kuckertz and Dr Hans-Peter Übleis. Thank you for giving me, in years to come, what other people can only dream of: money. No! I mean, of course, a home at your splendid publishing house, Droemer Knaur.

Klaus Kluge, who never shrinks from trying out crazy new marketing ideas. You're heaped with praise for it, by me as well as by your colleagues – not that my moist handshake will buy you any groceries.

Sibylle Dietzel. Many thanks for enhancing my ideas by means of your creative work in the production department.

Once again, I've nearly come to the end of my acknowledgements before paying the most important tribute of all: to the host of people working in production and sales, bookshops and libraries, without whom you wouldn't be holding this book in your hands right now.

* * *

Last but not least, I must apologise to several people whom I have brazenly robbed in order to write this book. Helmut Rassfeld, for example, with whom I was privileged to work for years in radio, and who has had to surrender his surname to a character to whom he fortunately bears not the faintest resemblance. Frau Patzwalk was the popular cook at my kindergarten (many thanks for never forcing me to eat liver!). Fruti, I'm sorry your son's first name had to go to such a memorably weird character. Marc, you're the only one who's not entitled to complain because you expressly requested me to use your surname sometime. How does the old saying go? 'Be careful what you wish for.' Well, Herr Haberland, your wish came true!

Sebastian Fitzek,
Berlin, April 2008

P.S. Never fear, you've only been reading a novel, not a genuine patient's record. At least, I think so…

About the author

SEBASTIAN FITZEK is one of Europe's most
successful authors of psychological thrillers. His
books have sold 12 million copies, been translated
into more than thirty-six languages and are the basis
for international cinema and theatre adaptations.
Sebastian Fitzek was the first German author to be
awarded the European Prize for Criminal Literature.
He lives with his family in Berlin.

sebastianfitzek.de

About the translator

JOHN BROWNJOHN was a British literary
translator. Over his career, he translated more
than 160 books and won the Schlegel-Tieck Prize
for German translation three times.
He died in January 2020 at the age of 90.